The 5th Realm

Constance Gillam

ISBN:
ISBN-13:978-1479231744

Dedicated to:

Jim Gillam

Acknowledgements:

Thanks to my critique partners, Mary Barfield, Pamela Varnado, and Tamara DeStefano for their dedication to making this manuscript the best it could be.

Cover Art by:

Tamera LeBlanc

Chapter 1

Huge and menacing, Haverford Academy looms in front of me like something out of a Stephen King movie. A bolt of lightning rips across the sky. With the wind whipping at my back, I stand at the bottom of the steep steps, trying to decide if I'm going to ditch school.

Like an omen, the rain, which has been threatening all morning, blows in accompanied by jagged claps of thunder, drenching me immediately. I make a dash for the building, the decision taken out of my hands.

Haverford, home to more rich snotty kids than 90210, is a private high school on the west side of New Orleans. Unfortunately, after someone said scholarship with all expenses paid to my *Grand'mere*, I found myself here before the ink dried on the transfer papers.

This place doesn't even smell like a school. Instead of sweat, mold and Pine-sol, it smells like beeswax and flowers. The floors are too shiny, the kids too preppy and the fluorescent lights hurt my tired sleep deprived eyes.

At my old school years of crud were crammed into crevices where the linoleum tiles met the dingy grey-blue walls, and the student's attire was an expression of their personality not of <u>Teen Vogue</u>.

Hair bedraggled and sneakers squeaking, I walk like a prisoner on death row toward my locker.

Just before I round the corner, I say a little prayer. "Please, don't let her be there." But the Gods plot against me. Michele Whitley, who has the locker next to mine, leans on *my* locker talking to her boyfriend, Eric.

Maybe I can carry my books around all day. Even empty the muscles in my arm start to cramp in protest. My English Lit book alone must weigh twenty pounds.

"Excuse me." At first, I don't think she hears me. "Excuse me," I say again.

Her conversation with her boyfriend trails off, and she turns to check me out.

Wrinkling her snub nose, she asks, "What *are* you wearing? Wal-Mart rejects?"

My tongue is stuck to the roof of my mouth and threatens to choke me.

Eric shifts, drawing her away from my locker. I throw him a grateful look. His black hair brushes his shoulders, and his brown eyes give nothing of what he's thinking away. No sympathy, no scorn. There's enough scorn in Michele's gaze to make me want to cower. I wish I had a comeback for her put down, but my brain is locked up tighter than my tongue.

Pretending to be oblivious to her sneer, I pull my books from my locker.

"She's too weird," Michele says as I merge into the crowd rushing to class.

The bell rings just as I slide into my seat in English Lit. Eric, who saunters in a moment later, only earns one of Mr. Bridges famous eyebrow raises.

Tall and slender, Eric sits two rows over and one seat up from me, making it easy to watch him without his being aware. He seems so much older than the other boys in school-silent and mature while they push and shove and tell stupid jokes. He enrolled at the Academy a couple of weeks before me, but he fits in so effortlessly. Instead of opening his book to today's assignment, he stares out the window at the storm whipping the trees against the panes. What is he thinking about?

"Today, we're discussing <u>Dante's Inferno</u>," Mr. Bridges drones.

My book is open to a page that shows Dante's descent through Hell. I trace my finger over the picture.

This Hell is nothing like the one in my nightmare- the dreams that wake me up, heart pounding and drenched in sweat almost every night.

"Lisette, what do you think Dante meant?"

Thirty pairs of eyes focus on me. "Uh-" I haven't a clue what led up to his question. Someone snickers.

Mr. Bridges looks disappointed. Until this moment I'd been his star student, always ready with an answer. In the short time I've been here, doing well in this class has been the only bright spot in my school day. I want to sink through the floor.

He moves on. "What do you think Dante means, Brittany?"

I slink down into my chair and stare at the massive literature book. It's going to be a long day.

Outside, thunder booms so close the windows rattle. The sound makes me jumpy and my skin supersensitive like an electric current runs over it. A second later the lights flicker, and the room is plunged into darkness. A couple of girls scream, then the room breaks into nervous chatter.

"Okay everyone, calm down," Mr. Bridges demands. "The lights should be back on in a second."

He's right. The lights flash back on in less than a minute and after the whispers die down, Mr. Bridges continues with the lecture.

Everything seems back to normal-with one exception.

Eric Gabriel is no longer in the classroom.

**

Eric stood in the school's courtyard, head turned up to the sky as the full force of the storm beat down on him. Cool rain sluiced over his skin, soaked his clothes, and embedded into the creases and folds of his body that were thirsty for the moisture.

Thunder boomed in the distance. He didn't flinch, just reveled in the sound. Stretching his arms up to the sky, he tried to capture the power of the storm. Maybe he could use that energy to turn back time, to recapture that long ago era of his innocence. It had been such a long time. The clap of the thunder reminded him of thousands of horses' hooves pounding over rocky soil. The sound vibrated in his body, in his soul.

New Orleans was a long way from his home of the past. That home high in the mountains where the day started out cold during the morning training sessions, but warmed during the afternoon until a glorious sun stood at its zenith. A sun that beat down on the heads of the warriors, making them sweat. He longed for those lost times-longed for the cries of the little ones and the scolding of the mothers- his mother, and his grandmother, the toothless old crone who loved him so dearly. Those people he had failed.

Dropping to his knees in the mud, he buried his head in his hands and let the storm absorb his cries of misery and pain.

**

Instead of getting off at the bus stop close to home, I hop off at Canal Street. The day looks like night and the rain continues to fall without an end in sight. Knowing I can't possibly get any wetter, I hike further into the mass of tourists that swarm the city for Mardi Gras. The smell of damp earth, diesel fumes and rotting vegetation lie like a wet, moldy cloth over the French Quarter. But it's still one of my favorite places.

I cross the railroad tracks and stop at the head of the steps as I catch sight of the Mississippi River. It never fails to take my breath away. After another suck butt day--

things didn't improve after English Lit-- I need the tranquil affect of the river. Except today it's anything but calm.

Usually the river is a big lazy alligator sunning itself as it makes its way toward the Gulf, but today it's a raging tiger that throws itself at the wooden ties, part of the city defenses. I hop down three steps to get closer.

The brown eddies of whirling water battering the ties reminds me of myself, battering at the stubbornness of my *Grand'mere*. If she's so crazy about Haverford, why doesn't *she* go there?

I live with her in a small house fifteen minutes from here. I always go straight home from school, but not today. Today I've got to come up with a plan to get away from Haverford and back to Easton. The idea of spending two more years at that stuck up school being tortured by Michele is enough to make me want to throw myself into the river. Maybe Father Patrick can make *Grand'mere* understand.

Suddenly I'm not alone. Tourists have invaded my sanctuary. Standing, I make my way out to Decatur Street past the Café de Monde. Because it's February, it's dark at 5 pm. Away from the bright lights of the bars, the dark streets on the Quarter's periphery pull me like a magnet.

The rain beats on my back, as I walk down one street of the Quarter to another. When the beat fades, I'm standing in front of a shop crowded with junk. I've been here many times before. Now the display window is dark. The store is closed.

My shoulders sag under the weight of my drenched sweatshirt. I turn and make my way home through the heavy rain.

Away from the historical district, the streets are deserted and most of the cottages are boarded up. They've never been renovated after Hurricane Katrina.

Our small bungalow is lit like a Christmas tree. *Grand'mere*'s small body is silhouetted in the open door.

"Lisette, where have you been?" Her golden eyes, dark with worry, take in my rain-soaked appearance.

"At the river." I try to squeeze by her, but she won't budge.

She grips my face between the palms of her soft hands. "What is it, *pi petite*?" She searches my eyes that are so like hers.

"Nothing." Wriggling out of her grasp, I hurry down the hall. She follows me. Her slippers make a soft pattering sound against the linoleum floors of our four room house.

Ducking into the bathroom, I strip out of my wet clothes, then step beneath the sting of the shower's hot spray, hoping to wash away the confusion and fear that clings to me like a second skin.

Grand'mere is waiting for me when I finish, her arms folded across her chest. I quickly grab a towel and wrap it around my body. With another, I wipe the steam from the cracked mirror, avoiding her gaze.

"Something is not right with you. Tell me what's wrong."

Everything- the new school, the dreams. But I don't tell her that. She's so excited about my acceptance to Haverford Academy. "Nothing is wrong."

I continue to wipe the mirror until the squeak of the towel against the glass makes me stop. Resisting the urge to throw myself into her arms, I try to smile. "You said it yourself. It's the new school."

She follows me to my bedroom. My *Grand'pere*, when he was alive, used to say a good stiff wind would knock her down, but what she lacks in size, she makes up for in stubbornness. I should know after living with her for twelve of my almost sixteen years, she doesn't give up.

"I made jambalaya."

"Ate something at Scooter's." It's a lie, but it will keep her from worrying.

After pulling on my pajamas, I climb into bed.

All the time, she hovers in the open door. "Lisette-" Some emotion spasms across her face. But then her expression shuts down. "Good night, *pi petite*." With a sigh, she turns off the light and closes my bedroom door.

Pulling the covers over my head, I wish for the first time since I was five she'd left the light on.

**

The dream comes again. The same shadowy figure leads me to an elevator that takes us to the 33rd floor. The face is shrouded in the deep folds of the black hood, but its image flickers in and out of focus like sucky cable reception.

Once off the elevator, the figure shows me to the same double doors.

"Himself awaits." My guide's voice is the deep baritone of a male. Then his form dissolves, and he's gone.

As I step into a large cavernous space, small six-legged creatures scurry away like cockroaches. From their midst emerges a tall hulking blond man with brilliant blue eyes.

As he moves toward me, I know what's going to happen, but I can't stop it.

"Ah, my bride." He raises my limp hand to his lips. I want to jerk my arm away, but I can't. His mouth opens wide to reveal the razor-like teeth of a prehistoric animal. They graze across my skin, drawing blood that gushes up dark and thick. A serpent-like tongue darts out of his mouth. Dripping saliva that burns like acid, he licks greedily at my blood. I scream in pain.

"Lisette, Lisette." The monster shakes me.

"Lisette, wake up."

My eyes fly open. I'm in my bed, but this time my screams were loud enough to bring *Grand'mere*.

She wraps me in her thin arms, and my tears stain her nightgown.

"A dream, *pi petite*. Just a dream."

Trembling, I rest my head in the cradle of her bosom like a child. *What's happening to me?*

She gently pushes me away and stares down into my face. "Do you want to tell me what has probably wakened the neighbors?" She smiles, but her eyes are worried.

Something holds me back from telling her about the nightmare. It was just a dream, a scary one, but still just a dream. "I'm okay. Must have been something I ate."

She lifts an eyebrow and studies my face.

Faking a yawn, I scoot down into the bed.

She touches my cheek. "Sleep. We'll talk in the morning." Pulling the sheet up to my chin, something I hate, she gives me one last look, then rises. She stands in the doorway and watches me for a moment.

As soon as the door closes, I turn on my bedside lamp and scan the room, expecting the demon to step out of the shadows. Rain beats against the window and the howl of the wind taunts me, but I'm all alone.

I don't turn off the light.

Chapter 2

Sometime during the pre-dawn hour, voices wake me.

"Tell her."

The voice is female-lilting and musical.

My head throbs from the tears I've shed earlier. I close my eyes against the pain and drift in a half sleep.

"Get out." *Grand'mere's* voice.

The front door slams. That brings me fully awake. "*Grand-mere?* Who's that?"

"It's no one. Go back to sleep, Lisette."

I wait, hoping she'll come to my room, but I hear her bedroom door close. Pulling the blanket up to my chin, I try and remember the conversation I heard. The woman's voice sounded familiar, but before I can remember sleep claims me again.

When the alarm buzzes, I rise.

As I dress for school, I can still feel the cold, clammy touch of the demon from my nightmare. My stomach heaves. I lean my head on the wardrobe door and concentrate on not throwing up. *It's just a dream.* And then, I remember another dream, someone shouting at *Grand'mere.* That had been real. But it couldn't, because the voice sounded like my mother's and she's dead.

Lifting my head, I start to ask *Grand'mere* about her early morning visitor, but I realize I've got a bigger problem.

"*Grand'mere,* where are my hoodies?"

"They're hanging in the kitchen. I just washed them," she shouts back.

"All of them?"

"Yes. Hurry up, Lisette. You're going to miss the bus."

I can't go to school without a hoodie. My hand goes to my hair. Nothing will make this bronze bush disappear. "I don't feel good."

Grand'mere appears in my bedroom door with a yellow rain slicker that I wore in middle school.

"I can't wear that. It's hideous."

With her lips compressed and that glint in her eye that says, "You're going out of here," she hands me the slicker.

I take it and stomp out almost tripping over a small form huddled at my front door.

My second best friend, eight-year-old Leticia Summers-how pathetic is it that an eight-year-old is one of my best friends- slips her small hand into mine. For such a tiny thing, she has a strong grip.

Rain has turned the street into a whirlpool and the grassless yards into a mud bath. It hasn't stopped Mrs. Joyner from putting her Chihuahua, Nappy, out in the front yard. He's running from one end of the fence to the other, yapping at the neighborhood kids as they head toward their bus stop.

"He really is a sweet dog," I tell Leticia for the millionth time. "He's just excited and wants to be friends."

She doesn't respond, just keeps her gaze on Nappy as we hurry toward her bus stop and away from the dog.

When we get there, I squat so we're face-to-face. "If you'd just pat him-"

She shakes her head so violently her corn-rowed braids hit her cheeks and fear makes her brown eyes almost black in her narrow face.

"It's okay, maybe later." I give her hand a squeeze just before she climbs on the school bus.

For me, the ride across the river passes in a flash. One minute I'm staring down at the churning brown water below, and the next, the city bus driver tells me it's my stop. The stop from Hell.

Luck is with me today. Michele isn't at her locker. I grab my books and head for English Lit, wondering if Eric will be there.

He isn't.

Letting out a sigh, I sink into my seat. The rest of the morning drags.

At lunch I peer through the rain streaked glass door leading to the palm tree courtyard.

"Ms. Beaulieu, where are you going?"

Caught red handed with my brown paper lunch clutched in my hand, I release the door's handle.

Ms. Matheson, the headmistress, stands not twenty feet behind me, vein prominent hand on her bony hip.

"Uh…"

"The courtyard is off limits. You've have to eat in the cafeteria today." She rushes toward me, ushering me away from the door. As though she doubts I know the way, she leads me to the lunch room. Her back is so straight you think she had a stick up her...

I glance longingly at the library as we pass.

She must have seen my look because she says, "You know there's no eating in the library. Ever."

She deposits me at the cafeteria. There's no door, just one large arched entrance. I feel like I should be announced by a footman.

The smell of meatloaf almost makes me gag. I hate meatloaf. We've had it too many times at home. Yes, here they serve it buffet style in fancy warming dishes, but it's still meatloaf. You'd think there'd be a better selection of food.

Michele and her circle of friends sit around one of the bigger tables. Eric, sitting next to her, whispers something in her ear when he spots me. She looks at him strangely, then in my direction. The tips of my ears burn. I crunch my lunch against my chest to hide it and head for a small unoccupied table in the back of the cafeteria.

"Lisette." The last syllable of my name is drawn out in Michele's Southern drawl. Her voice-like ice tea with too much sugar- is loud enough to be heard over the clamor in the cafeteria. All heads turn in my direction.

Why is today turning into such a nightmare? That's usually reserved for my nights.

"Come join us," she calls out.

The room is so quiet I can hear "I Kissed a Girl" playing on someone's iPod. They're waiting to see if I'm going to diss her. This is their entertainment for the day.

Why does she want me to eat with her? So she can torture me some more? I continue walking toward the table in the back.

A pair of tan loafers appears in my path. My gaze travels up the khaki pants to the Polo shirt to Eric Gabriel's thick lashed brown eyes. "Join us." He gestures back toward Michele's table. It's the first time I've heard his voice. It sounds rusty, like he doesn't use it often.

"Why?" I'm not going to be made fun of by a bunch of spoiled rich kids.

Whispering, he says, "Because I'd like you to." My stomach does a nose dive.

I glance over my shoulder in Michele's direction. Does she want me at their table that badly, or is this all Eric? Is he following her directions, or does he think on his own?

He touches my elbow and turns me around.

I don't know why, but I allow him to lead me toward their table. I'm so stupid. I said I'd never be swayed by a pretty face. Now look at me.

Michele glares pointedly at Ashley Crandall, the boy sitting to her right, and he rises quickly and finds another chair. She pats the recently vacated seat. There's no other seat available. I sit.

She smiles her phony smile. "I love your hair."

Her manicured fingers move toward my head, but I lean out of range. No one touches my hair.

"I love blonde twists. Is it peroxide?"

The other kids giggle, but Eric doesn't crack a smile.

My heritage is none of her business, so I don't dignify her question with an answer.

"Hey, Lisette," Ashley shouts from the other side of the round table. "I heard you're into Voodoo."

My body jerks. Where had he heard that?

More giggling. "Yeah," another boy shouts. "Put a spell on Rick." With a goofy grin, he points to a lanky kid next to him.

Michele's bright green eyes study me with renewed interest. "Voodoo, huh?"

I'm descended on my mother's side from a great Voodoo priestess, Claudette Toussaint, a disciple of Marie Laveau. The only things I know about her are what I've gotten from books and the Internet. My *Grand'mere* never talks about my mother's family. In fact, she never talks about my mother at all, who was killed, along with my father, when I was four.

"*Are* you into Voodoo?" Michele eyes are bright, probing. This is the first interest she's shown in me since I arrived two months ago.

She leans in so close her cloying perfume swirls around me like a malevolent cloud, making me feel like a cornered rabbit. My head swims. I don't know anything about Claudette or Voodoo, but it doesn't stop me from saying, "I can put a spell on you."

"Oooo." The two boys on the other side of her cover their mouths in mock fright.

For a moment, I feel good. I got one up on her, but the next moment I feel petty.

Michele grabs my arm. "Prove it," she says.

Her French manicured fingernails dig into my t-shirt. Too bad I can't turn her into the pig she is.

I shake her hand off. "I don't have to prove it." Not meeting anyone's gaze, I push away from the table and try to make a dignified exit to the accompanying laughter.

**

The library, the one place Michele and her friends won't enter, is my place of solace.

I'm wrong. Ashley Crandall slides into the seat next to mine.

"About what they said in the cafeteria," he says, lowering his voice to keep the librarian, Ms. Summers, off his case. "Is it true? Are you into Voodoo?"

He doesn't give me a chance to deny it. "Can you make me a charm? I'll pay you." From his pocket, he pulls out a wad of twenties and fifties.

My mouth falls open. I've never seen so much money. Coming to my senses, I cover his hand with mine and look wildly around the library. No one is paying attention to us. "Put that away," I whisper.

He stuffs all the money except a single fifty dollar bill back in his pocket. It lies forlornly on the table between us. That could buy a lot of food. I may be on a free ride here, but *Grand'mere* has other bills to pay, bills I should be helping her with. She's getting older, and moves so slowly and looks so fragile. A little extra money would help.

Another thought pops into my head. Something I try not to think about. How long will she be with me?

Ashley watches me. "Will you do it?"

"Do what?"

He slides the money in my direction. "Make a love charm."

I draw back in surprise. "What?"

"A love charm," he repeats. "I want Michele to like me as much as I like her."

This black-haired boy's got everything-- looks, money-- and, I thought until now, class. But Michele? Come on. Plus, she's got Eric.

"I don't..."

He pulls another fifty out of his pocket and places it in my hand. My gaze is glued on the money.

"Thanks, Lisette."

Before I can tell him I don't know anything about charms, he's gone.

Chapter 3

Dark clouds part and for a moment, a pale crescent moon hangs in the sky, casting a weak glow on the mausoleums in St. Louis Cemetery #1. A steady sheet of rain falls as I wait for Ashley. We've agree to meet here at midnight. I chose this place because I know it really well- my relatives are buried here-and because I wanted to impress Ashley. Okay, scare him a little.

Because I don't want to be seen from the road-the police patrol the area frequently-I wear *Grand'mere*'s dark rain coat.

An owl hoots in the distance. It's not really an owl. It's my best friend, Scooter. He's my lookout. Everyone knows these cemeteries are loaded with thugs out to rip off tourists or anyone stupid enough to come to the cemeteries at night. And there's always somebody. Scooter hoots twice. Ashley's coming.

I touch the cloth sack in my pocket. I did some research on the internet into *gris-gris* charms and used a little imagination to come up with this one. It contains Michele's hair, stolen from her brush while we were both in the gym locker room, some of Ashley's hair, chicken bones, which I scavenged from the parking lot of KFC, and a little dirt from one of *Grand'mere*'s potted plants. If Ashley wants to throw his money away, *Grand'mere* and I could use it.

"Lisette?"

The fool is standing in the open wearing a neon rain slicker. Why doesn't he just put up a billboard? What if someone else is here other than Scooter and me?

I step out from behind a grave stone. "Shh. Do you want to wake the dead?"

Ashley's laugh comes out squeaky. Glancing around he says, "It's kinda creepy, but cool."

That's what I wanted him to think, but now the place is giving me the creeps. "Let's get this over with." I pull the charm from my pocket, keeping it close to my body to protect it from the rain.

Ashley's eyes are glued to my hand. "Is that it? How does it work?"

When I grab his hand, he flinches.

"It won't bite." I transfer the charm to his large palm and step back.

"Aren't you going to say something?" he whispers. "Like a spell." His eyes are bright.

I was afraid he'd ask something like this. Without thought, I wave my hand over the charm. "As the descendant of the great Claudette, Spirits, I call upon you..."

Lightning flashes in the sky to the east, illuminating the cemetery with a gray cast. Head stones of demons and angels stand out against a sky bright as day. The earth begins to quake, then roll like a giant worm is passing beneath our feet. I stumble backward, and hit my elbow on corner of the mausoleum. Pain shoots from my funny bone to my wrist, numbing the whole arm. *What the heck?*

Where Ashley and I once stood, a fissure cracks the earth, and steam erupts from the break. We stare at each other. The fear I feel is mirrored in his face. He looks like a spooked horse; the whites of his eyes are huge.

Pushing away from the crypt, I hold my arms out for balance. My heart pounds against my ribs like a caged bird trying to break free.

"What's happening?" Ashley's voice has lost that mellow coolness he's known for. "An earthquake?"

New Orleans doesn't have earthquakes-hurricanes, yes, earthquakes, no. Another flash of lightning. To my right, a large ornamental stone angel topples off its pedestal. It lands with its head buried in the mud, its wings sticking out like some grotesque giant bug.

A loud grinding noise makes me jump. I turn just in time to see the mausoleum door explode, releasing a blast of funky, sulfurous air.

From the corner of one stinging, watering eye, I see the flash of Ashley's raincoat in the distance. I want to run too, but my feet won't move.

A pinpoint of bright, white light fizzes from the crypt's center, splitting the blackness in a zipper like motion.

"Hail... Hail Mary full of grace..." My hand goes to the cross I usually wear around my neck. It isn't there. My legs tremble as I try to back away, but my knees buckle and I fall on my butt, mud flying. My head swivels when an inhuman grunt comes from the direction of the fissure in the ground. Thick scaly fingers emerge out of the cavity, gripping the edge of the opening.

"Scooooter…" But my voice comes out in a croak instead of a shout. *Where is he?*

A long snout-green and scaly like the arm-is visible now above the hole. Hooded black eyes protrude from a face that resembles an alligator. I notice all this in a flash. The creature lets loose another roar that makes my scalp tingle and my breath come in ragged gasps.

My head ping pongs between the light display from inside the mausoleum and the ground cavity from which the reptile is trying to escape.

Move.

I put another hand behind me, trying in vain to crawl away.

My backward progress is stop by something solid.

OMG! The creature has a friend.

Chapter 4

"Come with me."

A very human hand is extended toward me. Grasping it, I pull myself up out of the mud, then stare in shock at Eric Gabriel.

"Hurry," he demands. Pushing me in front of him, I can almost feel his breath on my neck as we race toward the cemetery's entrance. My legs feel like cooked Ramen noodles.

When I begin to fall behind, he grabs my arm and pulls me along. We continue to run, zig zagging down one street after another until we blend in with the crowds still mingling in the Quarter. I look over my shoulder, then blow out a sigh of relief. We've lost it. Behind us are only drunk and costumed humans.

"Wait." I bend at the waist, hands resting on my thighs and try to catch my breath. A stitch of pain shoots up my side. My throat is sore and raw from panting.

"We shouldn't stop. It could be on us in a second."

Ignoring the partiers moving around us, I stare up at my rescuer. "How do you know so much about what's following us? And what is it?"

"Later." He pulls me upright, then grabs my hand and plows through the mass of partiers.

We jog until we reach the ghostly streets of my neighborhood. A large leafless pecan tree forlornly guards two phantom houses flattened by Hurricane Katrina. The only noise is the splatter of our feet through the puddles and the whine of an occasional car's engine as it passes.

Out of the corner of my eye, I study the tall guy walking beside me. His wet dark hair hangs down in his face, shielding his eyes, and his white Nautica shirt molds to his lean, but buffed chest. I can't believe he's the one that saved me. He doesn't know I exist unless Michele tells him I do.

We don't speak, which is fine with me. I'm too busy trying to make sense of what happened in the cemetery. I can still hear the scrape of stone on stone as the mausoleum door opened. I still feel bits of flying rock scraping my face. Am I bleeding? I touch my cheek. My fingers come away streaked with mud. No blood.

"Are you okay?"

"Yeah, yeah, I'm fine." Liar. I'm shaking so hard my bones might fly apart.

"What were you doing at the cemetery?" he asks.

What were you doing there? "Hmm, I was meeting a friend." Right. By lunch, it will be all over school. I bet when Ashley tells the story, he won't admit that he ran out of the cemetery like a five-year-old girl.

"Ashley Crandall?"

My head jerks up in surprise. "How...?"

"He almost knocked me down getting out of the cemetery."

I've heard him talk more tonight than ever before, and he speaks like he's from another country.

My house comes into view. "Thanks for helping me."

"Stay out of the graveyard, Lisette." He turns and starts to walk away.

"Wait."

He stops, but doesn't face me.

"What were you doing there?"

"I live nearby," he says, then continues walking, his hands in his pockets, his head lowered against the rain that is suddenly heavier.

It's only later that I realize that he didn't answer my question.

**

Pebbles hit my bedroom window. When I open it, Scooter slides over the sill and onto the floor like a snake, bringing the scent of rain into the room.

He rises slowly to his feet, which should've been a warning that something was up. Scooter is usually like a Jack Russell terrier on speed. But to give myself credit, I was still tripping on my own fear.

Hands on my hips, I glare at him. "Where were you? I thought you had my back."

He frowns. "Standing out in the rain in a creepy cemetery isn't having your back?" Moving away from me, he opens and closes my desk drawers.

He's looking for food. He's always looking for food.

"Bottom drawer," I say.

He extracts a package of Twizzlers, stares into the bag and only removes one, replacing the rest of the candy in the drawer.

"Did you see anything…weird?"

Taking a bite of the licorice, he chews then throws the stick in the trashcan. "Just dickhead with the raincoat running for all he was worth."

"Didn't you think it *that* was strange?"

Scooter cocked his head in thought. "Naw. I figured you scared the shit out of him. That's what you were planning to do, wasn't it?"

My cheeks burn. "I guess," I whisper.

Didn't he feel the quake? Didn't he see the crypt opening? How could he have missed everything?

"Why didn't you come and see if I was okay?"

"I did." He takes a seat on the floor, his back against the wall. "You were gone. I figured you just went home." Silence fills the room. The only noise is the patter of rain hitting the window.

What about the hole in the ground… the crypt door, didn't he see those?

"Scooter…"

My best friend has his head buried in his hands.

"What's wrong, Scoot?"

"Aw, Lis?"

Recognizing his tone, I lean back against the headboard and settle in. "What is it?"

"Boogie's in jail."

Boogie is Scooter's older brother-in and out of trouble. All petty stuff, but still...

"It's the third strike for him."

"I'm sorry." I want to go to him and touch his arm, but he wouldn't like that.

"But the funny thing is he didn't do it."

He must see the doubt on my face.

"Ya, ya. I know he says that every time, but this time I believe him."

By the lines that crease Scooter's broad forehead, I know he's trying to work something out.

He turns toward me. "Boogie needs a good lawyer. And that means big bucks."

Icy fingers creep up my spine. "You aren't going to do something stupid, are you?"

He grins. "Of course not. Why do you think I'd do something stupid? 'Cause I stand lookout in a cemetery at midnight while my best friend hands out Voodoo charms?"

I laugh for the first time in forever. "Okay, it was retarded."

"Damn right. How much money did you make?"

"Too much."

"Huh?" He stares at me as though I lost my mind. "You can never make too much."

Shuddering, I think about the last few hours, wishing I'd never agree to make the charm. What does *Grand'mere* say, "Money is the root of all evil?" She's right.

"I can use a little too much moolah right now." Scooter shrugs, then smirks. "And no, I'm not going to trap. What kinda example is that for Boogie?"

I don't bother telling him that Boogie is older and should be setting the example.

"Tomorrow," he glances at the clock on my desk. "Today when mama gets home from work, we're meeting with a lawyer who's supposed to be good with cases like Boogie's."

"Everything will work out," I say. I know it sounds lame, but right now I've got my own problems.

As though sensing my preoccupation, he rises. "Better go."

I follow him. He lifts the window and jumps. Staring out at the street, he flips up the hood on his sweatshirt. "This damn rain is getting on my nerves."

"Stay out of trouble," I say.

"You too." And he disappears into the darkness.

After lowering the window, I climb into bed, but don't turn off the lights.

**

A hush falls over the crowded hallway as I walk toward my locker Monday morning. Conversations resume when I pass, a buzzing like a hornet of bees. My eyes are focused straight ahead. Michele and Ashley are at my locker. I search the crowd lining both sides of the hall. Eric leans casually against the lockers on the opposite side of the hall. Why is he over there?

"Lisette, Saturday night was so cool," Ashley says.

I ignore him and try to open my locker. My fingers fumble with the lock, for a moment I've forgotten the combination.

"When that door exploded-" His voice is loud and seems to reverberate off the walls.

"Shut up, Ashley." I glance around. The other students make no pretense of looking away. They're hanging onto his words like bystanders at a fatal car wreck. They've probably heard the story already. They just want me to embellish his version.

Fingers too slippery with sweat, I give up on opening my locker.

"What did you say to make the ground tremble?" Ashley's eyes are bright with an insatiable curiosity now that he's safely on hallowed ground.

I don't answer.

Michele's hand rests possessively on Ashley's shoulder, her gaze glued to his face. His arm is hooked around her waist.

"Love you, babe," Michele whispers to Ashley.

He puckers his lips and sends her a mock kiss.

It takes a moment for me to interpret what I see and hear, then a wave of nausea hits me. Bolting, I practically run over students who stand between me and the bathroom.

Hiding in the stall, I fight the urge to vomit.

Chapter 5

The frantic flapping of wings draws my attention upward. A pigeon is trapped in the wooden beams above my head. He flies from one beam to another without the sense to fly out through the door he entered. I feel his pain.

Weak sunlight leaks through stained glass windows and falls on the first rows of wooden pews. The rest of the church is in shadow.

I don't remember how I got here or anything after I ran into the girl's bathroom. My arms tighten around my waist. My fingers cramp from the pressure.

I jump when a hand touches my shoulder.

"Are you alright, my child?"

A priest with a fringe of snow white hair around his bald crown smiles kindly down on me.

"Where- where am I?"

"You're in St. Louis Cathedral."

Jackson Square. I'm in the center of the Quarter. I've passed it many times, but had never been inside.

"Are you lost, child?"

Yes. "Forgive me, Father, for I have sinned."

"Do you want me to take your confession?" He points to the dark wooden stall in the front corner of the church.

"God won't forgive what I've done."

"God always forgives." The priest soft hand pats mine. "Nothing could be that terrible. Maybe it would help if you talk about it."

I shake my head. *No way*. He'll have me taken out of here in a strait jacket like they did Mr. Liebowski down the street when he found his mama in the house after the flood waters went down.

Easing down onto the pew beside me, he asks, "Would you like me to call your parents?"

I wish you could. I probably wouldn't be in this mess if my parents were still alive. There would've been money, and I wouldn't have made that jacked up charm. "My parents are dead."

He clucks his tongue in sympathy. "Is there someone else I can call?" He sits quietly, hands folded peacefully in his lap, waiting. His gaze is non-judgmental. I decide to take a chance.

"Father, do you believe that some people have special abilities?" I hold my breath, waiting for his answer. Not that I believe for one minute that all the chaos in the cemetery and Michele ditching Eric was because of me. It couldn't be.

"Of course, my dear. We all have gifts in the eyes of God."

"No." I struggle to find the words to describe what I mean. "You know- special like magical."

He frowns.

I've caught him off guard, then he smiles. "Well, Jesus did turn water into wine."

Remembering the Harry Potter books I read last summer, I say, "No, Father, dark magic."

His smile withers, and his eyes cloud in confusion. "Black magic?" he repeats.

I nod. "Do you believe that demons walk among us?"

He stares at me, probably debating whether I'm joking. "I believe that spirits dwell among us, those unfortunate ones who can't move on, but the average person can't sense them."

I go for it. "I raised a demon, Father."

He blinks once, twice, then suspicion enters his eyes. "Young lady-"

"I'm not lying! I made a gris-gris that made a girl a love slave and caused a creature to crawl up from..."

From where? Hell? It definitely wasn't human, so it couldn't have been buried.

"Young lady," he rises and stands over me. "This church is not the place to play games. I must ask you to refrain from such talk."

Tears fill my eyes, and my throat swells. If God's representative on earth won't believe me, who will?

Got to get out of here. Jumping up, I catch the priest by surprise. He stumbles backwards. Not checking to see if he is okay, I rush out the church's massive doors. I almost trip over something huddled underneath the Cathedral's overhang. Like the unfolding of a bird from the protection of its wing, Eric Gabriel lifts his head. His eyes go from brown to green. Strange.

Why is he here?

"I was worried about you."

He answered a question I didn't ask.

Did he follow me? His statement takes me out of my misery for a moment. He and his friends hate me. Now he's worried about me?

Not buying his sudden concern, I pull my jacket tighter and move around him. The rain makes me shiver. In fact, my whole body seems to be encased in ice. "I'm fine." I run down the rest of the steps and out to the street.

Forgetting the rain, I tilt my face up to the heavens, praying for forgiveness. To obtain absolution from my sins, I have to undo the charm.

**

Rain splattered against the boarded buildings, echoing off the tin rooftops with a constant metallic ping. Dressed in black, Eric walked down an isolated street in the French Quarter just after 11pm. Dirty rainwater lapped at the silver chains of his boots.

In the distance, the muted amber light from a streetlamp made him think of Lisette Beaulieu's eyes. He steeled his mind against the desolation and despair he'd seen in her face this afternoon at the church. Her pain was not his problem. She was not his problem. He was here to do a job, and he'd do it.

As he rounded a corner, the dark shadows separated into three hulking forms. He cursed.

"Himself wants you," one of the figures growled.

"And he sent you brainless twits?"

One of the minions snarled, showing yellow fangs, then dropped to all fours and charged. Without taking his eyes off the figure that had spoken, and was obviously the leader of this pathetic trio, Eric pulled a ten inch rapier from the scabbard concealed by the leather jacket he wore.

Sparks flew from the blade as it plowed through the leathery skin of the charging beast. The half-human, half-animal form imploded into hundreds of pieces that blew into the rain soaked night and hissed when they splattered onto the pavement. The pungent odor of sulfur singed the air.

The smell never failed to sting Eric's nostrils.

"Himself will not be happy," the leader said. He and his companion stepped back into the inky shadows and disappeared.

Eric sighed. He didn't want to see Saarel. He had nothing to report. He took a few steps toward his intended destination, then stopped. If he didn't go and see him now, he'd just send another group of his mindless slaves.

Eric grunted in frustration. He walked to the next block and turned down a dark alley. The smell of rotting garbage, urine and booze lingered in the air. Moonlight glistened in the puddles that shone iridescent with motor oil. Something moved on the periphery of his vision. He paused, then relaxed when a bottle of MD 20/20 rolled out of a cardboard lean-to. A grizzled face peered out between the cracks of the make-shift hovel.

"Where ya goin, buddy?" a whiskey graveled voice asked.

"To Hell," Eric said.

"Me too," the drunk agreed.

Eric strode to the end of the alley and entered an abandoned warehouse. Here the stench of urine and stale sweat from unwashed bodies was no worse than where he'd spend the last millennium. Stepping over the broken wine bottles, used condoms and drug paraphernalia, he made his way to the building's basement, an oddity in New Orleans since digging a basement could put you in the Gulf. The steps ended at a brick wall. Touching the bricks, a portal opened and he stepped through. It resealed with a hiss. The faint stench of sulfur, burning flesh and fear reached him. Home, sweet home.

Hell, of which the fifth Realm was a part, was not some mythical entity. It existed, just in another plane, another dimension.

As Eric descended, fingers reached out and snagged at his clothes. Without looking at the wrenched creatures, he detached their bony hands and ignored their pathetic cries for mercy. He was not the one they should be begging to, only Saarel could grant their wishes. But Saarel wouldn't. He fed on their pain and suffering.

"Looking for me?"

Saarcl sat atop a burnt out shell of an automobile. Behind him was a crumbling high rise Eric knew was the demon's lair. Eric had never been inside, never wanted to go inside.

Saarel leapt off the car, spewing ash when his hoofs landed inches from Eric.

He didn't move. Saarel liked to intimidate. Show him you were afraid and your life, such as it was in this hell hole, became intolerable.

"Where is she?" The demon's voice was rough and gravely as though air passed over rocks.

Eric didn't say a word. He didn't need to. The fact that Lisette wasn't with him said it all.

Saarel circled Eric, the heat of his breath like flames on Eric's skin. His breath smelled like something had died and putrefied in his stomach.

"One fifteen-year-old girl too much for you?" Saarel's laughter echoed around the sulfur-laden air and rebounded to whirl around Eric like a tornado.

"No."

His lord and master stopped pacing and stood within six inches of Eric. He didn't flinch, even as Saarel's face morphed into one of its many forms. His red skin wrinkled and wavered as hundreds of snakes hissed and spat around his head.

"She is mine," Saarel said.

A long tongue belonging to one of the snakes flicked out and licked Eric's skin.

"Mine. And if you can't deliver her, you'll be back there with the rest of these miserable beings." He pointed to the mass of bodies that crawled and slithered as they made their way toward him to beg for a crumb of his mercy. "For the next milieu and the next."

Eric struggled against the rising panic. He'd been imprisoned in this nether world for two millenniums. He'd felt as though he suffocated each day of his existence here. He couldn't take another thousand years in this limbo. He didn't even have the option of killing himself. He was already dead.

**

Although it's early, the Quarter is crowded. The rain, which is still falling, hasn't kept the partiers inside. I walk in the streets, partly to avoid the people, but also to avoid any drunks that stumble out of the bars.

I have to know why the charm worked. Skipping school, I'm in the Quarter again. The Voodoo shop is open.

When I enter the store, a few tourists are milling about, picking up Voodoo dolls, laughing and clowning. The man behind the counter smiles indulgently at them, but his dark eyes follow me as I wander around the store. Does he think I'm going to steal something? His skin is the color of walnut stain, and his bald head gleams, as though polished with oil. From his right ear, dangles a small silver cross.

When his store finally clears of customers, he turns his full attention on me. "So you finally got up the courage to come in to see me, little sister."

With a shaky hand, I place the Voodoo doll I'm holding back on the shelf. *He knows me?*

"I've watched you peek in the windows for the last two years." His deep rumbling voice vibrates through my body.

I started haunting the Quarter and this shop about the time I overheard *Grand'mere*'s conversation with her friend about my mother and Voodoo.

Walking to the counter, I finger some small pouches enclosed in fine netting. Now that I'm inside the store and face to face with the owner, all the questions I want to ask fly out of my head.

"Is it a love charm you want?"

I glance up to see if he's laughing at me.

His dark eyes hold mine, serious as death. "You are a special one," he said. "You don't need such things." His long dark fingers flick over the charms dismissively.

How does he know what I need? I don't even know that.

He sticks out a dark hand. "Let me introduce myself. I'm Henri Toussaint."

At hearing my mother's maiden name, my breath catches in my throat. Is he a distant relative? Searching his face, I don't find any resemblance to the one worn picture I have of my mother.

I take his hand. "I'm Lisette."

"Yes, I know. Your mother was my sister."

The words explode like a bomb in the silence of the shop. I drop his hand and back away. "That's not possible. My mother—my mother had no living relatives."

He laughs, the sound rumbles around in my head. "Oh, but you're wrong. You have a whole lot of family in the bayou."

"You must be confusing me with someone else." Turning, I make for the exit. I made a mistake by coming here.

"Your mother was Sherrilyn Toussaint Beaulieu." He calls after me, his voice holding certainty and conviction.

Hearing my mother's full name, I stop. I don't look at him, but instead study the shop with its African masks, its bottles of mysterious liquids and its smell of incense. Why was I so drawn to this place? Had my mother's spirit pulled me here?

"Have you ever been to a Voodoo ceremony?"

A thrill of excitement pokes its head through my confusion. I turn to face him, his dark eyes are mesmerizing. He glances toward the shop's entrance as though he expects someone to enter. "Have you?"

I shake my head.

No, I'd never been to a ceremony or spoken the word, Voodoo, within my *Grand'mere*'s hearing. But, I was curious about this religion she'd spoken of in such hushed tones when she thought I wasn't around. Curious about this religion I knew my mother had practiced. But most of all I wanted answers to the dark and dangerous disturbance I'd created in the cemetery. I needed to know what I'd done.

"Would you like to attend one?"

My heart is jack-hammering now and my mouth is dry, making it hard to get the words out. "Yes. Where?"

"The bayou."

If my eyes were wide before, they must be huge now. "The bayou?" I whisper. I've never been there. In fact, I've never traveled outside the city of New Orleans. I want to go, but…

He watches me with a look of expectancy in his eyes.

"When is it?" The real question is how I will get there.

"Meet me here tomorrow night at eleven."

Grand'mere will never let me out of the house. *Sneak out. You've done it before.* But that was with Scooter. As much as I want to attend this ceremony, I'm afraid to go by myself.

"I'll be here," I say. And hope I can get Scooter to agree to come.

**

The next day in school after the last bell rings, I head to the library. My goal: to use one of the library's computers. Haverford has a computer lab, but for what I'm about to do, I need privacy.

"May I help you, Lisette?"

I like Ms. Summers. She's an older woman, probably in her thirties. From Michele and her crew's comments about Ms. Summers, she has fashion sense. Since I have none, I have to take their word for it. I like her because she has a gentle smile and she seems to care about the students.

"I'm doing a research paper and the computer lab is pretty noisy. I don't have a computer at home."

I'm aware that all the teachers know which students are on scholarship, so, I add the last part, which is true, to ensure she doesn't say no.

"Of course you can." She smiles and waves a hand toward the computers that line the back wall.

It takes me a few minutes to locate the News Library site and to select the *Times Picayune* as the newspaper I want to search.

The only thing I know is the year 1997. Since that would bring up everything written that year, I abandon that possibility and plug my last name, Beaulieu, into a search window. That also brings up too many articles, so I narrow the search by typing in my father's name and the year 1997.

My father was a fireman, so my search yields five articles with his name, but it's the last story I'm interested in.

Couple Dies in Crash.

A motorist discovered an overturned vehicle just off I-10 westbound near the Teche Bayou exit. Edouard Beaulieu and his wife, Sherrilyn, were killed in the crash. Police speculate that Beaulieu was traveling too fast for the rainy conditions and lost control of his car, hitting a tree.

Impatient, I skip the rest of the article and read the last paragraph.

Edouard Beaulieu is survived by his mother, Evangeline nee Moriel. Sherrilyn nee Toussaint is survived by her mother, Chante, grandmother, Odette and brother, Henri Toussaint.

I stop reading and sit back in my chair. *Grand'mere* lied to me. My mother does have family. Or at least, as of twelve years ago, she did. Why would she lie?

Going back to the beginning, I take my time and read the whole article.

There is one line that knocks the air out of my lungs.

The Beaulieu's three-year-old daughter, Lisette, was found wandering near the car, unharmed.

**

Out of breath, I barrel into my house. *Grand'mere* appears in the kitchen's doorway, a reprimand forming on her lips.

I stand in the middle of the living room, tears falling, chest heaving. "Why--?" I take two shuttering breaths. "Why didn't you tell me I was in the car?"

Her narrow shoulders slump. She doesn't even ask me what I'm talking about. She knows. Turning, she heads back into the kitchen. I follow. My feet are heavy like I'm moving through quicksand.

She's sits at the kitchen table and worries her rosary, her amber eyes glisten with unshed tears.

"Why, *Grand'mere*?"

"I was trying to protect you."

I take a seat next to her. "From what?"

Reaching out, she clasps my cold fingers in her work-rough hands. "When they brought you to me and you didn't seem to remember the accident, I thought, God has given you a blessing. I didn't want you to remember. I didn't know what horrors you'd seen. I didn't want your life to be damaged by the accident. So I kept it a secret."

I want to be mad at her for a little while longer, but I can't. She loves me and it shines from her eyes. Noisy sobs rack my body. Her chair scrapes against the worn linoleum floor as she rises and comes to me. She brings my head to her bosom. "Shh."

I cry until my throat feels scratchy and raw.

"How did you find out?" she asks.

I almost blurt out about meeting Henri, but stop just in time. "I was doing research in the library at school and decided to look up Papa's name."

She nods, excepting my lie. I wrap my arms more tightly around her body. She's fragile like a bird. Like a bird, she can easily be hurt. I can't tell her about meeting Henri Toussaint and definitely not about my plans to go to the bayou. Because I'm going. I need to find out about the other side of my family. Maybe they can tell me what happened in the cemetery the other night.

Chapter 6

The bayou at night is alive. I see very little in the darkness, but my hearing is heightened. Insects buzz, creatures call to each other, and fish splash in this byway cesspool. Like the kinky gray hair of an old lady, Spanish moss trails in the dirty water of the swamp, eerily beautiful. I shudder to think what is caught in the tangles of her hair.

My head jerks in the direction of a huge splash. Something large slithers into the water.

"Alligators," my uncle says, piloting the pirogue with a long pole around another bend in the waterway.

Shivering, I strain to make out more, but can only see darkness behind us. I sit on my hands, more to still their trembling than for warmth. I wish Scooter could be with me, but since he's dropped out of school, he has other friends and other interest.

Long before the canoe reaches the spot, I feel the drums. The pounding travels through my nerve endings until my whole body is pulsating. I feel the same as I did several nights ago when I wandered the Quarter, restless and possessed.

The rhythm grows louder until it drowns out the songs of the bayou's night life. My blood leaps in recognition.

The bonfire slides slowly into view. Sparks flitter up to the sky like fireflies, each dancing and twirling before dying and falling back to the pyre, but no bodies gyrate in time to the drums. I'm disappointed. In the few Voodoo movies I've seen, there's always wild, frenzied dancing.

I look up at Henri, "Where's everyone?"

"They are there."

Suddenly his voice has taken on a Caribbean accent that wasn't present in the shop.

He maneuvers the canoe to the dock, ties it to a post and hoists his slender body out of the boat and onto the landing. He reaches down for me and pulls me up. His hands are rough and calloused.

Like what I've seen in the movies, the pathway from the dock is lit with flaming torches. Strangely, the drum still beats, but the tempo is now sluggish.

Déjà vu. Henri is leading the way, and for one insane minute, I feel like I'm reliving my nightmare, the one where I follow a dark cloaked figure to the demon's lair. I stop. Henri turns and motions for me to come. As though I have no will of my own, I walk toward him. He grips my hand in his warm one, the drums stop, and this feeling of apprehension disappears. Time resumes its normal speed.

"Welcome home," he says. He opens the screen door of a small house and beckons me inside.

I'm immediately surrounded by at least twenty people. Hands touch my face and arms. Warm smiles light the brown faces. They are happy to see me, but not one face is familiar. The three-year-old child that was me has blocked out everything associated with her mother.

The crowd parts and I'm ushered to the front of the room. An old woman is seated in a large fan backed chair. Her skin is dark, like Henri's, and her faced is creased by wrinkles. Her eyes are bright as she studies me.

"Come here, child." She reaches out a bony hand, the fingers swollen and crooked with arthritis.

Feeling awkward because I'm standing and she's sitting, I kneel at her feet. She touches my hair and then my face. "You are like your father." She turns and glances behind her at a younger woman. This woman nods in agreement.

If I'm supposed to know these two, I don't. "You knew my father?"

"Yes, but I knew your mother better," the old woman says. "Sherrilyn was my granddaughter."

The old woman points to the young one behind her, "Her daughter. And you have met my grandson, Henri."

So this is my great-grandmother, Odette.

My grandmother, Chante, the grandmother I thought dead, smiles gently at me; tears swim in her brown eyes. She looks nothing like me. Is it my mother she resembles? Questions race through my mind, too many to get out. "My *Grand'mere* told me you were dead."

The old woman sighs. "That is partly for your protection and partly because your father's mother is afraid."

I wet my lips, my mouth suddenly dry. I study the old woman, then my grandmother behind her. "Afraid of what?"

"Of us, the religion, and of other things."

I stare at my great-grandmother, fragile and twisted with her illness and the others who've touched me with kindness. *How could Grand'mere be afraid of them? So afraid she's kept me away from them for twelve years.*

"What things?"

But my great-grandmother only pats my face with cool dry fingers. "In time." She rises from her chair with the help of my grandmother. "Come," she says. A path opens for her like the parting of the seas for Moses.

She walks outside with everyone in step behind her.

White candles in all types of vessels circle the bonfire. Their flames sputter in the rising wind. For the moment, the rain has stopped, but the dark clouds move sluggishly across the sky, promising more showers. The fire burns bright as the worshipers form a circle around the candles.

Two men and one woman find seats on the wet grass outside the circle, pulling tall cylindrical drums between their legs. Their brown fingered hands rest on the once white skin. My great grandmother steps into the circle's center. She raises her hands to the sky. Lightening flashes in the distance.

"Brothers and sisters," she says, her eyes closed, "one of our lambs has return to the flock."

One loud beat of the drum fills the silence, vibrating through me like an electrical shock.

"Help me gather the spirits to welcome her."

Two beats of the drum. The hair on my neck quivers.

I'm pushed into the center of the circle. Everyone else joins hands. Their eyes are closed. As one, they start to sway to some unheard music.

My great-grandmother places both her small, twisted fingers on my shoulders. "Oh, Loa, spirit of our ancestors, thank you for bringing this child back to her people. Come into her heart and show her the way. Let her see the love we feel for her."

She fumbles, then pulls a knife from the pocket of her skirt. Before I can protest, she hacks off one of my bronze curls, holding it high for everyone to see.

"A symbol of our future," she said.

Huh?

The drums are beating faster now, their rhythm taken up by the worshipers who move their feet in a jerky movement, shoulders swaying.

My great-grandmother walks to the bonfire and tosses my hair into the blaze, then she pulls something from the other pocket of her skirt and tosses it into the fire. Like magic, the flames shoot higher into the sky their color tinge with blue.

Now this is like something out of the movies.

My grandmother is behind me, pushing me further into the circle to my great-grandmother. I'm sandwich between them. They each touch a shoulder. The two women hold me tight in their grip. My great grandmother's eyes are locked with mine. I want to look away, but I can't.

A silly thought flies through my mind. I bet Ashley Crandall would be freaked out. I am.

My stomach cramps. I want to go home. This is too…too out there. As I continue to stare into my great grandmother's eyes, the thought vanishes. I feel woozy. The faces of the people in the circle move in and out of focus.

Whoa.

The drum beat is louder, pulsing through my blood like-like fire. My body tingles. Strange, but I want to dance, even though I don't know how to dance. I have no rhythm. But my feet don't know that, because they move in time to the drum beat.

Someone starts to clap. More hands join in. I close my eyes and let the beat seep into my organs, my skin, my brain and finally my soul. My shoulders twitch. The motion becomes larger and I sway to the drum beat. A low wail fills the air. Startled, I realize it's coming from me. I can't stop it. Detached from my body, I stand in the crowd and watch this person who's me dance. I close my eyes again and this time I see flashes of another time.

A brown-skinned woman dances for a man seated on the ground. The river is behind them. I remember those faces. They're my mother and father. My mother is making love to him with her dancing. She sways toward him, and he toward her. And then a small sandy-haired toddler lumbers into the scene. I know instinctively it's me. My mother sweeps me up into her arms and continues the dance with me pressed to her chest.

The teenage me feels tears slide down my face and tastes their salt. I'm no longer dancing. The overwhelming love that flows between mother, baby and father is too much. Sobs well up in my chest and burst from my lips in loud gasps.

I don't want to leave my parents. I miss them so. Reluctantly, I open my eyes.

My grandmother's arms encircle me. "Don't cry my little one."

This is the first time she's spoken and her voice jars a memory loose. *Ask her about the prophecy.*

I can only stare at her in surprise. "It was you."

A slight smile flickers across her face. "Come," she says. "It is time. We must talk."

Until this moment, I've forgotten why I came. "I need to know-"

"We will answer all your questions."

Up ahead, hobbling from side to side on swollen knees, my great-grandmother moves toward the house.

Once inside the front door, she turns left down a dimly lit hall and then right into a small bedroom. I follow with my grandmother trailing behind me. The air in the room is humid and cloyed with the odors of stale perfume and dried flowers.

My great-grandmother sinks onto the side of the bed. The mattress springs sigh under her weight. My grandmother goes to her, lifts her thin legs and places them gently on the duvet. My great-grandmother pats a spot on the bed for me. I sit. She takes both my hands in hers.

"You must be strong, daughter of Sherrilyn. Stronger than you've ever been before." Her black eyes bore into my mine. "Something is coming that will test your strength."

Ghostly fingers trail a path down my skin, and my pulse pounds hard and sluggish through my body.

My great-grandmother looks over my head to her daughter. I feel the bed dip as my grandmother sits down behind me.

She places her hands on my shoulders. "Lisette, daughter of my daughter, you are the promised bride of a powerful demon, one of the Overlords of hell."

At first the words are foreign and incomprehensible, then images of my nightmare flash through my brain like fire crackers on a hot July night.

"-but you can defeat him. You will one day be the greatest priestess of all time, but you must trust your instincts and not be afraid when the Voodoo spirits call."

I want to face her, but her hands are strong and my body feels as though it's encased in ice. If I turn and see the truth in her eyes, I might splinter into tiny pieces.

My great-grandmother opens the drawer of her nightstand and pulls out two grey lumpy pouches. "Gris gris." She puts them in the palm of my hand and curves my nerveless fingers around them.

"Keep them close. You'll need them."

Are they crazy?

I jump to my feet, laughing because the tension is too much. "You guys..." I look between the two, waiting for their smiles. Their faces remain blank and solemn, although, I do detect compassion in my grandmother's brown eyes.

Neither woman says a word. My stomach by this time is twisting and churning. "You guys are nuts." I pivot and stare at my great-grandmother. "Nuts. There's no such thing as spirits or demons or-or spells."

But what about the cemetery and the love charm? A voice in my head whispers. I can't breathe. The air in the room, already heavy, has become suffocating. I turn ready to bolt.

"Lisette, what did you come here to ask?"

The voice belongs to my great-grandmother. I stop. I cannot possibly tell her about the upheaval in the cemetery. I can't admit they are right and something supernatural has already occurred.

The last thing I hear as I dash toward the front door and escape is my grandmother's voice.

"You can't outrun your destiny."

Chapter 7

Henri is waiting for me at the boat. One of the men of the congregation lowers me into the pirogue.

The blackness of the night is now tinged with grey. Dawn approaches. Silent, Henri pushes the boat away from the dock. I don't look back, but instead stare at the ripples in the water made by the rain.

We float into the murkiness of the bayou with my grandmother's words ringing in my ears. *"You can't outrun your destiny."* What is my destiny, to be the bride of a demon, or to be the greatest Voodoo priestess of all time? Both of them suck.

Henri drapes a jacket over my shoulders.

"Thank you." I pull the edges of the material together, but it doesn't stop me from trembling.

He nods, but doesn't say a word. Muscles bulging, he pushes the pole through the murky water. His t-shirt is quickly drenched.

"Your mother did she…did she say anything about me? You know, before today." *Like about me and demons?*

"Yes."

Surprised, I hold my breath. He doesn't look at me, but studies the swollen bayou. When he doesn't answer right away, I let the air out of my lungs slowly.

"What did she say?" I raise my voice to be heard over the steady pounding of the rain on the water.

"That you will be our next priestess upon her death."

I strain to catch his words and then jerk in surprise when I do. *What? Is he whacked?* "I'm not a priestess. I'm Catholic. I don't know anything about Voodoo."

"My mother knows things the ordinary person cannot see."

He maneuvers around an inner tube in the boat's path. "Voodoo and Catholicism they are very similar. In Haiti in the old days, the people practiced both-Catholicism to please the Master and Voodoo to appease the spirits from the old country. So you see, you know more than you think you know about Voodoo."

"Well, she's still wrong."

His face never changes. "We shall see."

The trip back to New Orleans seems to take forever. I don't want to talk anymore about Voodoo or becoming a priestess. It was a mistake to come. It serves me right if *Grand'mere* finds out I've snuck out. But I can't stop the ramblings of two old women from running through my mind. Too bad I can't wipe my memory clean.

After we leave the bayou, my uncle walks me home. We get within three houses of my front door, when he stops. His hand flies out, gripping my arm like a vise. "Wait." He lifts his head, nostrils flaring, and scents the night like a black panther. His eyes dart from house to house.

"What?"

"There is something dark and evil here."

Yes, me. I'm the evil one.

My stomach, already in turmoil from the ceremony and the prophecy, roils. I didn't find out how to undo the charm. I didn't even think about it while I was there. How can I be worthy of God's forgiveness if I don't make an attempt to undo the wrong I've done?

Sighing, I touch his arm. "It's okay. I need to get into the house before *Grand'mere* wakes."

Henri reluctantly releases my arm. "Be careful, little one."

"Go." I wave him away. When he disappears around a corner, I hurry toward my bedroom window.

The shadows move. A hand covers my mouth just as I open it to scream.

"Shh." Eric says, pulling me deeper into the darkness. "Who was that man?" He whispers in my ear.

Goosebumps break out over my skin as his warm breath fans my cheek. Snatching his hand from my mouth, I run my tongue over my dry lips. "My uncle. What are you doing here?" I'm surprised I can speak because my pounding heart seems stuck in my throat.

"Watching over you."

I decide to be real. "You don't like me. Why are you here? And at the crack of dawn."

Then it hits me. I'm so stupid. "I will not make another love charm so you can get Michele back. I'm so through with that business."

He doesn't deny it.

"I've got to go." Gripping the window frame to my bedroom, I hoist myself up.

He touches my shoulder.

My arms quiver as I hold myself poised to go over the windowsill. The rain has darkened his hair and it's slicked down over his perfectly shaped head.

"I'm not here because of Michele. It's you I wanted to see."

"Why?"

He shrugs. "I-"

A light goes on in the kitchen. "Crap." *Grand'mere*'s awake. "I've got to go." I tumble over the ledge, catching my foot and hitting my bedroom floor with a thud. Damn. No time for my p.js. I jump into bed fully clothed and pull the sheet up to my chin just as the door opens.

Breathing slowly, I turn, as though in sleep, so she can't see my eyelids twitch. After a long moment, the soft patter of her slippers sounds on my bedroom floor, then the faint screech of the window closing. My body tenses. Is Eric still outside? When she doesn't cry out in alarm, I realize he must be gone. After a minute, my bedroom door closes.

I relax into my mattress and try to sleep, willing myself to only think of what Eric could possibly want from me.

But his sudden interest in me isn't strong enough to chase away the fear of what I've learned in the bayou. Tossing and turning, I dream about my conversation with my mother's family. I wake up tired, cranky and even more determined to distance myself from the word Voodoo.

When I show up at breakfast, I must look as bad as I feel because *Grand'mere* stops dishing up oatmeal and frowns at me.

"Did you sleep okay, *pi petite*?"

"Yeah."

She raises an eyebrow.

I sit up straighter. "Yes, ma'am."

"Better." She adds another heaping spoonful to an already full bowl.

She knows I hate the stuff.

"I have made an appointment for you to see Father McCarran this afternoon."

My stomach plunges like the steep dive of the Scream Machine. I open my mouth to protest. She shuts me up with one of her 'don't mess with me' looks.

**

"Your grandmother is worried about you," Father McCarran says later than day. He's been at Our Lady of Guadalupe since before I was born.

I squirm in my seat. "I'm fine. She worries about everything."

Removing his purple vestment, he hangs it on a coat rack and pours a glass of water from a pitcher. He drinks long and hard, his large Adam's apple bobbing up and down with each swallow.

With a sigh, he places the glass back on the tray, then turns his full attention on me. "She loves you, Lisette. You're all she has left of Edouard. She wants you to be happy."

Yeah, right. If she loved me so much, why did she keep me away from my other family? In the next instant, I remember that they'll nuts, and I send out a silent prayer of thanks for *Grand'mere*.

"How's Haverford coming along?"

"Fine," I mumble. *I hate it. I hate it. I hate it.*

He smiles. "Good. I knew you would be the best candidate for the school."

I sit up in surprise. I thought it had been *Grand'mere*'s idea to pull me out of Easton and send me across the river. "You recommended me?"

He sits at his desk and immediately starts rearranging pens and pencils on his uncluttered desk. His fingers are long and thin like his body.

"Actually, a parishioner contacted me. He said Haverford was looking for a deserving student, one who was bright, but who might not have the financial means to attend their school. I immediately thought of you."

So Father Patrick is to blame for making my life miserable. He beams at me across the desk, so pleased he's done something wonderful for me. I don't have the heart to tell him I despise the school. I smile and clench my molars so hard I'll have muscle spasms later.

"So glad things are working out. When this person told me Haverford was interested in a young lady to even out the school numbers, I knew you were the one."

The girls at Haverford outnumber the boys three to one. So why would they want another female student?

"Everything else is going well?"

Other than releasing demons and finding out I have crazy relatives who think I'm destined to be a Voodoo priestess, everything is going fine. Of course, I don't say all that to him.

But maybe I should. Just because one priest thought I was crazy doesn't mean this one will. Father Patrick has known me all my life. Wouldn't he take me a little more seriously? "Father McCarran--"

A knock sounds at his office door.

Father Patrick's gaze shifts from my face to over my head. "Come in."

The door creaks open and his secretary's voice says, "Your next appointment is here."

"Just a moment." He looks pointedly at me. "Lisette, you wanted to say something?"

But I've lost my nerve. I shake my head and stand. "Thank you, Father, for what you've done for me."

He smiles and rises from behind his desk, unaware of the real meaning behind my words. "If you have any concerns, my door is always open."

"Thank you," I mumble, kicking myself because I'm too chicken to ask about the Voodoo thing.

As Father Patrick ushers me into the hall, a slender man turns from his study of a painting of Christ that hangs on the wall next to an indoor fountain.

Father Patrick greets him warmly, extending his hand to shake.

When their hands meet something strange happens. Sound is sucked out of the universe. Mrs. Montgomery, who's on the way back to her office, pauses in mid-stride.

The water in the fountain slows until each drop is delivered one plop at a time. Each plunk sounds like a cannon exploding.

Father Patrick's face is plastered with a smile more grimace than pleasure. The stranger removes his hand from the priest's and turns his gaze on me. White-haired, the stranger's face is young, except his eyes. They're old, black as rosary beads and twice as hard.

He moves toward me unaffected by whatever has stopped the secretary and Father. We seem to be the only two people in the world.

Time hangs motionless as the stranger studies me. Cold tentacles of fear snake out from my stomach to wrap around my limbs, leaving me paralyzed and stripped bare. I know what *Grand'mere* meant when she said she felt like someone was walking on her grave.

"So you are the priestess." His breath is ice cold and stings my cheek. His gaze travels over me, inspecting, weighing.

"When the time is right I will come for you." He snaps his fingers and Father Patrick drops his hand, and shakes his head in confusion.

At first I'm too stunned to move, then I turn on my heel and dash out of the Rectory. Father Patrick calls my name. I don't stop until I'm out the door.

For once, the pelting drops of rain feel like a blessing. I turn my face up to the dark sky, letting the rain downpour wash away a bone chilling fear.

**

As Eric stood at his bedroom window overlooking the courtyard, Hancock appeared from the street. He opened the wrought-iron gate, took off his shoes and walked barefoot over the wet stones toward the house. A minute later, he appeared at Eric's door.

"I assume this little incident in the Quarter is Saarel's way of making sure the job gets done with or without you?"

Eric turned. Hancock's pants were wet and his feet had made damp impressions on the wooden floor. "Looks that way."

"Remember why you're here. Himself would not approve of your taking so long. Your assignment-"

Keeping his words low and even, Eric said, "I know my assignment. But I'm going to enjoy this time out of that fetid smelling purgatory as long as I can. I'd advise you to do the same. We'll be back there soon enough."

He swung back to stare out the rain streaked window. He wouldn't let Hancock dictate to him how he was to do his job, and he would never tell Saarel's minion that he had no intentions of going back.

Hancock's fading steps were soon lost in the mammoth house.

Eric stared out over the rooftops of New Orleans- an old city, but one in its infancy compared to the region of his birth. A region he'd never see again unless he completed the task Saarel had set before him.

Lisette Beaulieu.

He'd blown his chance to make her comfortable with him. Would one of Saarel's beasts snatch her right from under his nose? He couldn't lose his one and only chance to get out from under the Overlord's control. He'd have to make another plan. One that would make Lisette trust him.

Chapter 8

"Jamal Gardner," the court bailiff calls.

Scooter's mom lets out a soft moan as Boogie, dressed in prison orange with his hands cuffed behind him, enters the courtroom. As he makes his way to stand in front of the judge, his ankle chains rattle.

I peek at Scooter. Unlike me, he's got his game face on, not showing the world a thing. Everything that's happened to me in the last few days, right down to that scary guy in the Rectory yesterday, is probably plastered on my face. I called Scooter to tell him about the guy. Before I could say a word, he asked me to come to court with him today, then hung up on me. The hanging up part ticked me off enough that I almost didn't come. But here I am, sandwiched between his skinny butt and Mrs. Gardner's humongous one.

A blue suited young man who doesn't appear to be much older than Boogie's nineteen years comes to stand next to him.

"I'm Lawrence Seaford, your honor, from the public defender's office. I would like to request a delay."

Judge Harold Cranks, a heavyset man sitting at his bench high above the courtroom, raises an eyebrow.

The young lawyer rushes on. "I've just been appointed and haven't had a chance to speak with my client." He glances up at Jamal, who's about six inches taller.

I poke Scooter in the ribs. "What about the big name lawyer?" I whisper.

"Too much money," Scooter says out of the side of his mouth.

"You understand, counselor, that this is Mr. Gardner's third offense," the judge says, glaring down at Boogie and his lawyer.

Seaford cuts Boogie a sideways glance, then clears his throat. "I wasn't aware of that, sir."

The judge grunts and places papers back in a folder. "Make sure you're well prepared when you show up in two days." He signals the Bailiff. "Escort Mr. Gardner back to the holding cell."

As the bailiff leads him out of the courtroom, Boogie searches the crowded room. His gaze locks on his mother's face, then on Scooter's.

Mrs. Gardner groans again and collapses on me. Feeling like a crushed ant, I look frantically at Scooter. His mouth is set in a tight line as he watches his brother disappear behind one of the side doors of the courtroom. He's also twitching. Not a good sign.

"Let's go, Mama." He moves to his mother's side, helping her to her feet. It's not an easy task, since Mrs. Gardner outweighs Scooter by a good hundred pounds.

"Oh, Marik, what are we going to do?" She leans heavily on him. I have to admire Scooter, because he shoulders her weight without stumbling.

His eyes are bright and hard. "I'll figure out something. Don't worry. I got this."

Short of robbing a bank, how is Scoot going to get the money?

When we get Mrs. G. outside, she collapses on a bench in the corridor, her noisy sobs attracting attention.

Scooter pats her awkwardly on the shoulder.

Not knowing what to say, I look away. The corridor is filled with a quiet despair, everyone waiting for their loved one's fates to be decided.

The space between my shoulder blades tinges. Turning slowly, I scan the room. My stomach takes a nosedive. Leaning against the opposite wall, the man from the Rectory watches us. I whirl around and pretend I don't see him. *What is he doing here?* I want to tell Scooter, but he's locked in a fear all his own-his brother going to prison. When I get up enough courage to look in the man's direction again, he's gone. My pulse slows to a gallop.

"We have to do something, Marik," Mrs. Gardner is saying.

"I know, Mama," Scooter whispers. "Help me get her up, Lis."

I glance around the hall one more time before gripping his mother's arm. With both of us supporting her, we lift her to her feet.

The short walk to the street seems to take forever. I open an umbrella and shelter her while he whistles down a taxi.

From the corner of my eye, I see the white-haired man step out of the courthouse and move toward Scooter.

"Scooter!"

Mrs. G. flinches.

Scooter looks in my direction, a quizzical expression on his face. What should I say? Run, because this guy is evil?

But the words stay frozen in my throat. My heart slams against my ribcage as the man stops in front of Scooter. They exchange words.

Seeing a cab pull to the curb, Mrs. Gardner, just by her sheer weight, drags me toward it. Unable to stop her progress, I twist my head to stare over my shoulder. The man hands Scooter a piece of paper, then watches as he walks away.

Scooter gets into the cab on the driver's side. As soon as he shuts the door, I ask, "What did he want?" My voice sounds loud and shrill in the small space.

"Says he can help Boogie."

A small ice ball forms in the pitch of my stomach. "May I see the card?"

He passes it over. There's no name, no address just a phone number in bold print. As I inspect the card, it grows warm.

I lean forward to see around Mrs. G's bulk. "What's his name?"

Scooter shrugs. "He didn't give it, and I didn't ask."

The edges of the card brown and curl.

"Don't call him, Scooter."

He draws back in surprise. "Why not?"

The card is now scorching my fingers. Remembering how this mystery man made time stand still in the church rectory, I'm almost not surprised to see smoke spiraling up from the center of the small piece of paper. I roll down the window and pitch it out into the rain. The card burst into flame just before it lands in the gutter.

Mrs. G. comes back to earth from where ever she's been and starts to shriek in high volume. She reaches over me and attempts to open my door. But it's too late. The card is nothing but ash.

"What's wrong with you, Lis?" Even as he asks, Scooter's climbing out of the cab.

"Where are you going?" I shout after him.

"He'd better be gettin' another card." Mrs. G. glares at me as she folds her arms across her massive chest.

Sure enough, when Scooter gets back in the cab, he has a card grasp between his thin fingers.

"Don't call him, Scoot," I plead, heartsick with a dread. If only I'd told him about my meeting with this man.

Nostrils flaring, Mrs. G. turns on me with a maliciousness I didn't know she felt. "You, missy, need to mind your own business. You and your bourgie *Grand'mere*-" She sneers when she says the word *Grand'mere*.

"Mama." Always respectful towards his mother, his sharp tone cuts off whatever nasty words she's about to spout.

She takes a deep breath and addresses the back of the taxi driver's head instead of looking at me. "He needs to get his brother out of that place."

Placing a brown pudgy finger on the card, she says to Scooter, "Call him."

Scooter stares out the rain streaked glass. "I will."

Leaning back against the cab's vinyl seats, I tell myself not to say another word.

"Where to, folks?"

We've completely forgotten the cab driver. Scooter gives his home address.

The white-haired man is still at the curb, watching as our cab pulls into traffic.

Please, God, make this be okay for Scooter and Boogie. I hope I'm wrong about this man.

I hope God's still listening to me.

Chapter 9

The next day at lunch, I avoid the cafeteria and go to my hiding place in the library.

Within two minutes someone takes the seat next to mine. Turning, I lock eyes with Eric.

Heat rises from my neck to my cheeks and my tongue seems to swell.

He leans in so close I can smell peppermint on his breath. "Would you like to hang out this afternoon?"

If he'd asked me to strip naked in the library, I wouldn't have been more surprised. He wants to hang out with me? I resist the urge to wipe my sweaty palms on my jeans.

Then my suspicious nature kicks in.

There's Annabel with her chestnut curls. She'd love to be Eric's new best friend. Then there's Jessica...

Why all of a sudden does he want to be my friend? I'm not tall and thin. I'm five two, short compared to these girls. My looks... well let's just say, I'm a mongrel: part Haitian, Choctaw Indian, French and Spanish. And I'm very proud of that, but the Eric's of the world usually like the Norwegian variety.

"Ahh..." Before I can say no, he interrupts.

"We're just going to study. I could use your help with English Lit, and I'll help you with Calculus."

Flushing, I drop my head. Does everyone know I'm flunking calculus? Scooter says the day they passed out the math gene, I ditched. The temptation is strong. I want to be a doctor and you can't get into medical school without being good in Calculus.

I won't admit this to *Grand'mere*, but I want to have friends, I want to belong. And here is this hot guy asking me to do something with him, even after I made his girlfriend fall in love with someone else.

Stupid, he's not asking you to be his girl, just to study. All the pain and loneliness of the past twelve years gushes out of my mouth. "Okay."

He smiles. "I'll meet you after school at the main entrance."

I can only nod. *Please God, don't let me say something retarded when we're together. And don't let me forget this is just a study session, nothing more.*

**

The bus's windows are fogged from the rain outside and the breath of forty odd people inside. When we reach my stop, I move into the aisle, swing my backpack over my shoulder and plod toward the rear door. It opens silently. I step out into the downpour and into ankle deep water. Cursing under my breath, I hop up on the curb, now in a hurry to get home and change into dry shoes.

"I thought we were meeting after school."

I yelp, and stagger backwards, my heart in my throat.

Leaning against a bright red sports car, Eric is deceptively casual, but the lines of his body are tense. He seems to be oblivious to the rain. His brown chinos and white shirt are drenched. He looks out of place in this neighborhood of baggy jeans and oversize t-shirts. Too preppy.

My mouth opens and closes like a fish snagged on a hook. I swallow. "I looked-"

He tilts his head. "Yes?"

"I thought-" *I was afraid you wouldn't be waiting outside school for me.*

He pushes away from the car and strolls around to the passenger side where he opens the door. With a wave of his hand, he invites me in.

Hesitating, I glance down the street. I'm only a half a block from home. Maybe *Grand'mere* needs me. I look back at Eric. The word 'no' hangs on my lips. Why am I so afraid of being with this guy? *Maybe because he's different. But I'm different. Take a chance.*

I slip into the leather seat of his car. Before I finish buckling my seat belt, Eric is peeling away from the curb.

He careens around a slow-moving city bus into oncoming traffic, then whips back into his lane. Horns blare.

I hug the passenger door handle.

"You're not scared, are you?" Eric glances over at me.

I shake my head, but watch the speedometer climb.

He steals another look at me, noting the death grip I have on the door. "Sorry." The car immediately decelerates. "I love the speed of these things. It beats the hell out of--out of anything else I have driven."

But it's not just the speed that bothers me. Something hangs on the periphery of my consciousness, something dark and frightening. Something set off by the rain, the speed and the smell of new leather.

The windshield wipers continue their hypnotic swipes across the glass, lulling me into a semi-conscious state. I hear Eric's voice talking about the car, but mentally I'm somewhere else.

It's raining. A woman turns from the front passenger seat and smiles at me. But the smile is not in her dark eyes. Her smile usually makes me happy, but today it makes me want to cry. I'm afraid because she's afraid.

"Lisette." Her voice is soft, but husky.

"Lisette." This time it's Eric's voice.

I open my eyes and straighten in my seat.

"You were asleep," he says.

Blinking, I stare around the car in confusion. These seats are cream-colored not black. The seats in my father's car were black. I remember that now. Strange. And that was my mother's voice. I must've been dreaming.

Eric's car is parked in front of a black iron gate. Through the misted windshield, a huge house looms. It's beyond old. God, he must be really rich.

"Maybe I should just go home."

He frowns.

"I mean--your parents..."

"They're in Europe."

"You're home alone?" As soon as the words are out, I want to kick myself. I sound like a baby. He's obviously much more mature and sophisticated than me. He doesn't need his Maman and Papa like I need mine. The sound of my mother's voice still echoes in my head.

His mouth twists into something that's a cross between a smile and a grimace. "I've been alone for a long time."

I'm just about to ask him what he means, when my attention is captured by the gate opening. He drives the car up a brick paved path that ends in front of two large wooden doors.

When the car stops, I step out into the rain. He ushers me through the wooden doors into a lush garden brightly lit by security lamps. The courtyard centers around a fountain with a cherub pouring water into a basin, its original color lost to the green patina of age. Around the perimeter of the garden, bushes follow the line of a tall wooden fence. A huge magnolia tree probably shades the courtyard on a sunny day. But today, the wind and rain force us to jog toward French doors on the opposite side of the courtyard.

Eric closes the doors behind me as we step into a brightly lit room with a roaring fire going in the fireplace. I'm dripping water onto the hardwood floor. Grimacing, I say, "Sorry."

For the first time, he smiles. He has a beautiful smile, with a dimple at the corner of his mouth. "Don't worry about it."

"Would you and the young lady like a towel?"

Ice water fills my veins. The same iciness I felt in the Rectory. I turn slowly in the direction of the voice.

The white-haired man stands in the door with towels draped over his arm.

I try to swallow, but can't. I try to speak, but can't. *What's he doing here?* I try to ask the question out loud, but the words stay locked in my throat.

Without speaking, the man hands me a thick towel and gives another to Eric.

"This is Hancock, my-our butler," Eric says to me, oblivious to my horror. "Hancock, Lisette."

His butler? No Way?

Hancock bows his head, a mocking smile hovering around his thin lips. His dead eyes hold mine for a long beat, a beat that I hear loud and deafening in my head.

I clumsily dry my face and hair. Ignoring the butler's outstretched hand, I give the towel to Eric. I can't look at-let alone touch-this man I now know as Hancock.

"Can you bring us something to drink? We'll be in the media room," Eric says, turning and heading for the door.

"Huh, Eric..." I'm not staying in this house.

"Right away, young master."

Eric halts in midstride and faces the butler. "I've asked you not to call me that."

Hancock's eyes are like black diamonds, hard and cold. The look he gives Eric is very unemployee-like. The hard knot in my stomach tightens even more.

"Come, Lisette." Eric turns and reaches for my hand, pulling me into the black marbled foyer.

"I want to go home."

"Why?"

"Because..." I look back at the room we just left. Eric follows the direction of my gaze.

"Everything is fine. Sometimes Hancock thinks he's my father." Eric takes the curving staircase two steps at a time, dragging me along with him.

It's not his relationship with his butler that concerns me. It's my fear of the man. He's the Satan's spawn. Evil oozes out of him like black slime. I pull my hand from Eric's and stare down at the shiny foyer. Hancock watches our progress. That's enough to send me scurrying to catch up.

As I trail Eric, my eyes take in everything. Green plants are everywhere. "What's with all the vegetation?"

"They keep the air fresh."

The air fresh? He's strange. I don't know a single guy who thinks about the environment. I was in Scooter's room once. Once was enough. It smelled like dirty socks and sweat. His idea of clean air was spraying Lysol to cover up the odor.

Like the rest of the house, the media room is over the top. First, it's huge. My entire house could almost fit into this space. Against one paneled wall are four different brands of laptops arranged on a massive wooden desk. Their screen savers flash bright geometric patterns in tandem.

A flat screen television is mounted over the fireplace. I itch to take a look at the DVDs aligned like books in a built-in glass case, but I don't give in to the urge.

I jump when Lil Wayne's "A Milli" booms from skinny high-tech speakers tucked in each corner of the room. The bass pounds in my chest like a kettle drum.

I'm glad I didn't invite him to my house. I shift my backpack off my shoulder. "I thought we were going to study?" I shout over the music.

Eric picks up the remote, clicks a button, and the room falls depressingly silent.

He gestures to a round game table in the center of the room.

Placing my pack down on the leather table, I pull out the English Lit book.

Feeling his gaze on me, a flush spreads over my face. *Stop it. Yes, he's cute, but remember last week he was with Michele. He's not interested in you.* I wish he did feel that way, but I'm smart enough to know something else is going on here. I just can't figure out what it is. Trying to understand his motives, hearing my mother's voice and now finding the white-haired man here in this house has scared the crap out of me. "What is it with you? You're always staring."

"Sorry."

He looks away, but not before I see a flash of curiosity in his eyes.

"Why did you invite me to study? I know you have better things to do than hang with me. I'm sure there are gazillion girls willing to take Michele's place."

There it is. It's out there. Now, he'll tell me how he really feels about what I've done. Do I tell him I'm planning to undo the love charm? That he'll be back with Michele soon? No, not yet.

"I don't want anyone taking Michele's place."

His face is full of shadows, and a little bit of sadness. Is he down because he's lost Michele? "Look, I'm sorry about the charm. I didn't know..."

"That you had the ability to raise the dead?"

I jerk in surprise. It's the first time he's mentioned what happened at the cemetery. His eyes hold mine, unflinching. They're dark eyes full of their own secrets. A realization comes to me. He doesn't think I'm a freak, because there's something freaky about him. Wonder what it is?

"I don't know—how-" I shudder as I remember. "I don't know how I did it."

"Are you sure?" His voice is low, husky, his face intense.

"Hmm." Hancock stands in the open doorway, a tray of drinks in his hands.

A muscle bunches in Eric's jaw, then relaxes. He motions the butler into the room.

As Hancock places the drinks on the table, I stare blindly down at my unopened textbook.

"How long has he worked for your family?" I ask after Hancock leaves.

"A long time," Eric says.

"Is he religious?" I casually open the English lit book.

"What?"

Glancing up, I meet his puzzled gaze. "You know, does he go to church?"

Eric's laugh is a harsh, rusty sound. "As far as I know, Hancock has never set foot in a church. He'd probably turn to stone if he did."

If he only knew.

"Why all the questions?"

I move the ice cubes around in my drink with a straw, then glance up at him through my lashes. "Just curious."

With one eyebrow arched, he waits. He's not buying my disinterest.

"Okay! He gives me the creeps."

Eric's face hardens.

Thinking I've offended him, I wait for him to shout at me or tell me to leave.

"He gives me the creeps, too."

My mouth drops. "Then why keep him around?"

Eric shrugs. "I didn't hire him. Therefore, I can't fire him."

"Tell your parents that you don't like him."

He seems to weigh that option. "My opinion doesn't matter to my father."

Grand'mere has always cared about what I thought. She might not let me have what I want, but she always listens. I feel a moment of sympathy for him, until I remember this expensive house he lives in and the fancy car.

Flipping through pages of the text book, I stop at the section I want. "We should be finishing up Dante's Inferno soon. It seems like we've been discussing it forever."

His face goes still.

"Have you read it?"

Shifting in his seat, he says, "I don't have to. I'm living it."

Yeah, me too. But I don't ask him what he means, because if I do, he might ask me to personal stuff. And I don't want to discuss me-now or ever.

So I avoid his gaze. I look down at the book. A man trudges through a mass of bodies. The bodies appear to move. I close my eyes. When I open them again, all is as it should be. The picture is just a picture.

Shaken, I glance up to see if Eric noticed, but he's staring out the window at the rain. It gives me a chance to study him. He's gorgeous, dark hair, dark eyes, full lips. He turns. I look away.

What does a beautiful boy who has everything know about Hell? Of course, I don't say that out loud. I don't have the nerve. "Well, according to Dante-"

Eric reaches across the desk and slams the book shut, making me jump.

"I don't want to talk about Dante." Lips pinched, his dark eyes are clouded. "Or Hell. Let's do Calculus."

When I don't pull out my book, he jumps up. "I've got a better idea. Let's get out of here."

He doesn't have to ask me twice. I cram my English Lit book back into my pack and hurry to catch up with him. He's half way out the door.

Out in the courtyard, we make a dash for the car. Before climbing in, I glance back at the house. Hancock watches us from one of the upstairs windows.

**

Eric maneuvered the car through the dark streets of New Orleans. The Mardi Gras revelers were left far behind. The dark forlorn streets of this port city reeked of the despair of lost souls. He and Lisette were two of those souls. As he turned a corner, he glanced over at her. She pretended to be asleep, but he wasn't fooled. She sat too straight in her seat, her breathing too fast. He shouldn't have brought her to the house. Hancock frightened her. The bastard frightened him at times. But thinking of the butler brought Eric back on task.

"Tell me about yourself." He knew most of the answers, but if she was comfortable he might learn something he didn't already know. Something he could use.

At first he thought she wasn't going to answer, then she shifted in her seat. The subtle scent of strawberries filled the air.

"I live with my *Grand'mere*."

He felt her gaze.

"That's French for grandmother."

He suppressed a smile. She went silent, so he prompted, "Your parents?"

"Dead." A wealth of emotion leaked around and through the single word. She was definitely a lost soul.

"How?" This he didn't know.

"A car crash. My father was speeding. Rain."

Rain streaked the windshield. Eric eased off the accelerator and shifted from fourth to third. The engine growled a protest, but adjusted quickly, purring as it glided down the deserted street. She leaned back against the head rest. Her golden hair contrasted sharply against the black leather.

Silence again. Just the rain and the wind as the wheels of the car sliced through the water. Instead of taking a left at the traffic signal, a turn that would take them directly to her house, he turned right. She didn't seem to notice, or at least didn't comment.

"Your parents...?" he prompted.

"They were so different." She hesitated. "At least *Grand'mere* thought they were different."

"Different how?"

"I'm not really sure." She glanced at him. He took his gaze off the road and gave her what he hoped passed for a reassuring smile. "Grand'mere always talks about her family. How they've been in New Orleans for hundreds of years. The founding fathers almost. But I don't—didn't know a lot about my mother's family. Just that they were from Haiti."

"Do they still live in Haiti?"

Again that hesitation. Maybe she didn't trust him. But why should she? If she knew why he was here, she'd run from him.

"No. They live here," she almost whispered the words.

He thought back to the other night when he'd waited for her outside her house. He'd followed her to a boat ramp and watched her get into a canoe. "Who was that man you were with the other night?"

She shifted in her seat to face him. "The night you were outside my bedroom window?"

"Yes. That night."

Her hands traced invisible patterns on her damp jeans. "My uncle."

He'd seen her grandmother from a distance. Light skinned with curly gray hair. This man had been dark. "Your mother's brother?"

She nodded.

"Where did you go? It was late." He added the last sentence to make it seem more natural that he'd asked.

"To visit my mother's family." There was something in her voice. Pain? Fear? He wasn't sure.

Eric took his gaze off the road. "Not a good visit?"

She shook her head. "I don't want to talk about it."

She'd learned something on that trip into the bayou. Something she didn't like, maybe something that had frightened her.

"Ok." But it was far from okay. He needed answers.

She'd met the uncle around 11pm and returned just before dawn. She'd slipped back into her house through her bedroom window, which told him, her grandmother didn't know she'd gone to meet her mother's people. Why would she go to them in secret? And what about them or the visit frightened her?

They rode in silent for a few minutes.

"What keeps your parents out of the country?"

His brain froze. When he'd started this little game looking for answers, he never thought she'd ask about his family.

"Ah… My father is a diplomat."

Her gaze felt warm on his face, but he didn't dare look at her. She'd see the lie in his eyes. But part of that answer was true. His father had traveled from village to village trying to maintain peace among the warring tribes.

"Don't you get lonely living in that house alone?"

"I'm not alone. Hancock is there." That was laughable. Hancock was the gatekeeper not a friend.

Something in her stillness made him take his attention off the road to glance over at her. She stared out the window at the darkness beyond. "Lisette?"

She didn't respond.

"Lisette?"

She jerked and swiveled in the seat to face him. "Yes?"

"What's wrong?"

"Nothing."

He didn't ask any more questions. To do so would require he answer some of hers- something he wasn't ready to do. Maybe later when his assignment was over. If they both lived.

Chapter 10

"Who was that?" Scooter squints between the slats of the blinds, trying to see out to the street as I walk in my front door.

"A friend." Thank God, the streetlight is out so he couldn't see Eric's face. I'm not ready to talk about my new friendship with him just yet.

He grunts in disbelief.

The smells of sizzling onions and peppers pull me toward the kitchen-toward my *Grand'mere*.

"What are you doing here?" I ask him.

"Your grandmother invited me to dinner."

"Right. More like you invited yourself."

"Same difference," he says.

I sense rather than see him shrug.

Face flush from the heat of the stove *Grand'mere* stirs a skillet, while rice boils in another pot. Her gold eyes meet mine, and she smiles. Wrapping my arms around her neck, I hug her tightly. For the moment, her love chases away the fear and uncertainty I felt in Eric's car. When she pulls back to give me a questioning look, I hide my face in her neck.

Behind me, Scooter says, "Awww, ain't that sweet."

Ignoring him, I pretend to inspect the pots on the stove. Usually, the smell of *Grand'mere*'s cooking makes me hungry, but not tonight. Hearing my mother's voice and seeing Hancock has taken away every bit of appetite I have. Too much has happened to me in a few short days. I'm on overload.

"Some dude brought Lisette home," Scooter says. "Looks to me like she's got a boyfriend."

I round on him. "I don't."

"Do too." He sits at the kitchen table, egging me on with a grin. "And he's got a nice set of wheels."

"Is this true, Lisette?" She stops stirring and pins me with a look.

"No. It isn't," My teeth are clenched so tight it's hard to get the words out. "He—he just gave me a ride home."

"Why didn't you invite him in?" she asks.

No way. "He had to get home."

"Well, the next time ask him to stay for dinner. There's always plenty."

"Yes, ma'am." Somehow I can't see Eric chowing down on dirty rice.

Feeling Scooter's eyes on me and knowing he hasn't fallen for the *friend dropping me* off routine, I try and change the subject. "How's Boogie?"

He loses his easy going smile. "The same."

"Have you talked to his lawyer?" I ask.

Scooter snorts. "I know more law than that dude." He watches *Grand'mere* at the stove, but he has a far off look in his eyes.

"Set the table, Lisette."

"Yes, ma'am." For a minute, the only sound is the clatter of dishes and the rain hitting the tin roof.

When I turn, Scoot is staring at a card gripped tightly between two fingers. My breath hitches in my throat.

He looks up and catches my eye. "I'm calling him tonight."

"Tonight!" My voice comes out in a squeak.

Scooter cocks his head. "Yeah, tonight."

His chair scraping across the kitchen linoleum catches *Grand'mere* by surprise and she stiffens as she places a dish of rice on the table. "Where're you going?"

"I got to go."

"I *have* to go," *Grand'mere* corrects.

When I smirk at Scooter behind *Grand'mere*'s back, he doesn't smile. She's big on diction, correct pronunciation and grammar. He says I sound like a news anchor. But her language lesson doesn't make him smile tonight.

"What about your dinner?" She asks.

"I'm not hungry. Sorry." He stalks out of the kitchen toward the front door. It opens and rain scented air rushes through the house.

My natural response is to follow him, but what do I say? "Don't meet this man. I know who he is and he can't possible help you." Somehow I don't see Scooter listening to me.

"Jamal may not get out of this one," *Grand'mere* says, shaking her head. She takes the seat across from me at the table and starts spooning rice into her plate.

My stomach gives a queer little flip. I'm glad she waited until after Scooter left to make her prediction. He's feeling pretty down as it is, that would send him over the edge.

"Maybe Scooter should talk with Father--"

But I'm pushing away from the table before she can finish her sentence. I can't let Scooter face this man alone. This man is the devil himself or at least his right hand man. He means Scooter harm. I feel it. I've always thought the best of people, but this time... this time all bets are off.

"Where are *you* going?" *Grand'mere*'s lips are compressed into a thin line. She looks pointedly at my plate.

If I tell her I'm not hungry, she'll want to fix something else. "I need to see Scooter. I'll be right back, promise." The last part is said as I escape down the hall to the front door.

"Lisette, you're wasting away to nothing," she shouts after me.

The last week has robbed me of all desire to eat. For one insane moment, I think if I waste away, the prophecy won't come true.

**

"I want to go with you."

Placing the house phone back in its cradle, Scooter turns, frowning at me. "Go with me where?"

"To meet him," I point at the phone as though it's turned into the creepy butler.

Cocking his head to one side, he asks, "Why?"

I can't tell him it's because I'm afraid for him. That's absolutely the wrong thing to say to Scooter. "I just want to know what he's going to say."

"Why? Cause you think I'm not smart enough to do this on my own?"

That shuts me up. For the first time since I've known Scooter, I don't know what to say. *Is that what he really thinks?* "Scoot—"

He turns and walks stiffly down the narrow dark hall that smells of cooked cabbage. Running to catch up with him, I grab his arm, but he shakes me off.

"Scooter, you're the smartest person I know. I just-" *Honesty is the best policy, Grand'mere says.* Okay, in this case almost honesty. "We don't know this guy. He's come out of the blue, offering help. Aren't you the least bit suspicious?"

Scooter stares at me for one awfully long minute. "Can't afford to be. This might be Boogie's only chance."

"I'd feel better if you took me along to watch your back."

His lips twitch, but he has the good sense not to laugh off my offer. "Okay, you can come."

I breathe a sigh of relief. "When are you meeting him?"

"Tomorrow evening at eight."

"Where?"

"The Riverwalk. Outside the Aquarium."

I nod. Good. Someplace open with lots of people around. "I'll be here at seven fifteen."

"Okay." Scooter's fingers beat out a light rhythm on his pants leg.

"Well, I guess I should get back home." I point in the direction of my house. "*Grand'mere* will be waiting to torture me with food."

He doesn't laugh, only nods his head a couple of times. "Yeah, you do that. See you tomorrow."

As I turn to leave, he raises his voice. "Hey, Lisette?"

"Yeah?"

"Don't be late."

"I won't," relieved that he's agreed to let me go.

Darkness comes early in February and the heavy clouds don't help. Standing in front of Scooter's house wind and rain blowing in my face, I smile, glad I can help him.

I step out into the flooded road, then stop. My mind flashes back on the scene with Scooter-his twitching fingers. Heat floods my face and my hands curl into fists. Without looking back, I continue across the street.

He lied to me.

I know when he's sad, happy, faking it or lying. Now he's lying.

Time is running out and he knows it. Boogie has to appear before the judge in less than twenty four hours. Scooter has to get something in place *now*.

The meeting with Hancock is tonight. I feel it in my bones. The location and time are probably right, just the date is wrong.

Why'd he lie to me?

Flipping up the hood of *Grand-mere*'s slicker to conceal my bright hair, I walk around to Mrs. J.'s backyard where I melt into the shadows. Anyone watching from Scooter's house will think I've continued on to my mine.

I settle in and prepare to wait. It's already 7:30, so if I'm right, it won't take long.

A loud bang makes me jump. "Crap." Nappy, crashes through his doggy door into the backyard. Immediately sensing someone in his territory, the three pound burglar alarm starts yapping.

"Shh...Be quiet."

When he hears my voice, his bark turns from menacing-as menacing as a Chihuahua can be-to yaps of excitement. My head jerks toward Mrs. J.'s kitchen window. I'm expecting the lights to flash on. They don't. She must be watching television in her living room with the volume turned up to maximum, as usual.

Nappy pulls on my pants leg, wanting to play. I try to shake him off. "Not now." He continues to bark until I pick him up and rub his head. Body pressed to my raincoat, he lets me stroke him, while I keep one eye trained on Scooter's house.

Sure enough fifteen long sneaker-soaked minutes later, Scooter opens the front door and walks out bold as you please. I want to wring his neck. That sob story about me thinking he wasn't very smart echoes in my head. He played me. He's the one who thinks *I'm* not very smart.

I set Nappy on Ms. J.'s back steps and start out after Scooter.

Okay, Marik Rashad Gardner, we'll see who's smarter.

**

Ten minutes later, I realize he's right. I'm not very bright. Yes, I was right about the meeting place, Scooter is within five minutes of the River Walk. And yes, I've done a great job of mingling with the partiers so he can't spot me. But I won't be able to get close enough to hear what Scooter and Hancock say, and that's the whole purpose of being there.

But luck is with me. As I get closer to the River, fog rolls in, making the area like something in a dream. People move in and out of the patchy mist like actors entering and leaving a stage, their speech distorted by the smog.

Scooter doesn't look around as he makes for one of the areas not too far from the River's edge. Pulling the folds of the slicker around me, I take a seat on a bench next to a sleeping homeless man-at least I think it's a man.

Somewhere out on the River, a tugboat's horn blares, the fog amplifying the sound as though I'm seated on its deck.

Scooter paces back and forth as he waits for Hancock. My guess is that he'll come from my right since that's the direction of Eric's house. I'm right. He steps out of the mist like a ghost and passes within five feet of me. I pull the folds of the slicker's hood down over my head, but his eyes are fixed on Scooter.

I take a deep breath, and when I do, I inhale wine fumes and the smell of urine and sweat from my companion who snores next to me.

Neither man is very tall. Scooter is only about five foot seven or so. I would guess that Hancock is only an inch or two taller, but the butler seems to loom over him. Maybe it's just my fear at work, but I want Scooter to get as far away from Hancock as he can.

The older man seems to be doing all the talking. His voice comes to me through the fog, distorted and sometimes loud. "—lawyer—" There's an intensity to his body as he stands in front of Scooter. "—repay—" The only indication of Scooter's feelings is his twitching fingers. Then Hancock turns and stalks toward me. I lean back against the bench and huddle closer to my stinky companion. The man shifts in his sleep and drops his head on my shoulder, his funky garbage breath blowing in my face. Suppressing the urge to heave, I don't move as Hancock approaches, then passes out of sight.

Scooter is on the move. I jump up. As I do, I hear what sounds like a baseball bat connecting with a ripe melon.

"Hey!"

My bench companion has fallen over. He sits up and rubs his greasy black hair with a grubby paw.

I catch up with Scooter at a stop sign on the periphery of the Quarter. The streets are quieter, the fog thinner. Sounds of a parade can be heard in the distance.

"You lied to me, you rat turd."

He jumps and spins around in a defensive crouch. Scooter would never let anyone sneak up on him, which tells me he was so lost in thought he never heard me.

"Lisette?!" He glances around us like he's expecting an army of a thousand people to be with me. "What—what-"

"What am I doing here?" I place my hands on my non-existent hips. "Because I should be at home waiting for tomorrow so I can go with my best friend to meet a suspicious stranger. Right? But oh no, my best friend snuck off without me."

He flashes a shit-eating grin. "I was only looking out for you."

"Right." I glare at him. "So what did he say?"

Turning, he steps off the curb. I fall in beside him.

"Nothing much. Just that he'll hire a good lawyer for Boogie."

I want to tell Scooter that Hancock can't possibly hire a good lawyer because he works as a butler, and butlers don't make a lot of money. But that would mean I'd have to tell him how I know Hancock. I don't want to share that part of my life with Scooter. He'll think I'm forgetting about my old friends and neighborhood.

"Do you believe him?" I ask.

He shrugs. "I'll know tomorrow."

Chapter 11

At 7:30 the next morning, I pass through a gate and into the Rectory's garden courtyard. I've never come willingly before, but these are not normal times.

I try the door. Locked. Ringing the bell, I wait impatiently for Mrs. Montgomery.

Rain collects in puddles on the cobblestone terrace and seeps into my damp sneakers. I wiggle my toes. This endless rain is getting old.

Shivering, I press the doorbell one more time. As I do, I notice for the first time the Rectory hours posted to the right of the door. Eight to six pm.

I stalk out through the courtyard and slam the gate in frustration. With a loud clatter, it shuts behind me.

For the moment, the rain is lighter, and I can see the other houses on the block. This was a wasted trip. I'm going to be late for school with nothing to show for it. After all, how much can Father Patrick tell me?

"Lisette?"

Father Patrick stands at the gate, one hand resting on the black iron spikes.

My heart gives a panicked hiccup. All of a sudden I've lost my nerve. He's going to think I'm crazy. "Never mind, Father. It wasn't important."

"Come, child. You didn't come all this way so early in the morning for nothing. Come in." He motions with his hand. "Mrs. Montgomery is here, and I'll have her make us some hot chocolate."

After no dinner and no breakfast, hot chocolate sounds good. Maybe his secretary brought donuts. She's addicted to Krispy Kremes.

A few minutes later, seated in his office with the cup warming my hands, I watch him water his plants.

"How is your grandmother?"

He moves to another plant carefully moving the leaves aside to moisten the soil.

"She's fine."

"And school?"

"It's fine." *Liar. Liar.*

He puts the watering can on the window sill and sits at his desk. Pale morning light filters through the glass and reflects off water droplets on an African violet, *Grand'mere's* favorite plant. Lifting his cup, Father

Patrick takes a sip and glances at me over the rim. "So, what's brought you out so early?"

"Scooter—"

He lowers his cup slightly. "Scooter?"

"Marik Gardner."

He nods. "Yes, I was sorry to learn his brother was in jail."

"Do you remember when I came to see you a couple of days ago?"

"Yes." He draws the word out, as though he's reliving our meeting in his mind.

I take another sip of hot chocolate. The drink suddenly tastes like sludge. "Do you remember the man who was outside your office waiting to see you?" *The one who put you in a* trance?

"Mr. Hancock. He's a new parishioner."

Gripping the cup so tightly my knuckles are white, I lean forward. "What do you know about him?"

Father places his cup on his desk and rubs his hands together as he stares over my head, thinking. His watery blued-eyed gaze shifts back to mine. "Not much. I think he's a businessman. Why?"

My thoughts chase each other, trying to find an acceptable answer for the priest. I settle on honesty.

"Nothing. I... Well, he offered to help Boogie-Jamal, and I just want to make sure he's not jerking Scooter's-Marik's-chain. That he can deliver."

Smiling, Father stands. "You're a good friend to be so concerned. Marik has nothing to worry about. I'm sure if Mr. Hancock promised to help, then he'll help." The priest makes his way around his desk and pats my shoulder, then pulls me to my feet. "Come, you'll be late for school."

"What do you know about this man?"

Father Patrick studies the ceiling for a moment then looks down at me. "I'm sure the good Lord wouldn't mind me telling you this. Mr. Hancock informed me Haverford Academy was looking for a needy female student. And I recommended you. He--" Father Patrick stares at me for a moment as though debating what he's about to say. "Mr. Hancock has been kind enough to pay your tuition."

My stomach clenches into a cold knot and threatens to bring the donut and hot chocolate back up. First me and now Scooter. Why is Hancock helping us? The blackness of his aura tells me he's not doing this out of the goodness of his heart. He wants something in return.

I just need to find out what that something is before it's too late.

**

Later that afternoon, I dash down the school steps. Rain pounds my back and soaks through my jeans. As I wait at the bus stop, my classmates jam the street with their Beamers. Not fazed by the rain, they lean out of their cars and shout at each other. The air is filled with horns as the morons tie up traffic.

Shivering, I cram my cold fingers into the pockets of my slicker. At least they'll stay dry, if not warm. I strain my eyes to see if I can spot the bus. I've got to tell Scooter about my conversation with Father Patrick this morning. Not that I think it would change Scooter's mind about accepting help for Boogie. Scooter would make a deal with the devil if he could keep his brother out of jail. And my instincts tell me Hancock is definitely the devil's right hand man.

A red convertible pulls to the curb. I jump back before I'm drenched by a deluge of water. Another moron.

The passenger window slides down. "Get in," a faceless voice shouts.

It's Eric. I ignore him.

"Do you want to drown?"

When I don't answer, he says, "I can have you home in fifteen minutes. It'll be forty-five on the bus."

As though my toes have ears, they start cramping in my drenched sneakers. Telling myself that this is a good time to ask him about Hancock, I open the car door and slide in. The leather seats are warm. I've heard of cars with seat warmers. Without speaking, he pulls smoothly away from the curb and into traffic.

Dark clouds hover over the city, making the day seem like night.

As the car speeds through the Westside of the city, I turn to face him, and for a brief moment our gazes lock. His eyes burn me they're so intense. I bite my lip and turn away, staring down at my hands locked in my lap.

I want to know if his parents are paying my tuition, but I can't bring myself to ask. Then something occurs to me that make my hands go icy cold and my stomach cramp. Is he hanging around with me because I'm the family's pet project? Without thinking my hand grips the door handle. But then I relax my death grip. This isn't about me. This is about Scooter. Can Hancock really get a lawyer for Boogie? Is he acting for Eric's parents, or is he playing some kind of game?

I turn back to face Eric. "I need—" Clearing my throat I try again. "I have to ask you something."

He pins me with his dark blue gaze before concentrating on the road. "What?"

"Your butler—Hancock—offered to help a friend of mine with a problem."

Frowning, Eric takes his attention off the road, his gaze probing mine.

"He says he'll hire a lawyer for my friend—" Out of the corner of my eye, I catch a blur of movement just outside the car-then a thud. "Eric!"

"What was that?" His face screws up in alarm.

"Stop, stop, stop." I bang on his arm.

He brakes hard. I'm out of the car almost before it comes to a screeching halt.

"Lisette?" I hear his footsteps behind me, the concern in his voice.

I shut him out as I race back down the street, scanning the darkness with all my senses.

I don't know how it's possible, but I smell the animal's fear before I spot it. The smell is a dark, musky brown with a tinge of yellow. I shake my head in confusion and the smell is gone.

I almost miss the dog, its fur so dark it blends in with the night. A small terrier lies in a puddle of rainwater at the curb.

It whimpers as I draw near, its breath coming out in bloody bubbles. Its rear leg juts out at an impossible angle. Crouching, I coo to the dog. "It's okay."

Eric squats next to me and reaches out to touch the animal. I grasp his hand, stopping him.

"Don't touch him. You might make things worse."

White bone protrudes from beneath the dog's matted dark fur. Blood is everywhere. It runs in pink diluted rivulets down the street and into the gutter.

"I think his head..." Eric says.

He's right. Some of the blood that streams away from the body comes from around the dog's head.

"Call a vet." But even as I say the words, I know time is against us. The animal's belly rises and falls in rapid pants.

It whines and the sound catches at my heart.

"Shh," I whisper. "It's going to be okay."

"Hurry," I say when I realize Eric hasn't left.

Heart wrenching whimpers draw my attention back to the injured animal.

How do I stop the bleeding? I search my memory for all the medical shows I've seen. And the only thing I remember is applying pressure.

Before I remove my slicker and pull off my shirt, I twirl around to make sure Eric is gone. Rain immediately soaks my bra and funnels down my chest before I can get my slicker back on. I fold the fabric into a wad and press it just above the gash in the leg. I can't do anything for the head wound. The animal whimpers and feebly twists its neck and snaps at my fingers.

Wind and rain start again after a lull. I hear my name. Turning, I look around. But there's no one there.

"*Lisette.*" This time I can tell it's a female voice. "*Heal it.*"

I whirl around in surprise. It's my mother. Why am I hearing her now? I haven't heard her voice in twelve years, and now, I've heard it twice in the last twenty-four hours. Am I losing my mind?

The animal's whimpers have stopped. I place my hand on its small belly. *Oh, shit*. It isn't breathing.

"Heal him, Lisette."

How am I supposed to do that, Maman?" I don't know how." My tears blend with the rain running down my face. "And it's too late. He's dead."

"Heallll." The word fades away on the wind.

I glance down at the small limp body. What can I do for a dead dog? Nothing. I'm not a miracle worker.

Wiping my eyes to clear my vision, I place my hand on the still warm form. "I'm sorry. We didn't see you in time. I'm so sorry."

The rain continues to beat down on me and the small scrap of life lying in the gutter. I sit with my hand on the dog for what seems like a lifetime, until a small vibration starts building in my stomach. The tremor grows and pulsates to my arm and out to my fingertips. I close my eyes against the tidal wave, but it wants to consume me. Panting, I lean over the dog. I feel like puking.

On some primal wave, words burst from my throat. Words that run together and make no sense-like another language, but one I've never heard before.

While I chant, images of women with long dresses and tignons wrapped around their heads flash through my mind. I don't know how long I pray. Eventually my vision clears and the dog's body comes back into sharp focus.

Beneath my hand, I feel the rise and fall ever so slightly of its chest. I feel its warmth.

Did I do that? No, no way. I just made a mistake thinking it was dead.

Shaking my head at how foolish I must have looked, and glad no one was around to see me chanting like a witch doctor, I sit back on my heels and examine the animal. A cold chill runs over my body. The bone no longer protrudes from the dog's leg. And the head wound-the head wound, well, there isn't a mark on the animal.

Even if it wasn't dead, the dog couldn't have healed itself.

A hand touches my shoulder. I turn slowly to find Eric kneeling by my side. Has he been here the whole time? I flush in mortification. "I was just-"

The look of wonder and respect blazing from his eyes stops any lie I'm about to tell.

I've just brought this poor being back to life.

Chapter 12

"You say he was hit by a car?" The veterinarian squints as he holds the dog's X-ray up to the light. He turns a curious gaze on me and Eric. "Are you sure? There's no indication of any break."

Images of white bone poking through blood matted fur flash through my mind. I shudder. "I hea-"

Eric's hand clamps down hard on my shoulder. "He was limping, so, we brought him here."

The dog watches us with bright eyes that are almost lost in its fur.

"And he doesn't belong to either of you?"

We shake our heads.

"He ran in front of our car in the Quarter, and he doesn't have a collar," I say.

As though we haven't told him the truth, the vet walks to the table and searches the area under the dog's chin. The ball of fur flips over and exposes his belly. Laughing, the vet rubs the dog's exposed stomach, then pulls a stethoscope from around his neck and places it on the animal's chest.

"Everything seems fine. In fact, he's in the peak of health." The doctor shakes his head. "I don't see how a small thing like this could have survived without some injury." He strokes the dog's head.

It lets out an energetic bark.

"Unfortunately, he can't stay," the doctor says. "I don't have room to board him. You'll have to take him with you."

Eric looks at me.

"I can't. *Grand'mere* is allergic to dogs."

Eric shakes his head. "I don't know anything about dogs."

"No problem." The doctor walks toward a door at the rear of the exam room. "You two just wait here."

We hear the barking of excited dogs and the pungent odor of dog crap as he steps into the kennel. Our miracle dog starts to yap in response to the greetings of the other dogs.

The vet returns with a package of dog food. "Until you can get to the store, this ought to do you." He pushes the food into Eric's reluctant hands.

"And for you, young lady," he puts a leash on the dog and deposits him into my arms. "Your Cairn terrier."

He ushers us toward the entrance and practically pushes us out the door. "Good luck."

He flips the hours sign to closed, and shuts the door, leaving us standing in the rain.

"I think we have a dog," I say, nuzzling the dog's wet nose.

"We need to take this animal back to the Quarter and try and find its owner." Eric doesn't look at me, but peers out into the parking lot where his car is just visible in the heavy downpour.

Those aren't the words I expect to hear. I stare down at the dog. He stares back. As though he can read his fate in my eyes, he places his paws on my shoulder and licks my face. I touch my forehead to his.

"How do we do that? It's chaos down there. And we can't just leave him," I say in a rush.

Eric is silent for a long moment. When he finally speaks, his words also make my heart stop in my chest.

"I can take him home with me for-"

"No!"

His head swivels in my direction. "What-"

I don't look at him. I don't want him to see the fear in my face. Not meeting his gaze, I say, "Hancock probably doesn't like animals." *And I wouldn't leave a cockroach in his care.*

Eric runs his large hands over the animals back. "So what do we do with him?"

"I might have a home for him. But I've got to work on it."

"What does that mean?"

I tell him about Leticia.

"That might take time. Where will you keep him while you 'work on it'?"

Mrs. Gardner doesn't like dogs, so I couldn't ask Scooter. I could hide him in my bedroom and let Leticia come over--.

The terrier gave a bark as though reading my thoughts. I laughed. Well, I guess that idea wouldn't work. He'd bark all day while I was at school. Plus *Grand'mere* would start sneezing as soon as I brought the dog into the house. I needed someone who liked dogs. Someone who might already have a dog. A light bulb went on in my head. Of course, Mrs. Joyner would be the perfect person.

If I told her it was only for a little while, I'm sure she'd agree.

"Take me home. I've figured out who can help."

Taking the dog from my arms, Eric places him in the space behind the seats. The terrier snuggles in and lays its head on its paws.

"What should we call him?" I ask when we're both seated.

Eric shrugs. "How about Dog?"

"Funny, ha ha." I study the dog and he tilts his head in question.

"What's your name?" I ask him. He kinda looks like Toto from The Wizard of Oz.

"How about Toto?" I say as I ruffle his fur. He gives an enthusiastic bark.

"Toto it is." I like the name it suits him.

Giving Toto a final pat, I turn in my seat. "I think I had a pet when my parents were alive." I feel a blush creep up my neck. I hadn't meant to say anything about my parents. I glance at Eric out of the corner of my eye. People treat you so differently when they know you're an orphan. And I definitely don't want Eric feeling sorry for me.

But he doesn't say anything, which is just as weird as him probing into my life. Instead he's staring off into the distance, his fingers so tightly clenched on the steering wheel the knuckles are bone white. Then his shoulder's slump as the tension leaves his body. He loosens his grip on the wheel and puts the car in gear.

As he pulls out of the Animal Hospital's parking lot, the streetlamp brightens the car's interior, creating harsh shadows on his face. I get a glimpse of another Eric. An Eric that seems more like the boys in my neighborhood-tough, old, like he's lived longer than his sixteen or seventeen years.

He takes his eyes off the road briefly to glance over at me. "You were about to ask me something about Hancock just before the dog ran under my car. What was it?"

I reach between the seats and pet Toto, running my fingers through his now clean fur. He licks at my hand, his tongue warm against my chilled skin.

In the hour since we hit this precious animal, I'd put Hancock out of my mind. Okay, that's a lie. His presence has lingered in the back of my mind like my nightmares.

"Lisette?"

Sighing, I face him. "Does Hancock have lots of money?"

"You've been very curious about my butler. Why?"

Hurt by the sharpness of his voice, I almost don't answer, but I've got to stop being so easily offended. "He offered to hire a lawyer for a friend. I'm wondering why?"

"Is this someone from our school?"

I shake my head. I don't want to mention Scooter's name. It's like I'm betraying his confidence.

As though sensing my reluctance, Eric shakes his head. "His name doesn't matter. What matters is your friend's character."

Puzzled, I pick the sentence apart, looking for the hidden meaning. I can't figure it out. "Do you mean can he pay Hancock back for hiring the lawyer?" I shake my head. "Probably not. Scooter-" I mentally kick myself. "He doesn't have a lot of money."

Eric stares at the road as he maneuver's the car around some party stragglers. "Hancock may not be looking for payment in money."

I frown. "What else is there? Does he want my friend to work off his debt?"

Eric doesn't say anything for a long time. "Don't let him accept the offer."

"Why not?"

"Just trust me. He shouldn't accept the offer."

I stare blindly out the car's window, my hands locked in my lap and my throat dry with fear. What does Eric know that he's not telling me?

By the time he pulls up to my house, I'm shaking. "He's desperate."

Eric nods. "Yes, that is usually the case."

"Huh?" I lean forward to get a better look at his face, thinking I misunderstood what he said. "I don't get it."

"Goodnight, Lisette."

I wait hoping for more explanation. But the stubborn line of Eric's mouth tells me he's not going to tell me more.

"Goodnight, Eric." I reach for Toto before opening the passenger door.

His hand on my shoulder makes me jump. "Hancock is dangerous. Tell that to your friend."

"How do you know this?" I whisper.

Eric's jaw tightens. "I just do. Goodnight, Lisette."

I get out of the car, legs trembling as I watch the car drive away. I bury my face in Toto's fur. He must sense my fear because he gives a little whine. "Sorry, boy." I looked down into the dog's expressive dark eyes. "I don't think there's anything I can do to keep Scooter from accepting whatever Hancock proposes."

As though agreeing with me, Toto barks.

Sighing, I across the street toward Mrs. Joyner's house, wishing I had the power to change the future.

**

When Eric returned to the big house, it was empty. But he knew Hancock couldn't have gone far. The man was afraid of automobiles and found this world confusing. Eric strolled to the windows that overlooked the house's courtyard.

Oblivious to the downpour and the lightening, Hancock was in the garden, his face turned up to the sky. Rain pounded his pitted face. Clutched in his meaty palm were a bunch of flowers. If the sight weren't so sad, Eric would have laughed. If there was a scarier person other than Eric in the Fifth Realm, it was Black Hancock. He'd received his name for the condition of his soul not the color of his skin. And now he was cutting flowers and inhaling their scent.

Eric moved away from the window. He didn't have any illusions about Hancock. He was devoted to Saarel and loved his role as one of the chief torturers of the Realm. Eric had tortured because it was either inflict pain or be tortured. Two millennium of being on the receiving end of Saarel's sadistic pleasure was enough to drive a person mad. So when Saarel offered him a chance, Eric took it. He became one of the torturers of the Realm. But he hated every minute of it.

No, if he was to find out why Saarel wanted Lisette, he would have to do it without Hancock's help.

Eric took the steps two at a time, and moved swiftly down the hall to the sparse bedroom Hancock called his. Standing in the doorway, he surveyed the room. The bed was made and, in fact, had never been slept in. Hancock preferred sleeping on the floor.

Eric stepped into the room and opened the closet. A few pairs of dark trousers and white shirts hung from padded hangers. The only pair of shoes that Hancock possessed sat forlornly on the closet floor. He only wore them when it was absolutely necessary to leave the house, otherwise, he was shoeless. Eric knew very little about Hancock. He'd come to the Realm a millennium later than Eric.

There was very little in the closet that gave him a clue as to Hancock's purpose. Based on Lisette's friend's encounter with Hancock, Eric knew the man had other duties to the Overlord. He wanted something from Lisette's young friend, but what?

"Find what you were looking for?"

Hancock stood in the doorway. Rainwater dripped off his drenched pants and pooled around his bare feet. He had disposed of the flowers.

Instead of answering, Eric deflected Hancock's suspicious by asking a question of his own. "Why are you doing this?"

"Doing what?"

Eric eyed the older man coldly. "Being my nursemaid."

Hancock strode toward Eric and shut the closet door. "Saarel commanded me to."

"And you do whatever Saarel ask?"

Hancock spun around so fast Eric almost didn't see the move. Hancock's lips were pulled back into a feral grin, his eyes hard as stones.

"As long as I am here, I am my own master. And you do well to remember that *Eric.*" His mouth twisted in a snarl as he said Eric's name.

"For whatever reason, you are taking your time with this task. But if I find out that you plan to disobey Himself, I will have no compulsion about dragging you back to the Realm myself."

"Brave words," Eric said.

"True words." Hancock snapped his head from side to side, the bones in his neck cracking. He took a deep breath and tension seemed to flow out of his body. He pointed a finger at Eric. "A word of warning, don't be misled by this girl's innocence. She is a powerful entity."

Entity? Why had Hancock used that word to describe Lisette? She was just a girl, confused, alone, but still just a girl. "More power than Saarel?" Eric held his breath. Would Hancock reveal the truth behind why the Overlord wanted her?

Hancock opened the closet and pulled from its depths an identical pair of pants and shirt to the ones he wore. "Do your job and do not be concerned with matters beyond your understanding."

"How can I do my job if I don't know everything about her?"

Hancock's mouth turned up at the corners in a mockery of a smile. "It can be done." He marched to the bathing chamber, leaving Eric standing in the middle of the bedroom as clueless to Saarel's plan as when he'd entered the butler's room.

Eric would not so easily kowtow to Saarel. This would be his one and only chance to escape the demon's control. What had he learned from this exchange with

Hancock? That Lisette was a force to be reckoned with, possibly more powerful than Saarel. Also, the Overlord and Hancock were afraid if Eric had all the answers he wouldn't complete the assignment. They were right. Maybe it wasn't necessary to know the Overlord's plan just know Lisette's power. A power he would use to escape the Realm.

Chapter 13

I haven't talked to Scooter in a couple of days. Anxious to hear what happened in court today, I readily agree when he texts me to meet him outside the Voodoo Museum. He wants to meet at the cemetery, but I nix that idea. No way am I going back there.

A church bell bongs eleven times somewhere in the distance. "Where in the world is he?" Jogging in place to keep warm, all I manage to do is splash water over my jeans.

A sound like rats scurrying over dried leaves makes me swirl around. Icy fingers zip up my spine. There is nothing dry anywhere in the city. So what did I hear? Did something move in the shadows? Cursing Scooter, I back away from the building's entry.

Bump this! I turn and hurry toward home.

There's been nothing reported in the news about strange creatures roaming the city. But with Mardi Gras in full swing, if anyone saw something strange they'd think it was a very realistic costume. Shuddering, I pick up speed until I'm running full out.

Things have gotten too weird. First Eric's warning about Hancock-a warning I'd planned to give Scooter tonight-and then finding that article about my parent's death.

Why was my father driving so fast? I don't believe he was driving fast because he liked speed. From the fear in my mother's eyes, I think they were afraid of something-running from something or maybe someone. Or maybe I'm completely off base. Maybe I've transferred my own anxiety to everything and everybody I see.

The part about my parents, I wasn't planning to share with Scooter. This part of me I was going to keep to secret. Secrets. It seems my whole life has been about secrets-secrets about my family in the bayou. And if that family is to be believed, secrets about who I'm destined to be.

Feeling like I've put enough distance between me and the museum, I slow down. Near the edge of the Quarter an impromptu mini-parade has sprung up.

Spattering everyone around them with their plastic cups of beer and daiquiris, drunken tourists mingle and sing with the musicians. Unfazed by the rain, some of the partiers are dressed in nineteenth-century costumes with partial and even full masks covering their faces.

Fog rolls in from the river, giving the area a surreal appearance as I duck down a less crowded street. Without the benefit of cars zooming past, it could be New Orleans two hundred years ago.

The night is silent. I can almost hear the fog swirling around buildings and streetlights, the creak of a swinging door, the scrape and click of something on concrete. Turning, I see only trails of vapor. I continue walking. There it is again, a sound like nails on concrete.

The hairs on the back of my neck prickle. I stop. The clicking stops. I continue walking. I stop again, and the click stops also. My pulse leaps. Someone is following me. I walk faster. As I turn a corner, I glance behind me. Big mistake.

Something humongous is moving toward me on all fours, sleek and black. Two red orbs glow from a head like a hippopotamus, long and thick.

This can't be real, but I have enough sense to run. My mouth is dry as I gulp air. My legs, weak from fear, threaten to collapse. I turn a corner, then another. I'm lost. Whatever is behind me is gaining. I can almost feel its breath on my neck.

Dear God. Please help me.

And then the unthinkable happens. The thing that only happens in bad movies. A brick wall looms in front of me. I've turned down a dead end street. I have no option but to face whatever this is that's chasing me.

I stop. I sense it stops also. I turn, and, sure enough, it waits, a big ugly obstacle between me and the street. It's the size of a small elephant. Its skin is pitted, and from within the black hide, something glows green like stagnant swamp water.

I shake my head, trying to make myself wake up. I'm dreaming. Creatures like this don't exist outside of nightmares. Please let me wake up. When my slicker scrapes against the bricks at my back, I know that this is no dream. There's nowhere to go.

The buildings that will witness my death are abandoned or closed for the night. No help from that quarter.

"What do you want?" I whisper more to myself than this hideous creature in front of me.

"Himself wants you."

Stunned, I can only stare. It spoke. I want to laugh, but I can't. I have visions of the commercials where they make cats and dogs talk, their jaws moving in comical gestures.

"Himself? Who the hell is Himself?"

"Saarel." The word comes out in a guttural growl, the s extending into a long hiss.

Vapor carries the animal's fetid breath to me on a wave. Once I had to walk past a dead dog that lay rotting at the curb. The beast's breath smelled like that, sweet and sickening, a combination of decaying flesh and rotten eggs. I want to puke.

"I don't know a Saarel. You have the wrong person." I can't believe I'm having a conversation with something out of a nightmare.

"Himself-"

But whatever the creature is about to say is cut short by two steel objects flying through the air. They embed themselves in its rough hide. Sparks fly and the creature bellows, then deflates like a punctured hot air balloon. Embers shoot up from the spot and then disappear. So does any evidence of the animal.

A tall, featureless figure dressed in black walks toward me. The light from the cross street shines behind him. He stops at the now smoldering spot, picks up the steel objects that shine brightly, even though there is little light, and sheaths them in a pouch at his back.

My pulse thuds in my ears as he comes within touching distance, and then my jaw drops. Eric Gabriel stands in front of me, his face hard and dangerous.

Chapter 14

My knees buckle, and I slide down the brick wall until my butt hits asphalt.

Hovering over me like a menacing angel, he extends his hand.

I cringe and shrink away, my feet backpedaling, fruitlessly trying to put distance between us. But my back is against the wall. I have no place to go.

He drops his hand. "I'm not going to hurt you."

Who is he? Who walks around with swords and kills talking monsters. I will myself to wake up and be back in my own bed. But he doesn't disappear, nor do the swords peeking out beyond his shoulders.

Without taking my eyes off him, I ask, "What was that?" I point behind him.

He doesn't turn around. "A Nian."

"What?"

"A beast of prey from the Fifth Realm of Hell."

Mouth ajar, I can only stare up at him. Which one of us is crazier? "Hell?"

"Later. Come." He extends his hand again. "We must leave."

I shake my head. "I'm not going with you. What-what are you?"

"Call me your guardian angel." Frowning, he glances around. "Come on, Lisette. We've got to hurry. Let me take you to safety."

His eyes are dark with concern. Just when I think I know him and kinda like him, he confirms what I believed all along. He's weird, he's scary, and he's not from this world. How can he be? The guys I know can't handle swords like they're extensions of their arms. They don't talk about demon creatures as though they're real.

Struggling to my feet, I avoid his out-stretched hand. Right now he's about as alien to me as the monster he just destroyed.

What's happening to me? A few days ago, I was a misfit, trying to make it at a school where I didn't belong. Now, I've raised the dead, made a classmate a love slave of another, attended a Voodoo ceremony and been chased by a beast from Hell. My life is all out of whack. But through my confused haze, I sense his unease. I have enough brain cells left to realize if he's uneasy after killing that- that Nian thing, it's time to leave.

I follow him, but keep a safe distance between us. I want maneuvering room in case I need to run. Right now he's the lesser of two evils. Or is he?

When I get to the spot where the creature died, I see nothing but an oily black residue floating on top of a puddle of rainwater.

"Hurry," Eric calls. He's now several feet away, moving fast.

My legs tremble like stalks in a strong wind as I race to catch up with him.

At the mouth of the alley, he holds up a hand for me to wait. After scanning the street, he leaves the shelter of the alley and motions for me to follow.

We walk several minutes in silence until the bizarreness of what's happened forces me to speak. "You knew how to kill—"

"Hush." He moves quickly, forcing me to almost run to keep up.

"It talked. It actually talked."

"What?" He glances back at me, a deep crease between his eyebrows.

"That Nian thing. It said something."

There's a small hesitation in Eric's stride. "What did it say?"

"That Saarel wants me."

This time he stops. I have to do a little dance to keep from plowing into him. He looks at me, but it's like he doesn't see me. Something about his stillness makes the hairs on my arms stand straight up, as though a cold arctic wind has blown across my body.

"Saarel," he whispers, but it's not a question. He says the name as though he knows this person.

The name seems to echo around the deserted street, bouncing around and between the old buildings until I swear I hear the bricks groan. I shiver.

When Eric doesn't speak, I grab his arm. "I have a right to know who this Saarel is, especially since this thing tried to kidnap me."

Indecision plays across his features.

There's so much I don't know about him. I always thought he was weird, but his knowledge of demons is beyond anything I could have imagined.

"Who is he?"

Two forms step out of the shelter of a building up ahead. Eric's muscles tense under my hand. The rain and the darkness make it difficult to determine anything about them.

Before I can blink, Eric's swords are in his hands.

The two forms merge. Their lips meet, then part.

He sheaths his swords.

Arm in arm, the couple walk away, totally oblivious to the fact they almost lost their lives.

Shocked, I stare stupidly at Eric's retreating back. "Wait."

I catch up with him, but this time I don't touch him. "You didn't answer my question. Who is Saarel?"

He glances at me then looks away. "I've heard he rules a Realm of Hell."

I blink once, twice, unable to believe what I hear. This isn't a Dungeons and Dragons game to him. He's talking as though this is real- that there are actually divisions of Hell. Like Dante's essay in English Lit. But that was fiction, this is not.

Then an ice cold hand grips my heart, slowing the beat until all I can hear is the slow thudding pulse of my blood. "Is he-" I swallow and try to speak again. "Is he a demon Overlord?"

Eric's dark gaze rakes my face. I can feel the tension radiating from him. "Yes. How did you know?"

I move away from him, and as I do, I step into a puddle of water that splashes my jeans, drenching them to the knee. But it's not the wet pants making me shiver. "My family spoke of him."

"What do they know about Saarel?"

I can't tell him about the prophecy. He'll think I'm crazy. "Just that he exists."

We walk in silence for the rest of the trip with me looking over my shoulder the whole way.

We round the corner and my house comes into view. All the windows are dark. I breathe a sigh of relief. *Grand'mere* is still asleep.

Eric touches my arm. "I'll go in first."

My head swivels from Eric's face to my house. Mouth dry, I ask, "Do you think that thing was here? Here with my *Grand'mere*?"

He hesitates too long. I run toward my house.

"Lisette." His voice is just above a whisper, but I hear the anxiety in it.

He catches up with me and places a hand over mine just before I open the front door. "Wait." He stares down into my eyes. His expression softens as his gaze travels over my face. Then immediately the softness is replaced by an intense fierceness. Maybe I imagined the gentleness.

He pulls the blades from their pouch in one smooth motion. I jump back in alarm. He steps into the house and sniffs. What's up with the sniffing? Glancing at me over his shoulder, he mouths the word "stay." I grind my teeth. I'm not a dog to be commanded. But in the next instant, I remember what chased me into the alley, and I don't move.

He seems to take forever. What if something has happened to her? Ignoring his warning, I step over the threshold and tiptoe down the hall. A lamp glows softly. Nothing appears disturbed. When I find him, he's standing in *Grand'mere's* bedroom, as still as a statue.

Please don't let her be hurt. Chanting the words, I move slowly into the room. *Grand'mere* lets out a soft snort. I almost giggle in relief. I must have made a sound, because Eric turns and gently, but firmly, pushes me out into the hall.

"Why didn't you listen to me?"

My mouth tightens in anger. "She's my grandmother. I couldn't just stay outside when she might need me."

He blows his breath out through his nose, then points to my room. "Don't leave until morning."

How did he know that was my room? He's been in there. Then my face grows warm with humiliation as I remember the stuff animals and the fairy tale posters on the walls.

Before I can accuse him, he's standing at the kitchen door. "Bolt the entry behind me."

Irritated by his bossy command, I almost don't obey. But common sense and fear finally take over and I flip the dead bolt.

I watch from the kitchen window as he vanishes into the darkness.

Chapter 15

The next morning just at dawn, I leap off the front porch, avoiding the creaky boards so I don't wake *Grand'mere*.

Thunder booms in the distance. As I race across the street, I peer through sheets of water looking for Eric. Breathing a sigh of relief when I don't spot him, I open Mrs. J's chain link gate and dash through her yard.

I didn't sleep well last night. Actually, I didn't sleep much at all, and when I did, I dreamed of silver blades tumbling end over end in the blackness, and Eric stepping out of the darkness. Who is he? How did he know how to kill that beast?

I made a decision in the wee hours. I'm not going to have anything to do with Eric Gabriel. If he tries to seek me out in school, I'll turn and go the other way. I don't want whatever is associated with him to touch me.

Wishing I owned a pair of boots, I dash through the standing water in Mrs. J's backyard. I've put on another pair of sneakers and now they're drenched.

Scooter didn't answer my texts I sent early this morning. I'm afraid maybe the creature got to him before it came for me.

Using the throw away Scooter bought me at Wal-Mart. I sit on his porch swing and dial his number. It's too early to knock on his front door. I'm prepared to wait until someone comes out of the house or Scooter answers. Thinking the worst makes me want to cry, so I push the thought that he doesn't answer because he can't, out of my mind.

On the tenth call, he picks up.

"What!"

Relieved that he's okay, I'm not even mad that he's shouting obscenities in my ear.

"I'm on your front porch."

"Why?" he grumbles.

"Just come out."

In five minutes he opens the door and steps out onto the porch. He's barefooted and wears wrinkled jeans and a t-shirt.

"Did you sleep in those?" I point to his clothes.

"What's it to you?" He yawns so wide, his jaw cracks.

He sits on the swing next to me, reeking of old sweat, and cigarettes. I screw up my nose.

He's so relaxed and casual I start to get angry, remembering my terror filled run through the Quarter. "Why didn't you show up last night?"

His eyes blink open in surprise then his brow knits in confusion. "Show up where?"

I punch him in the shoulder. "At the museum."

"What museum?"

"The Voodoo museum, you idiot. You told me to meet you there."

"I didn't."

"Yes, you did. I texted and you texted back and said meet you there at 11pm."

He stares at me as though I've lost my mind. "You're nuts."

"Give me your phone."

Frowning, he pulls his cell from his back pocket. I snatch it out of his hand and scroll through the messages. It's not there. *But it's got to be here.* Maybe I missed it. I start from the beginning. Nothing.

Fear swirls around me like a funnel cloud, black and humid. If it wasn't Scooter, who was it?

"Well, I never saw your message and no one's had my phone but me." He stares at me. "Did you go?"

"Of course, I went. I thought I was meeting you."

"And..."

"You weren't there." I'm at a loss for words. I had so much to tell him, but now in the light of day, it's not that easy. The demons, Nian beasts and the evil Hancock are all well and good in the movies, but not in real life.

"What if I tell you something strange happened?"

With his head still braced on the back of the swing, he turns toward me. "Stranger than us passing out charms?"

I nod. "Yeah. Stranger than that."

"Shoot. I'm all ears."

He closes his eyes. I wonder if he's fallen asleep. I poke him in the ribs.

"Oww." He rubs his side. "I'm just resting my eyes. I was listening."

In a way, I'm glad he's not looking at me. It makes it easier to speak. After a short silence, Scooter sets the swing in motion with his bare foot.

"Ashley asked me to say some words over the charm. You know, to bless it."

I glance at Scooter. His eyes are still closed. The swing has a gentle motion.

"I just made up some words to get it over with." I pause and try to swallow, but my mouth is too dry. My tongue seems to be stuck to the roof of my mouth. I clear my throat. "I raised the dead with those words."

The swing stops moving.

I don't look at Scooter. I don't want to see the look of horror on his face.

He starts to laugh. Not just chuckles, but double over, touch your face to your knees howling. It's not the reaction I expect.

"That's good, Lis." He wipes his eyes. "Now, let's eat." He rises from the swing and heads for the front door, shaking his head.

"Scoot?"

"Yeah." He's still wiping his eyes.

"It's not a joke. It really happened."

One hand on the front door knob, he turns, frowning. "What really happened?"

"I raised the dead."

He shakes his head. "Lis, you're getting stranger and stranger. Why do you think you raised the dead?"

I hesitate. Do I tell him about the lizard creature? Do I want the only true friend I have to think I'm crazy?

Plowing on without waiting for my answer, he asks, "What possessed you to make the charm in the first place?"

He raises his hand to stop my words. "The money. I forgot." His gaze roams over my face. "You know what your problem is? You're too goody-goody. When you do something a good Catholic girl wouldn't do, you can't handle it and you freak out."

He comes back to the swing. "Lis, you're freaking out, that's all. Spend the money and don't feel guilty. I'm sure dickhead has more where that came from."

He heads back to the front door. "Now, let's eat."

I don't follow him inside. Am I losing my mind? I feel like I'm living in two different realities. The world with Scooter and *Grand'mere* and this nightmare dimension with Eric and demons. What scares me is that

Eric's reality is becoming more real than my life a few days ago.

**

I invite Scooter to my house for breakfast since there's no food in his kitchen. He doesn't refuse. He prefers *Grand'mere*'s cooking over his mother's. He says his mother's has no imagination. When I ask him why he doesn't take over the cooking, he stares at me as though I've cursed in church. I retreat to the shower and leave him with *Grand'mere* in the kitchen.

Bathed, and dressed, I walk toward the kitchen. I hear their voices, but the whispered tones slow my steps.

"-acting weird," he says.

There's a low response from *Grand'mere* that I can't heard, then silence.

"She's gotten interested in Voodoo."

Grand'mere gasps.

A chair scrapes against linoleum.

"Are you okay, Mrs. Beaulieu?"

I rush into the kitchen. *Grand'mere* is slumped in a chair, her pale face drained of color.

"What's wrong?" I ask, rushing to her side.

Scooter looks guilty.

"Nothing," *Grand'mere* says, struggling to rise. "Must be the heat in here."

I know that's a lie because she walks to the stove and turns on the burner under the griddle iron, creating more heat.

I glare at Scooter. "What'd you say to her?" I whisper.

"Nothing," he whispers back. He doesn't look at me.

Narrowing my eyes, I walk to the refrigerator and take out a carton of orange juice. I pour myself a glass. The tension is thick. All I can hear is the sizzle of pancake batter cooking in oil and the sound of thunder rocking the house. I take my glass of O.J. and stroll over to the kitchen door, which *Grand'mere* has propped open. This weather is crazy. One minute it's cold and rainy and the next it's hot and humid enough to be July instead of February.

Standing in the open door staring out at the backyard, I can't see the grass. The yard is buried under at least six inches of water. Raindrops dimple the standing water. You would think with so much thunder the rain would be torrential. It isn't. The sky is a black mass of clouds lit from within by flashes of lightning.

I turn back to face the room. *Grand'mere* places a mile high pile of griddle cakes in front of Scooter. He attacks them with a vengeance, shoving an overloaded forkful into his mouth. He nods with pleasure, moving his upper body to a rhythm only he can hear.

Grand'mere comes to me and places a warm hand on my shoulder. We are the same height, so I can stare into her amber eyes. Scooter calls me *Grand'mere*'s mini-me.

"What's wrong, *pi petite?*"

Respecting her too much, I don't shrug off her hand, but the urge is there.

Scooter watches us, his fork never pausing on its journey from plate to mouth.

"Nothing."

"Bullshit," he mumbles, the word almost lost in a mouthful of food.

Grand'mere glances at him. "Will someone tell me what's going on?" Her cheeks are now flushed with color. "What is this about you and Voodoo?"

If my eyes could shoot daggers, Scooter's body would be pinned to the wall behind him. I wanted to tell her in my own way and in my own time.

But, Scooter being here might work in my favor. Maybe she'll be more relaxed and more open.

My stomach, already tightly coiled, twists like a pit full of snakes. "Did my mother practice Voodoo?"

Not the question I want to ask, but a start. Will she be truthful or evade the question?

She opens then closes her mouth. Slowly she lowers her body into one of the kitchen chairs. I want to run to her and beg her to forgive me and tell her I really don't need to know. But something holds me still- rooted to the spot.

Scooter stops eating and stares at us.

"She- your mother converted to Catholicism when she married my son, your father." *Grand'mere* picks up her rosary that's always close by. "She only paid lip service to it. She would sneak away when your father stayed nights at the fire station. She would leave you with me, but I knew where she went. She'd go to the bayou to see her family to worship those heathen saints." *Grand'mere*'s face twists in a mask of disgust and anger.

With dawning realization, I suddenly understand something that's been staring me in my face for the last twelve years. *Grand'mere* hated my mother.

Does that mean *Grand'mere* doesn't love me? I am my mother's daughter.

My feelings must be plainly painted on my face, because she straightens and moves toward me. I back away.

"*Pi petite*, I never blamed you for your mother's ungodly ways. You were just a child. And my son..." She raises her hands and lets them fall to her side. "My son was bewitched by her."

My mind flashes to the vision of my mother dancing for my father on the lawn in the bayou-his rapt face full of love for her.

I can't breathe. I need to get out of here, but *Grand'mere*'s hands, like small talons, restrain me.

"I don't want you to turn out like her," she says, her eyes bright with memories.

"Turn out like her?" My forehead crinkles in confusion.

She struggles with some inner turmoil. Her eyes darken from light brown to almost black. "Your mother called herself a Voodoo priestess. She said that you would be one too. I couldn't let that happen. After her death, I told her family not to come around.

"Imagine a Voodoo priestess." *Grand'mere* laughs, but it's not a happy sound, more like the bark of a threatened animal. "You understand. I did it for you. I had to save you."

I can only stare at her. This woman isn't my beloved *Grand'mere*. The gentleness is gone from her face.

"Ms. Beaulieu?" Scooter stands behind *Grand'mere*.

She doesn't respond. Her eyes are locked on my face. God knows what's written on my features. Has this love I felt from her only been my imagination?

She raises her hand to touch me. I back out of reach. Turning, I run for the front door. I hear her shout my name as I dash out into the storm.

**

Rain smacks me in the face as I jump off the streetcar near Washington Ave. Between parades, the area is relatively quiet. Colorful remains of sodden streamers cling to my sneakers as I dash across the street and through the gates of Lafayette cemetery.

When I was last here, the massive oaks that guard the entrance were heavy with burnt orange leaves. Now, the tree's bare limbs weep rain droplets. I'm ashamed it's been so long.

I follow a path that winds between crypts until I come to the one marked, Beaulieu. My parents aren't interned here. I guess now I know why. At least *Grand'mere* hadn't separated them. Only my great-grandparents and my *Grand'pere* are here.

Although I was too young to remember my parent's death, I do remember when *Grand'pere* died. We were very close. I run my hand over the rough stone of the crypt. "Oh, *Grand'pere*. I wish you were here. My life's such a mess." I look up at the dark clouds pregnant with rain. I know he's in heaven. He was such a good man. He didn't always go to mass, but he always made me smile. I feel like I haven't smiled since he died. My eyes sting and fill with tears.

I want to lie down in front of the crypt and curl into a ball. I would give anything to be someone else.

You can't outrun your destiny.

My grandmother's words ring in my head until I clamp my hands to my ears to shut out her voice. "I'm not meant to be a priestess. Tell them, *Grand'pere*." I shout at the stone crypt. "Tell them I'm not the one."

A strong wind kicks up, showering me with more rain. Then a silence fills the cemetery. The faint traffic from the street recedes, and the wind dies down.

The hairs on my arm rise as I sense someone standing next to me. Heart pounding like a drum in my chest, I slowly turn, afraid of what I might see. My breath hitches in my throat. As though I've conjured him up, *Grand'pere* stands beside me. His white hair, once gold colored like mine, is smoothed down over his skull like after *Grand'mere* has run a brush over it. He's staring at the crypt. I stare at him. Is he real or just a figment of my pain? Did I need him so badly, I wished him here?

Did I raise him from his resting place? Please by the Virgin Mary, say it isn't true.

He's wearing his burial suit. Surprisingly, it looks as good as it did three years ago. I reach out and touch his sleeve. He feels very solid. "*Grand'pere?*" I whisper.

He turns at the sound of my voice and smiles down at me. He doesn't speak, just gives me the same smile that once filled me with comfort. For that one moment, all is right with my world.

"Why are you here, *Grand'pere?*"

He doesn't answer, but turns and gazes at the crypt. It's probably very strange to see your own burial site.

I don't care how he got here. I'm just glad he's here.

After several minutes when he doesn't disappear, I start to tell him about what's happened to me. I tell him about the Voodoo thing. About meeting my mother's family, and about *Grand'mere* lying to me about them. Then I stop talking, realizing he was also involved. Both he and *Grand'mere* kept this secret from me. For a brief moment, I get mad all over again, then I swallow my anger. For whatever reason, I have him back in my life. I don't want to waste this time. Does that mean I shouldn't be mad at *Grand'mere*? But the horrible things she said about my mother still ring in my ears. It's going to be harder to forgive her, if I ever can.

I glance up at *Grand'pere*. Why is he here? Why now? During his life, the only things he cared about were me and *Grand'mere*. Is he worried about us? He should be.

I've told him everything. Well, almost everything.

"There's this boy..." I swallow. What do I say about Eric? "He's—-he's different." What I don't say is that he's a demon slayer. I don't want *Grand'pere* to worry. But if what the priests teach us is true, *Grand'pere* knows this already. He's been watching over me from heaven.

"He scares me, but at the same time..." What? What am I trying to say? That I like Eric? No way.

Grand'pere still hasn't said a word, but his love for me radiates across the small distance between us, until I feel warm with it.

We stand this way until the long shadows of evening creep across the rainy lawn, bringing in its wake, the fog.

My breath gives a funny hiccup in my chest as I realize it's getting dark and I'll have to walk home alone. But would I have given up this time with my *Grand'pere*? No. "I guess it's time for me to go."

I turn toward him, but he's gone.

Chapter 16

I haven't taken two steps into the house, before *Grand'mere* rushes out of the kitchen, arms outstretched.

"Lisette. Lisette, I'm so sorry. I didn't mean-"

I back away from her until my body hits the front door.

"Don't," I say. "Don't." My voice cracks as I fight tears.

Dropping her arms, she doesn't try to touch me, but her eyes beg me to forgive her. How can I when she's said such awful things about my mother?

I move around her like a cornered animal afraid of being hurt again. I turn and run for my room. Once there, I slam the door and press my back against it.

Something moves in the shadows.

"It's me. It's me." Scooter whispers before I can scream.

"What the hell are you doing here?" I go to the nightstand and switch on the lamp.

He grins. "I thought you'd need me."

"Traitor." The word comes out low, almost a growl.

He throws up his hand in defense. "I didn't-"

"Shut the--"

His eyes open wide in mock horror.

"Shut. Up." Pulling dry clothes from my dresser, I slam the drawers as hard as I can. It doesn't ease the pain or the anger. "Turn around."

He obeys.

I shed my wet jeans, but keep on my panties, pulling dry sweats over them.

"Are you mad at me?" Scooter asks.

I glance up and catch him watching my reflection in the mirror above the chest of drawers.

"What are you doing?" Without waiting for him to reply, I turn my back to him.

 I yank my shirt off, ripping out a few hairs in the process. My scalp tingles, but I don't care. What's a little more pain?

"Yes, I'm mad at you. Why'd you have to tell her about the Voodoo?" I pull on a t-shirt and face him. "I'm finished, but you already know that."

He turns, giving me a sheepish grin. "Sorry."

But I can tell he's not sorry, which makes me feel weird. Scooter's never done anything like that before. It makes me feel sad, like I'm losing my best friend.

"I told her cause you were scaring me. It's like you were freakin out. I said you were hanging out with a bunch of weirdos at your new school." He grins at me. "Thought it might make her send you back to Easton. How would I know Voodoo's a sore spot with her?"

"I didn't know, either." I plop down on the bed. Scooter joins me.

"She loves you, you know." He touches my arm, gently rather than the punch he usually gives me. That, too, makes me feel strange. He's never done that before-been all sensitive and stuff. I hold myself very still as though that will keep everything from changing, but I know it's a hopeless cause. For me things have been changing for months. I sense they're changing for Scooter also.

He's deep in thought, which is unusual for him. Normally, everything's a joke. It's his way of keeping everybody at a distance. I'm the only one he lets in, and I've failed him.

"What's happening with Boogie?" I ask, hoping it's not too late to save my best friend.

"Out on bail."

The bottom drops out of my stomach. "The new lawyer did that?"

Scooter nods.

"And how will you pay him?" My hand digs into the bed linen until my fingers cramp.

"It's all taken care of."

Heat rises up my neck and floods my face. I feel like steam is coming out of my ears. "How can you be so calm about all this? Lawyers are expensive, and I know this guy isn't doing this out of the kindness of his heart."

"Chill, Lis. I got this."

If he only knew, but even if I told him, he wouldn't believe me. He didn't believe me when I told him about raising the dead. How can I make him understand that Hancock is not what he seems? That he's the devil.

I study Scooter out of the corner of my eye. Do I dare tell him about *Grand'pere*? I need to tell someone. I feel like I'm losing my grip on reality.

Feeling like an unmanned boat floating away from a familiar dock, I take a deep breath and turn toward Scooter. "I saw *Grand'pere* today."

I hold my breath, waiting for his reaction. There's confusion on his face, then comprehension, then he draws back. Hurt, I close my eyes against his rejection.

"Aw, come on, Lis. You're weirding me out."

I shrug. "I'm weirding myself out."

We sit in uneasy silence for a few more minutes, while he tugs on the few scraggly hairs on his chin. "Did you really see him?"

I nod. "I touched him."

Scooter shivers. "I've heard of seeing dead people."

"You have?" Scooter isn't into the supernatural, the Sci-fi channel or anything otherworldly.

"Yeah, that Bruce Willis movie with the creepy kid."

I roll my eyes. "Be serious. Have you heard of *real* people seeing the dead?"

"Nope."

I take a deep breath. "I'm not sure why *Grand'pere* was there, but I think he was trying to tell me something."

I glance at Scooter out of the corner of my eye, trying to judge what he's thinking from his expression.

He's not smiling.

"You know how he felt about *Grand'mere* and me."

Scooter nods in agreement. "Yeah. He let you guys run the show."

I punch him on the shoulder. "He didn't."

"Did to." He rubs his shoulder and mouths the word "Oww" with a grimace.

"He just loved us."

"Like I said, he spoiled you."

I smile, knowing Scooter is right. We were *Grand'pere*'s world. He was ours. So for him to show up now, after being dead for three years, must mean something.

Scooter throws up a cautioning hand. "Don't get me wrong. I still think you're flipping out, imagining things and shit, but maybe if you thought you saw him—"

"I did see him!"

"Okay, okay." Scooter motions for me to be calm. "Chill," he says in a soft tone. "Let's just say he *was* there. Maybe it's because he's worried about you."

I cross my arms over my chest. "You're only saying that because *you're* worried about me."

"Well, yeah, but why else would he show up now? He didn't show up when you and me had that car accident."

I shudder, remembering the ride in the car Scooter said he "borrowed" from a friend, then the accident, and my overnight stay in the hospital for a concussion.

"He sure didn't show up when you were planning to run away because you had to go to Haverford. So this Voodoo thing must have him rattled. If you really saw him." The last he muttered under his breath.

I narrow my eyes at him. "I saw him."

"Okay. So like I said, he's worried."

Grand'pere is not the only one worried. I'm beyond worried. I'm scared shitless. This Overlord that my mother's people told me about is sending creatures to take me to hell. And if they succeed, what will happen to *Grand'mere*? As much as I want to hate her, I can't. She did take care of me when my parents died. So it's my turn to take care of her.

I can't tell Scooter about Saarel and the creatures from Hell. He already thinks I've lost it. I don't want to scare him away. He's the only friend I have. Eric's face flashes before my eyes. He's not a friend. I don't know what he is, but anyone who can kill hell beasts without breaking a sweat has to be dangerous. And those swords... The flash of light off those long blades of steel plays again in my mind. I shudder. No. He's not a friend. But why does he keep coming to my rescue?

"Strange things are going on in my life, Scooter. I think *Grand'pere* senses it."

Scooter raises his eyebrows. "He sensed it from the grave?" His tone is laced with disbelief.

I shrug. "I know it sounds crazy, but why else was he there?"

He shakes his head. "Lis, this is too strange. And I've seen some strange stuff."

"I've got to protect *Grand'mere*."

"Protect her from who?"

Things that go bump in the night. "I don't know." But I do. From Saarel.

"Well, you don't have to worry. I'll protect her," he says. "And if I need fire power, I'll call on my boys."

I want to laugh. How can I tell him I suspect guns will do nothing against what I've seen? Besides, you have to fight strangeness with strangeness.

"Thanks, Scoot, but I think I know who can help us." I realized from the moment I saw *Grand'pere* that I would have to, as *Grand'mere* says, tuck my tail between my legs and beg forgiveness.

"Who?" He frowns as though there isn't anyone who could possibly help me but him.

"My mother's people."

He pulls back from me in astonishment. "You're going to the bayou?"

"Yes."

Concern, then curiosity flits across his face. Before he can ask, I rush on, "I'm going alone."

His face falls. "Why?"

"I think it'll be better." Even though, I'm not sure I'll be welcomed.

"Are they really into Voodoo?"

I hear the excitement in his voice.

"Yeah."

"Do they sacrifice chickens and drink their blood?"

I look at him in disgust. "That's Hollywood crap. Voodoo isn't like that." At least I don't think it is. But I can't see my grandmother and great-grandmother doing something so disgusting.

"When are you going?"

"Soon." The sooner the better.

Chapter 17

The trip is different this time, maybe because it takes place during the day.

My uncle, unable to leave his shop, has sent a man to ferry me down the waterway.

My guide doesn't say a lot, which is fine with me since my thoughts are occupied with thoughts of Eric, Hancock and creatures from Hell.

After seeing *Grand'pere* in the cemetery, I realize how vulnerable *Grand'mere* is. As much as I want to hate her for her mean words against my mother, I can't bring myself to despise her. She thought she was protecting me. Now it's my turn to protect her.

For the hundredth time I wipe my hands on my jeans. My feet tap restlessly against the bottom of the pirogue, and I will myself to study the bayou to take my mind off the coming reunion.

The waterway is as beautiful during the day as it is eerie at night. Snow white pelicans perch on half-submerged tree limbs and watch as our boat floats through the marshy area. This time I see the scaly tail of an alligator as it slides into the brackish water. The birds, small and large, are too numerous to count. Their songs fill the air with a symphony of chirps. Even though it's technically still winter, the irises have opened and their purple and yellow color adds to the exotic feel of the area. The bayou is not bound by the laws of nature. Before a week ago, I never knew such beauty existed just miles from my front door.

I concentrate on breathing in and breathing out, unsure of what I'll say to my grandmother and great-grandmother. Will they be able to help me or will they refuse to see me because of my rudeness the other night?

My guide grunts as the landing pier comes into view. No one rushes out of the house to greet me. I glance uncertainly at the high dock. How will I climb up? There are no steps. I turn and study the small man who has brought me here. He seems to be unaware of my dilemma or unwilling to help me. I guess he feels, "I've gotten you here. How you get up on land is your business."

I grasp the wet wood of the pier and prepare to hoist myself up. I can do this. How many times have I crept back into my bedroom from some midnight excursion with Scooter? But this is different. Pieces of rotten wood break off in my hand. Okay this is going to be a little harder than I thought.

As I mentally prepare for another try, my guide gives a loud whistle. Within a minute two men appear at the pier and lift me up and onto the boardwalk. Why didn't he do that earlier? Was it to watch me sweat?

"Thanks," I say to the men.

They nod. I can feel them watching me as I walk toward the house. Before I reach the door, my grandmother steps out. I hesitate.

"Lisette?"

"I'm sorry about what I said- how I acted..." The lump in my throat has grown so large I can barely speak around it. I blink several times and my grandmother's image swims. "I-"

She opens her arms and I run into them. She is a fit woman, but her body feels soft and comforting as she hugs me close.

"It is okay, little one. It was too much to take in all at once. We understand. Come." She turns me loose and gently pushes me through the open door.

It is silent inside the house that bustled with bodies and voices a few short nights go. "Where is my great-grandmother?"

"She is taking her afternoon nap. She is eighty-five and needs her rest. Let's have tea and we can talk."

She leads me to the back of the small house to a kitchen that looks out over the water. A small garden is marked off for planting. Behind me my grandmother runs water and I hear the tap of metal on metal and the click of the stove's burner igniting.

"We have lived in this spot for sixty years since your great-grandmother came from Haiti. I was born here and your mother also."

I open my mouth to ask a question.

She smiles and shakes her head. "No. You were born in New Orleans. My daughter wanted to please her new mother-in-law, so she gave in to your other grandmother's wishes that you be born there."

I felt a sharp pang of loss for the mother I didn't know. The mother I need so badly at this moment in my life.

"I..."

My grandmother smiles her encouragement.

"I think *Grand'mere* is in danger," I say in a rush.

She cocks her head as though listening to something I'm not saying. "In danger from whom?"

I remember the name the creature spoke. "I think from someone, something named Saarel."

My grandmother doesn't move. Her stillness scares me. She stares at me, but her eyes seem to see through me. My stomach twists and coils.

"Do not speak *that* name out loud," she whispers. "To speak his name gives him power."

I sink into one of the kitchen chairs. "So he's real."

The teapot whistles. She removes it from the burner and with trembling hands fills two cups. "Very real."

She places one of the cups in front of me, then fills a silver ball with loose tea leaves from a flowered canister. She plunges the ball into my cup of hot water.

"Your birth has been prophesied for thousands of years. It generated jealousy among the priestesses, especially Claudette."

Goosebumps raise on my arms. "Prophesied? My birth was prophesied?"

"Yes," she says simply. "Thousands of years ago."

I frown. "How? Why?"

She sits, and then takes both my hands in hers. "You will be the most powerful priestess in our lifetime." I try to extract my hands from hers. She shakes her head and squeezes my hands. "No, in all known lifetimes."

I can't make sense of what she's telling me. It's so unreal. I want to laugh, but the seriousness in her eyes stops the laughter dead in my throat.

"How do you know this?" I imagine a roomful of women sitting around telling old wives' tales.

"From The Book of Truths."

I frown. "From the *what*?"

"Book of Truths," she repeats. "It's a book as old as time. It tells the future."

"Tells whose future?"

"Everyone," she whispers.

I try and digest what she's saying. "Including me?"

She nods.

A chill runs over my body. "And this Claudette knew about me?"

"Yes- and the other one knew also."

I mentally supply Saarel's name for her.

"She made the pact, and offered you to... to the demon. He accepted her offer," my grandmother says.

I pull my hands from hers and wrap them around the tea cup for comfort, and I stare down into its brown depths, then up again at my grandmother. "How can she promise my soul? What about my will to choose?"

"When you make a bargain with a devil there is no free will. Claudette paid with her soul."

"But I didn't make the bargain, Claudette did."

My grandmother pushes her cup away. "It doesn't matter. You were yet to be born, a nonentity at that moment in time."

My head is fuzzy and her face swims in and out of focus. "So, I'm just to be sacrificed like a fatted calf?"

She covers my hand with hers. "Do not give up hope. This book might hold the answers you need to defeat *that* one."

I lean forward. My heart pounds so hard with excitement my voice comes out breathy. "How will the book help?"

She shakes her head. "I don't know. No one knows very much about it, but your great-grandmother assures me it exists."

Rising, she moves to the sink and empties her untouched cup of tea down the drain.

I force myself to calm down. I can't pin all my hopes on a book that might not exist. But something pops into my head. I turn to her. "If it tells your future, it must also tell your death, maybe even how you died."

She nods. "Maybe."

For the first time since I arrive, I feel hopeful. Now, I need all the information I can get about who I am, what my powers will be, and how I can defeat this Saarel. "You mentioned priestesses. What's that about?"

She stares out at the water. Her eyes take on a distance look. "We do not have male priests, only females. There has been a priestess in our line for thousands of years, before we came to this new land from Africa and took the name Toussaint."

"My mother..."

My grandmother nods. "Yes, my daughter was to be a priestess, but she died before her time."

The headlines from the New Orleans Times Picayune dance in front of my eyes. Couple Dies in Crash. I tell myself not to think about that. It's the past. I need to learn all I can about the future so I can protect *Grand'mere*. "Every female has been a priestess?"

She shakes her head. "No. Some have been ordinary women leading ordinary lives. Some have been good priestess, leading our flock. Only a few have been great."

She stares out the kitchen window. "Claudette was one of the good ones. But she was eaten up with jealousy. She knew sometime in the future you would be born, and in her present there was Marie Laveau. Her jealousy ate at her like a poison. She wanted to be as great as Marie and greater than you."

"So she sold my soul," I supply.

"Yes. She sold your soul to the devil. And I can see this devil using your father's mother to get to you."

I can't wrap my mind around all my grandmother is telling me. It's too much. Jumping up from the table, I pace the small kitchen.

"Lisette. Sit."

I throw my hands in the air. "I can't." But in the next instant I sink into a chair. "What if this is all a mistake. How... how do you know I'm this powerful priestess? It could be anyone in our family."

My grandmother grips my cold hands in hers. Her sad brown eyes hold mine. "It is prophesized that the priestess will be born in the seventh generation of the house of Toussaint. You-" she taps my hand-"are the only child born in this seventh generation. And there is the other..."

"The other?"

She nods. "You were born with a caul."

"What?" My voice rises to a squeak. "I was deformed?"

"No, no." She smiles slightly, rubbing my arms. "It is an old term that means at your birth the bag of waters was still intact."

I shake my head, still confused.

She sighs. "Before birth, babies live in a sac filled with fluid. It protects them."

I nod. "I learned that in Health class."

"Yes, yes," she says, nodding in agreement. "Usually it breaks during labor or the doctor breaks it. For whatever reason, the sac didn't break during your delivery. When you came out of your mother's womb, you were encased in an unbroken sac."

"Yuck." I draw back from her, disgusted.

She smiles slightly. "It is a very unusual thing. The nurses and doctor didn't understand the significance of what had happened, but your mother did. She knew that you were the one."

"So there's no chance that this priestess could be someone else?"

She shakes her head. "No. It is you."

Why is this happening to me? I feel this scream building like a volcano deep in my core, bubbling up until it erupts from my mouth in a long wail. "Noooo..."

My grandmother gathers me in her arms and lets me cry myself out. Finally throat raw and eyes swollen and itchy, I move out of her arms. Crying like a baby will not keep *Grand'mere* safe.

"Do you think this book will tell me how to protect *Grand'mere*?"

She shakes her head. "Like I said, I don't even know if it's real."

But the idea of this book, this lifeline, has made me excited, given me hope. "I've got to find this book," I say almost to myself.

"You can't. No one knows where it is, if it exists."

"I've got to find it. I just can't let him hurt her."

"You are still a caterpillar, not yet a butterfly. In your present stage you can do nothing to help her."

"How do I speed up the stages?"

She studies me, her gaze traveling over my face, my body. "Have you noticed any changes in your body, in your mind?"

In my mind? That confuses me, but I don't have the time to investigate that now. I tell her about the charm, raising the dead and the healing of Toto.

Her eyes widen. "I had no idea so much has occurred so soon. Normally the transformation to priestess occurs by the eighteenth year, but you, you are only fifteen."

"I'll be sixteen in a few days."

She smiles sadly. "Of course, *your* maturation would be different, faster."

"How many stages are there? What other skills will I possess?"

"I don't know. My guess is there are many stages to your transformation." Her eyes are dark and troubled. "Healing and the gift of sight are the only gifts we priestess have possessed."

I dance in place. "Maybe that's it. I can't see into the future. I didn't know the charm would work. Maybe that's the last and final one."

"How many of your friends know about you?"

Startled, I turn.

My great-grandmother stands in the kitchen door, her weight resting on a cane.

"What?" I ask, confused by her sudden appearance and this change in subject.

"How many of your friends know about you?" This time her voice is sharp and her words slow, as though she's talking to a mentally retarded child.

"They all know."

She draws back in surprise. "How can this be?"

I shake my head slowly. "I don't know. I never told them."

"It is the demon at work," she says. "He wants to create chaos, so you have no peace. He wants to keep you looking over your shoulder. Then when you least expect it, snap, the trap is set and he has you. These students, what do they know?"

"Just about the love charm. Only Eric knows about the healing."

"How does he know so much more?" my grandmother asks.

"He was there when I healed the dog."

"Do you trust him?" my grandmother asks, her eyes probing mine.

I remember the shadows in Eric's eyes, the unwillingness to answer my questions.

"You should trust no one," My great-grandmother snaps. "The people you put your faith in could be the devil's helpers, his slaves."

"What do you know of this boy?" My grandmother asks. She goes to my great-grandmother and helps her to a chair.

My mind swims with the doubts they've placed there. "Not much. His parents are in Europe and he lives with just one servant."

My great-grandmother snorts. "He probably has no parents, and this servant is probably the hand servant of the demon."

For once I agree with her. Hancock is spooky enough to be a demon.

"Mother," my grandmother says, "not everyone is in the devil's employee."

My great-grandmother lowers her body slowly into the chair before giving up and allowing gravity to pull her the rest of the distance. She lands with a grunt. "You're too trusting," she says to her daughter.

Then she turns her sharp eyes on me. "Trust no one." She took a sip of my tea and made a face. "Where's the honey?"

As my grandmother hunts in the pantry, my great-grandmother studies me. "So you came back. Are you ready to believe now?"

I nod. She's lost the gentleness from the other night. Now she's all sharpness and vinegar, as my *Grand'mere* would say.

"You will lead this flock when I'm gone."

From the corner of my eye, I see my grandmother's body stiffen, then she relaxes and continues her search for the honey.

My chest and throat tighten in a spasm. "I don't-"

"It doesn't matter what you want," my great-grandmother snaps. "They need you. Only you will have the strength to lead them out of the darkness to come."

My grandmother isn't searching the pantry any longer. She stares at her mother with pain in her eyes. "Lisette fears the demon is after her father's mother."

My great-grandmother puckers her lips after adding honey to the tea. She adds more. "She is probably right. He will use any means to get to our Lisette."

"How do I stop him?"

"You don't," great-grandmother says with a bluntness I find confusing. She was so sweet and gentle the other night. Now she's- she's an alligator with sharp teeth that cut to the bone.

"You will only be able to stop him when your journey to full priestess is complete."

"But no one knows when that will be," I say.

"And that's the way it should be," my great-grandmother says. "The transformation is shrouded in mystery. It's a safeguard against the evil one."

Was this trip a waste of time? No. At least I reestablished contact with my mother's family and I know about the Book.

But that doesn't help me keep *Grand'mere* safe. Of course, I could tell her everything. Will she believe me? Probably not. She'll rush me to Father Patrick and ask him to pray over me. Or better yet, and I almost giggle over this thought, ask him to do an exorcism.

My only hope is finding this all-knowing Book.

Chapter 18

The next morning I catch sight of Ashley and Michele strolling through the school corridor, making goo goo eyes at each other. Apparently the charm hasn't faded yet. It's sickening. But what's even more disturbing is I've created this nightmare.

"Hey, Lisette." Rick, one of Michele's groupies, is leaning on the locker to the right of mine. Watching from across the corridor are his friends. They stare at me with fascinated eyes. If I said boo they'd shit in their boxers.

I tune Rick out as I try to open my locker.

"There's this girl-"

I hold my hand in front of his face. "Don't-"

He doesn't say another word, just stands there silent as I get my books from my locker. Congratulating myself on how persuasive I've been, I turn to my left and run smack into Eric's chest.

"Are they bothering you?" he asks. His question is directed at me, but his gaze is focused on Rick and his friends.

Rick's face pales and he and his buddies scurry away like rats under the glare of bright lights.

"No." I try and put distance between Eric and myself by moving into the crowd of students making their way toward the next class.

It doesn't work. He falls into step beside me.

Do you miss me? I almost stumble as the words run through my mind. Why should I care whether he misses me? I stare at the other students in the hall rather than at him.

I've spent all day ducking down hallways not anywhere close to my classes just so I won't run into him. I ate lunch in the library stacks to avoid him.

"I can pick you up after school and drive you to my house to study."

"I'm busy tonight," I say, dashing into my classroom just as the bell rings and the teacher shuts the door in Eric's face.

I don't hear a word of the Biology lecture. Each time I attempt to take notes, my mind drifts off to the nightmarish scene in the alley. At some point, I look down at my notebook and find doodles of strange beasts being killed by a dark haired featureless male. Around the corners of my notebook *Grand'mere*'s name is traced over and over in black ink. I'm nowhere in the picture. What does that mean? My subconscious is telling me something, but what?

When I emerge from my class at the end of the hour, I half- expect Eric to be lounging against the wall waiting for me. He's not. Strangely, I'm disappointed.

At the end of school, I retrieve my books from my locker, close it, and come face to face with him.

"You need me," he says.

He doesn't say anything more. He doesn't have to. I've come to the same conclusion. I don't know how to protect *Grand'mere*. Only he does.

I give my agreement by falling into step beside him. We continue down the hall each in our own world, and then he turns to me. "I am going to pick you up in the morning and take you home in the evening."

I stop in my tracks and someone runs into me from behind.

"Sorry," I mumble, the student narrows her eyes at me as she walks around.

"Are you asking me or telling me?"

His face is blank, as though I'm speaking another language. Looking away, he seems to study the other students as they flow in the opposite direction. He turns back to me. "I'm telling you."

I see red. "Then the answer is no." I stomp away before he can say another word.

He catches up with me.

Traffic in the hall has stopped. We're causing a scene.

"Are you a Neanderthal?"

He blushes. "I've offended you, I apologize."

I can tell he doesn't use those words often. They sputter from his mouth like water from a rusted faucet.

"It is the only way I can protect you."

"Then ask me nicely."

He struggles with the words.

"Lisette..." I prompt.

"LisettecanIpickyouupinthemorning?"

It's the best I'm going to get, for now.

"Do you want to visit Toto?"

His dark eyes trace the outline of my face. "If it means spending time with you, yes, I do."

I stare down at the school's floor, trying hard not to smile. I can stop the smile, but I can't stop the flutter of my pulse.

Stay focused, Lisette. Find out about the Book. You've got to protect *Grand'mere*.

"I'll arrange it with Mrs. Joyner, then call you."

He nods.

I never make the call.

**

Rain beats down on my head as I knock on Eric's patio door later that evening. Tucked underneath my yellow rain slicker, Toto claws me trying to get free. There's no bell at this entrance so I pound on the door. I wonder if anyone can hear me over the heavy downpour. Shadows are growing in the garden. I shiver. After several minutes, I reach out a cold, wet hand and place it on the doorknob. It turns easily, and I step inside.

The house is strangely silent. Rain thuds on the roof. Somewhere a clock tics loudly. Conscious of my wet shoes, I toe them off, then pull Toto from under my slicker. I leave the raincoat on the floor by the door. Better a puddle in one place than rain all over the house.

"Shh," I whisper to the dog when he whimpers. I don't know why I whisper, but the house seems to demand it. I pad barefooted to the staircase.

My heart pounds like an amped up bass. "Eric? Are you there?" He doesn't answer.

I glance back at the patio door, judging the distance. At the first sign of Hancock, I'm out of here. Maybe bringing Toto here is not such a good idea, but what choice to I have? Mrs. Joyner asked me to take him because the dogs didn't get along. Nappy doesn't want to share his home. I can't take Toto to my place because of *Grand'mere*'s allergies, not that I care how she feels. I hope Eric will keep him here just long enough for me to talk to Mrs. Summers, Leticia's mother.

"Eric?" I place my foot on the bottom stair and then the one above it. Toto bumps my chin with his small head. His body trembles in my arms, but I continue upward. I don't know why I don't just go home, but something is keeping me here. Feeling like a stupid girl in a horror movie, I continue to climb.

At the top of the stairs, I hear Eric's voice. Relieved, I start down the corridor. I stop at an open door, light spills out into the dimmer hall.

"Do not disobey him," Hancock warns.

The butler's voice sends a chill through my body. His posture is that of a man in control, not a servant. He and Eric are equals. I can tell this by their body language, by the tension in the air. I don't know what the conversation is about, but there's definitely a challenge in their words.

I'm outside a bedroom. It contains a single piece of furniture. A mattress covered in a white sheet sits directly on the floor. Eric stands in front of an open closet. Hancock is just inside the door, his back to me. Glancing behind me, I wonder if I can get back down the stairs without their realizing I'm here.

"For whatever reason, you're taking your time with this task. If you're planning to-"

Toto barks. Hancock stops speaking, turns and sees me.

Dressed in dark slacks and a white shirt, he's shoeless. He's also drenched. Rain water collects in a pool at his bare feet. Clutched in his large hand is a bouquet of flowers. The petals are still wet. Dirt clings to the stems of the flowers.

Fear drives all sensible thought from my brain. All I can think about is where did he find flowers blooming in February?

"Your little friend is here."

The announcement isn't necessary. Eric spotted me long before Hancock did.

What're you doing here?" Eric's tone isn't welcoming as he steps around his butler.

I extend Toto toward him. "I brought Toto." My voice is soft, frightened. I try again. "Mrs. Joyner can't keep him. I thought—"

Eric grabs my arm and leads me down the hall to the media room. Once there, he moves away from me, his attention straying back to the room down the corridor.

Toto squirms in my arms, and I place him on the floor. He scampers away, glad to be on solid ground.

"What was that all about?" I tilt my chin in the direction of the stark bedroom.

Eric's lips thin. "Nothing that would interest you."

Oh, but it would.

Squatting, he calls to Toto. The dog tries to run on the shiny wood floors, but his legs splay. He comes to rest between Eric's legs.

"Why don't you tell your parents? Maybe they're fire him."

He laughs, there's no happiness in the sound. "My father is in Hancock's corner not mine."

I stoop so I can look in his eyes, then place a hand on his shoulder. "I'm sorry."

"Don't be. I'm use to it." He gives me a lopsided smile that doesn't reach his eyes.

Eric lifts the dog into his arms and Toto lathers his cheek with a pink tongue.

"Ugg.." Placing the dog on the floor, Eric stands and uses the bottom of his shirt to wipe his face.

"He likes you." I've heard animals can sense the goodness in people. Underneath Eric's layer of mystery and strangeness, there must be a good soul.

Toto runs off to look for new adventures.

"How did you heal him?" Eric doesn't look at me, but watches the dog.

A tidal wave of despair washes over me as his words sink in. I'm surprised he hasn't asked sooner. I wanted him to believe I'd done something based in modern medicine instead of rooted in dark magic. "I don't know." I can't tell him about the Voodoo thing. He'll really think I'm weird. "It just happened." My voice is strangled as I fight back tears. All I want is for him to see me as a normal girl. If I tell him the true, he'll never look at me the same.

He leans down and touches my arm. "Don't cry."

I search for my backpack. It takes me a moment to remember I didn't bring it. "I'm not crying." Cramming my hands into my jeans, I watch the terrier until I think I can speak without bawling like a baby. "Can you watch Toto for a couple of days until I see if Mrs. Summer's will take him?"

He nods.

"And Eric?"

His lifts an eyebrow.

"Don't let Hancock hurt him?"

Eric stares at me, his eyes probing. "I'll take good care of him."

I give a half hearted smile, then turn to leave the room. At the door, I pause, but don't face him. For some reason, I can't look in his eyes. I'm afraid of what I'll see. "What did you mean when you said you were my guardian angel?"

He hesitates so long I look over my shoulder.

A queer look passes over his face-like he swallowed something awful.

"Because that is what I am. I was sent to protect you."

Intrigued, I turn to face him fully. "Really? Who sent you?"

After what seems like forever, he opens his mouth to speak, but snaps it shut. He's stares over my shoulder. I sense Hancock before I turn to find him behind me, holding a tray.

"Would the young lady like some cookies?" He's changed his pants and now wears shoes.

He's asking me, but his eyes are locked on Eric. I can feel the tension. Toto must feel it too, because he whimpers and pees on the floor.

Scooping up the dog, Eric says in a cold voice, "She's leaving." He glides me around Hancock and out the door.

As Eric drives me home, I watch him from the corner of my eye. His hands grip the steering wheel until his knuckles show white beneath the skin. The only sound in the car is Toto panting in the back seat.

In my mind, I replay the last words Hancock said before he knew I was in the hall. He spoke of a task Eric hadn't completed and of disobeying. What was the task? He spoke to Eric as though they were not employee and employer's son, but equals. No, that's not right. Not equals, but almost as though Hancock was Eric's superior. His tone was commanding, and Eric's body was tense, ready for a fight. I don't trust Hancock. And because I'm no longer sure of the relationship between Eric and Hancock, I can't trust Eric.

I'm not going to speak of the Book. It's too dangerous to share its existence with someone who might mention it, even innocently, to Hancock.

**

The next morning I wait for Eric at the end of my street. I don't want *Grand'mere* to see him and ask questions. Because then I'll have to lie. I hate lying to her.

As our vehicle speeds toward school, Eric turns on the radio. Jazz drifts through the car, filling up the spaces left by our unspoken thoughts. The scent of his soap makes my nose tingle, though not in an unpleasant way. I want to ask him what he's wearing, but I don't want him to know I'm that aware of him.

We're sitting at a red light just before we go over the bridge to the Westside. The rain makes the morning commute as sluggish as my brain.

"Do you want to go to my house after school?" he asks.

I shake my head maybe a little too forcefully because he stares at me until a car horn blares behind us. He lets the clutch out, and the car eases forward only to come to a stop a few yards ahead.

"Why not?"

Because your butler scares the shit out of me. "I just don't want to."

His gaze darts to my face then back to the road. "We can go to your house."

I shake my head again. Even though there's a strong urge to protect her, I'm not back on speaking terms with *Grand'mere* yet. The two of us dance around each other, pretending her hateful words were never spoken.

"Then what do you want to do?" His voice is sharp, impatient.

"Look, it was your idea to drive me around," I lash out. 'We don't have to do this."

He breathes deeply through his nose, and I can almost imagine he's counting to ten in his head.

Sighing, I lean into the heated seat. "I'm sorry. I didn't mean to come off all wacked. I want things to be the way they were. I want you to go back to Michele, and I'll go back to..." I'm about to say, I'll go back to the way I was before I made the charm. Actually, I want things to be the way they were when I was at my old school. I wasn't a prom queen, but I was comfortable in my surroundings and no one noticed me.

"There's no going back, Lisette." His voice is flat and cold.

Though he speaks in riddles, my body understands and responds to the tone of his voice, causing a wave of nausea to roll over me, leaving me shaken and chilled.

We travel the rest of the way to school in silence. He pulls into an empty space in the school parking lot, then stares through the windshield at the passing students.

"What did you mean- there's no going back?"

Finally he turns to me. "We are both on a path with no exits."

"What—" My throat is dry. I swallow and try again. "What are you talking about?"

Students walk by the car, peering in. When he doesn't answer, I reach for the door handle, ready to jump out and run. Run from him, his words and my life.

He grabs my arm before I place a sneakered foot on the wet gravel.

"Meet me in the library after school," he says.

"Why?" I'm tired of his cryptic answers and his mysterious ways.

"We can talk."

Maybe my disbelief is mirrored in my eyes, because he says, "I promise."

I study him for a long moment, then nod.

He releases my hand. I'm out of the car and running for the school's door, ignoring the girls shocked looks as they take in me and Eric together.

**

The day drags. I see Eric from a distance, but I don't make an effort to seek him out. It's not that I don't want to be with him, I do, but here at school I'm always aware that he's Michele's boyfriend. If it wasn't for the charm, he'd be with her now and not giving me a second thought.

At the end of the day, I'm outside the library. I wasn't going to show, but he has answers I need.

As he approaches, three giggling girls trail behind him like he's Lil Boosie.

When he sees me, his face lights up like an over-decorated Christmas tree. Dazzled, I can only blink. Is that smile meant for me? He must really like me-maybe even love me.

Whoa. Sanity intrudes. How can he love Michele one week and me the next? He can't. In that moment, everything that stands between us flashes through my mind-the secret side of him that peeps out from time to time, Michele, demons, and Hancock. Now, I want to run in the opposite direction.

He must sense my indecision. Like an eclipse, a cloud passes over his face, and the smile is gone. Although I want to see it again, I know I have no right to it. That smile rightfully belongs to Michele, and I stole it from her.

I make a decision in that moment-it's time to undo the charm. No more hesitation. Tomorrow, I'll ask my uncle to help me break the love spell I've cast over Michele. Today, I'll enjoy Eric's company and find out what he knows about me.

We find a corner table, as far from Ms. Summers as we can get.

The silence of the library is broken by the sound of laughter. The girls have taken a table across the room from us, but close enough so they can still see Eric. They eye us now, or I should say, eye Eric. This makes me remember something.

"Eric, before—before the charm you didn't like me. Why are you hanging with me now?"

His gaze travels over my features. I can feel heat crept up my face.

"Because you're strong. And there's something special about you-something unique that I didn't expect."

Why do I find it so hard to believe him? "But you made fun of me."

He shakes his head. "I never made fun of you."

I remember those chilling brown eyes observing me, studying me like a cat sizing up a mouse. He's right. He didn't make fun of me, just spooked me with those eyes.

"I've always liked you. I just didn't know how to tell you. It is not easy to approach you. Not as easy as talking to them." He nods in the direction of his admirers.

As though they know they're the topic of our conversation, the trio starts another round of annoying giggles that brings Ms. Summers over to their table.

I have one more question I have to ask him before we all get kicked out of the library.

I wait until the librarian returns to her desk before I whisper. "What'd you mean this morning when you said my path had no exit?"

He stares down at the smooth, shiny table top, emotions playing across his face-emotions I can't put a name to. When he raises his gaze to mine, he's made some kind of decision. His eyes darken and his mouth thins.

"Whatever you were before I met you, you cannot go back down that road. You have or will have great power. People will want that power for themselves. And they will try to take it from you."

For a moment my vision blurs. His words echo those of my great-grandmother. "How—how do you know all this?

A muscle clenches in his jaw. I wonder if he's going to answer my question. I lay my smaller hand on top of his. My stomach does a funny little flip flop. It's the first time I've touched him. I don't know why I do it now. It just seems important that I do. His skin feels hot against the chill of my own. "Please tell me, Eric," I whisper.

Is Eric getting information from Hancock? Not for the first time, I feel Hancock knows a lot about me. Maybe more than I know about myself. But how could he? His only contact with anyone that orbits through my world has been with Father Patrick. And the priest knows nothing of my Voodoo roots.

"Did Hancock tell you about me?"

Eric jerks his hand away so quickly I think he'll fall out of his chair. "Hancock?"

His surprise is so genuine I know Hancock isn't the source. Then who is?

Eric recovers, glancing around to see who might be watching. "I can only tell you someone means you harm."

Who? Since it isn't Hancock that can leave only one other person. Chilly fingers run over my skin. "Is it Saarel?"

Eric's face is blank-so blank that it's telling.

But it doesn't matter whether it's Hancock or Saarel. Both are Satan's hand servants. "How—how can I protect myself?"

Eric's gaze bores into mine. "I don't know that you can."

Chapter 19

My Uncle Henri opens the door to his shop just wide enough for me to enter. To the waiting customers, he says. "We will open in fifteen minutes."

"So, little one, you come again." He shuts the door and flips the electric switch that start the large bamboo ceiling fans spinning.

The motion of the blades stirs up the scent of incense. The aroma is sharp and tickles my nose, making me sneeze.

Even if it means losing Eric as a friend, I have to undo the effects of the charm. "I have a problem."

His dark eyes study me as though he can see deep within my soul. "And what is this problem?"

Avoiding his eyes, I look around his body at the growing number of people waiting outside the shop. "I need to undo a charm."

"Ah." He nods his head calmly as though he gets that request every day.

I tell him about taking money from Ashley to make the love charm.

"And it worked?" He gives a little shake of his head and a slight smile lifts one corner of his wide mouth. "Of course it did." His brown eyes search my face. "And you feel guilty?"

"They thought I was a Voodoo priestess."

"The kids at school?"

I nod. "I shouldn't have done it. It- it wasn't right. I just want to give Ashley back his money."

Henri studies me with something like pity in his eyes. "And the fact that the charm worked doesn't tell you something?"

I keep my mouth shut and stare down at the old warped floors, refusing to admit I understand what he's saying.

He lifts my chin with a mahogany finger. His eyes are dark with an old knowledge I can't begin to understand. "One day you will be the greatest Voodoo priestess New Orleans has ever known."

Cold fingers trail down my spine. I jerk my face from his hands and back away. "I don't want to be a priestess." I turn and make for the door. This has been a mistake. Why did I even come?

"Lisette."

I stop with my hand on the handle, but I don't face him.

"It's the intent that counts," Henri says. "It doesn't matter what you make or put into the charm. It's what's in your heart that counts."

With his words ringing in my ears, I open the shop door and push my way through the waiting customers. I'm no closer to knowing how to undo the damage I've done than when I woke this morning. But what really eats away at me is the realization I don't want to break the charm's spell. I want Michele to stay in love with Ashley so I can have Eric all to myself.

**

I asked Eric to meet me at the river. As I wait, I think about my uncle's words. What is my intent? I want to return things to the way they were before I made the charm, but I don't want to lose Eric's friendship. And I surely will, but my Catholic upbringing eats away at my selfishness. I have to make things right, then after I do, I have to go in search of the Book of Truths. Remembering

Eric's words, I know I can only go forward, no more hiding in the past of my youth.

Lightning crackles and highlights the skyline on the west side of the river as rain continues to fall. Brown water laps at the third wooden tie from the bottom. The river is seriously rising. It's been raining forever. I can hear my *Grand'Pere's* voice in my head. *"Noah is coming."* I smile to myself. I miss him. He brought fun into our house to offset *Grand'mere's* seriousness.

"You are happy?"

I jump in surprise. Eric slides down onto the plank beside me. He appears unconcerned that he's sitting in a puddle of water.

I study his beautiful face. His eyes are a mystery to me. Sometimes they're blue and at other times they look brown. His normally coffee colored hair is wet and appears darker. Water slides down his pale cheeks and lingers at the corners of his mouth. His lips look so soft. I reach out to touch them, but then draw back. I have no right to touch him. He belongs to someone else.

"You were smiling until I sat next to you. Have I made you unhappy?"

No. The last few days we've been together have been the happiest I've been in... forever. But of course, I can't admit that to him. To say those words would let him know how important he's become to me. Giving him that knowledge would hurt almost as much as saying goodbye.

Instead, I shake my head and fake a smile. "I'm fine." I look into his eyes to complete my lie. I memorize the strong structure of his face, his ears that lie flat against his head and a dimple at the corner of his mouth. Forcing myself to be bolder than I am, I comb my fingers through the wet mass of his hair. Three fine strands come away and nestle between my fingers. I close my hand around the hair and tuck them into my jacket pocket.

"I like it when you touch me."

He studies me until my cheeks flush. It will be the one and only time I'll touch him.

I turn and stare out at the turbid water. A large log bobs in the current.

"What's happened? Have you seen more of the demons?" His voice is full of concern.

I shake my head. "No demons." Just the ones that live inside me. The evil ones that tell me I can keep you.

"Then why so sad?"

I give him what I hope passes for a convincing smile. "Just worried about *Grand'mere*." That's no lie.

"What can I do to make you smile?"

Just the question, a sign of his caring makes me smile. It fades as I remember what I have to do and how much I'm going to miss him.

"Eric, can I ask you something?"

He tilts his head and smiles at me. "Anytime."

Butterflies play in my stomach. "Can I kiss you?" I hold my breath waiting for his answer.

But he doesn't answer. Instead, he leans toward me and places his cool lips over mine. My eyes flutter closed and the sound of the river recedes. All I hear is my own pulse beating in my ears and feel the touch of his hands stroking my face. His tongue traces the contours of my lips.

"Open your mouth," he whispers.

I obey. When his tongue touches mine an electric current shoots across my skin, leaving it hypersensitive.

The world disappears. I'm not aware the kiss has ended until I hear my name whispered on the wind. As I slowly open my eyes, Eric's smiling brown eyes stare down into my mine.

Then the reality of my world returns. This is the last time we'll be together like this. Tomorrow I'll just be the weird girl with the clothes from Wal-Mart and he won't give me a second look.

Chapter 20

Today is Friday, five days before Ash Wednesday, which starts the season of Lent. People usually give up something meaningful during the season. This year I'm giving up Eric.

Ignoring the shouts and laughter of the other students, I rest my forehead on my locker and chant the words I've been saying all morning. "Michele and Eric belong together. Michele and Eric belong together." I must make myself believe it.

Since Michele is under the charm's power, I guess whatever I'm going to say needs to be said over her. But according to my uncle, the words don't mean as much.

I arrived at school early so I wouldn't miss her. There's only five minutes before the first bell, and she hasn't arrived at her locker. I have to do it today, since this is the last day of school before the break for Mardi Gras.

"You will be late for class."

I turn my head, never losing contact with the metal locker. Dressed in tan cargo pants and a black t-shirt, Eric leans against Michele's locker, his hair is still wet from either the shower or the rain or both.

"Hey." My voice quivers.

His lips turn up at the corners in a brief smile.

"Why so sad?" He trails a forefinger down the side of my face, leaving a trail of goose bumps along my skin.

Here is my chance to tell him how I feel about him. "Eric, I-"

The click of heels on the marbled floors drags my attention away from him to Michele who struts toward us.

"Hi, Eric." Her red painted nails clutch a Coach purse. She gives off a cool sophistication I'll never match.

He turns to face her. "Michele."

Now is the time. The corridor is almost empty of students. I can do it now. I fumble with my locker's combination. Michele continues to talk to Eric as I try to remember the stupid numbers. Why didn't I have the charm out and ready? *Because you didn't want to use it.*

Finally I spin to the last digit, yank open my locker and grab the charm from the shelf. When I turn with the charm clutched tight in my sweaty palm, I see Eric's retreating back. He's gone.

"What's wrong, freak?"

The charm may have made Michele Ashley's love slave, but it hasn't changed her feelings toward me. She still lives to torment me.

Her face twists into a sneer.

I don't have to give her back to Eric. I can let her stay just as she is and hope the spell doesn't fade.

"Can't speak?" She taunts.

But I can't do that. My soul will be forever damned. *But you'll have Eric.* Yes, I'll have Eric, but I want him to choose freely to be my friend, my...love. I don't want him to be with me because he can't have Michele.

I grab her hand. She lets out a squeak of surprise. I place the charm into her palm and close her fingers around the small cloth sack. She tries to pull away and looks surprised by my strength.

"You belong to Eric, Eric belongs to you. Let it be as it was," I intone.

For a moment nothing changes. But the hall now empty of students resonates with static energy.

Michele's eyes lose focus for the blink of an eye, then she glances down at our bound hands.

I release her, and she uncurls her fingers. The charm and her purse fall and land at her feet. "What the hell?" She stares at the charm for a moment and then a look of horror crosses her face.

"What have you done?" Hands to her face, she rushes around me to get to my open locker. "Where's the mirror?"

I stand mutely in front of her, trying to determine if the charm has worked.

"Where's the mirror, freak?" When she discovers there's no mirror, she pushes me out of the way and rushes down the hall. Her purse lies on the floor, forgotten.

**

Michele and I don't share any classes. So as much as I hate going to the cafeteria, I have to see if the charm worked.

I take a seat at one of the tables that's shielded by a column, and peer around it to check out Michele's table. The usual suspects are there minus her and Eric.

Are they together at this very moment? My stomach twists until the sight of the food on my tray makes me want to puke.

I bite my lip. If they don't show up soon, my mouth will be a bloody mess. As if on cue, Eric enters the cafeteria and moves toward his old table. Before taking a seat he glances around the cafeteria. I duck behind one of the white Doric columns. Why I don't know, because he's probably searching for Michele not me. Any feelings he might have for me will vanish the minute Michele appears.

And appear she does. She saunters into the cafeteria not one minute after Eric and moves toward him, bestowing fake smiles along the way.

Ashley, who's been watching the door, probably for her appearance, smiles and pats the chair next to him. She ignores him and signals to one of the girls sitting in a chair next to Eric to get up. The skinny red-headed girl, like all the students at the table, worships Michele and thinks nothing of giving up her seat and finding another. Michele slides into the chair and smiles brightly up at Eric. He smiles back.

Ashley frowns. But he's clueless and stupid, so he gets up and walks around to Michele's side. He pushes

Rick out of his chair, which is next to Michele, and takes that seat. It's like musical chairs.

Michele ignores him as she leans in close to Eric, touching his arm and staring fawn-like into his eyes.

I want to gag. My stomach churns and twists on itself. I've seen enough. Rising, I pick up my untouched lunch tray and move toward the exit. I don't bother trying to make myself invisible. There's too much action going on at that table for anyone to notice me.

But, I can't keep myself from glancing over just in the off chance Eric is looking for me and has seen through Michele's attempts to make love to him with her eyes. Fat chance.

Frowning and confused, Ashley grabs Michele's arm and says something I can't hear over the chatter in the cafeteria. She freezes him with one of her "how dare you" looks. When he tries to touch her again, she stands and glares down at him. She's quite tall at about five feet nine inches. Whatever she says makes him flush scarlet and the mouths of the group fall open in surprise.

I've seen enough. I dispose of my tray on the conveyor belt. The new charm has worked and Eric and Michele are back together. I can barely see the stairs leading out of the cafeteria for the tears pooling in my eyes.

**

After the last class I rush to my locker, trying to make it to the bus stop without running into Michele and Eric.

Someone grabs my arm and spins me around. "What happened?"

Ashley's eyes are slits of fury.

"Wh--What do you mean?"

"You know what I mean." There's spit at the corners of his mouth.

Traffic in the hall has slowed until there's a jam of gawking students in front of my locker.

"I mean-" For the first time he seems aware of the other kids milling around. "I mean," he lowers his voice. "The charm isn't working. You need to make another. And this time stronger."

Twisting out of his grip, I dig into my jeans pocket and pull out all his cash and shove it into his hands. Some of it flutters to the floor. I don't even care if everyone sees us making the exchange. "What we did was wrong."

He stares at the money and turns scarlet, then he tries to give it back to me.

Stepping out of reach, I back into the lockers. "I can't take your money. I won't make another charm."

"Listen to me, you mulatto, quadroon, whatever you are, freak. You took my money before, you take it now. I want Michele back."

"She's not yours," I whispered.

The crowd of students is growing. He grabs my arm and attempts to drag me away from the listening horde.

I resist, pulling my arm out of his hand. "We can't play with people's lives. It's wrong."

"It wasn't so wrong when you saw my money."

I blush, remembering how I felt when he plunked all those green bills in large denominations on the library table. "I know. I was greedy. I shouldn't have taken your money." It's hard for me to apologize. If he touches me or shouts at me one more time, I'm going to lose it.

"Listen-" Ashley grabs my arm. I can't say what happened next. One moment he's standing in front of me blowing his Dorito breath in my face, and the next, he's lying in a heap on the floor on the opposite side of the hall.

"You okay?"

Eric's voice flows over me like warm honey. Immediately I remember this isn't my Eric. I can't look at him. I don't want to see what's in his eyes. I don't want to see I'm back to my status as a non-entity and he's just being kind. I move around him to grab my backpack and get the hell out of Dodge.

"Hey stupid!" Ashley shouts as he rises awkwardly to his feet.

I groan. He doesn't have enough sense to stay down. Ashley doesn't want to mess with Eric. I've seen him slay monsters.

Like a tennis match, students' heads swivel between Ashley on one side of the corridor and Eric on the other. The energy level is enough to blow out the windows in the building. I can close my eyes and for this moment I could be at Easton. It's all the same. If there's a possibility of entertainment provided by a fight, all students, no matter how rich or poor, behave the same.

"What's going on here?" Mrs. Matheson's voice booms over the chatter in the hall, as she makes her way through the crowd.

I don't wait for the fall-out, but join the scattering masses.

I bolt out into the rain, running over students in my haste to put distance between, Eric, this suck butt school and me.

I leap down the front steps and charge after the city bus as the driver pulls away from the curb. I don't break stride, even though my jeans are soaked and flap around my sneakers like flags whipping in high wind. I'll run to the next bus stop if I have to.

Luckily, the driver sees me in the rearview mirror or some kindly soul on the bus tells him I'm trying to get on, because he slows to a stop. Breathless, I jump on.

"Thanks," I say as I show him my pass. He nods and I start down the aisle looking for an unoccupied seat.

The bus pulls away from the curb as I sit. After a few stops by the bus to pick up additional passengers, my pulse rate slows and I turn to stare out the window. Humidity clouds the glass. Using the palm of my hand, I wipe the moisture away.

A red convertible pulls up to the light. The car is on the left side of the bus, so I can't see the driver only the passenger. Michele Whitley stares up at the bus and like some heat-seeking missile her eyes find mine and she smiles smugly.

**

Rain pelting my bedroom window wakes me later that night. My legs are tangled in the sheets, and I'm breathless as though I've been running. I lay motionless, trying not to think about the events of the day, trying not to see Michele's self-satisfied smile as the car, in a burst of speed so typical of Eric, shoots away from the traffic light.

I did the right thing by reversing the charm's spell. But why don't I feel better? Why does my heart sit in my chest like a lump of clay?

My other problem also keeps me awake. How can I get my hands on the Book of Truths? I mean it's not like I can waltz up to Saarel and say "May I see the book?" First, I don't know how to find Saarel, and second, what if the book doesn't exist?

The rain against the window seems louder. It takes me a moment to realize it's not rain.

Eric. A stupid grin splits my face. I throw back the sheet and dash to the window. Only it's Scooter.

"What do you want?"

"Come out." His attempt at a whisper sounds loud in the silent night.

I don't want to. I'm not in the mood for his antics. I just want to climb back in bed and sleep my life away. "Why?"

"I've got news."

Wrapped in my own despair I failed to realize Scooter's body is twitching, a sure sign that something's up. And I know him. He'll just keep hurling rocks at my window until I give in or *Grand'mere* hears and comes to investigate. "Give me a minute."

I slip into jeans, a sweatshirt and sneakers, then climb out the window. I land with a plop in standing water. Great.

Scooter is buzzing around me before I have time to indulge in anymore self-pity.

"Boogie's out."

I frown. "What?"

"The judge dismissed the case on some technicality."

"That's great, Scoot."

He's so excited he doesn't realize I'm only half there. I stare out at the quiet street, expecting Eric to come walking out of the fog. Is he with Michele? Is she playing with Toto?

"Hey."

Scooter's sullen features are up in my face.

"I know he's not your brother, but you could at least pretend that you're interested."

"Sorry." I shift my attention from the street to my best friend, the friend who's been there for me since we were six. "I'm listening."

He stares at me as though he doesn't believe me.

"Let's walk," I say. Needing to get away from the house, I grab his arm and start pulling him toward the street.

"Where are we going?"

"Let's go down to the river."

He stops. "That's two miles away and it's late."

With one hand on my hip, I stare him down. "You afraid of the dark?"

His lips twitch as he tries not to laugh. "Hell, naw. Let's rock."

"So what was the technicality?"

"Okay, it was like this..."

I sighed. Scooter can drag a story out until you just want to scream. We walk. I try to listen and nod at the appropriate times. Scooter's such a good brother. It's too bad Boogie isn't worthy of that concern.

He continues with this long tale, but I'm only listening with one ear. The other part of my brain has picked up a smell that causes the hair on my neck to stand up and quiver.

I grab his arm. "Scoot?"

"What?" His voice is irritated. I've stopped him right in the middle of his story.

"Scoot?" I say again as I turn in a circle trying to see through the fog. I swear it's thicker than when we left my house. "I think we have company."

Chapter 21

Two figures-or I should say one figure and one creature walking upright-step out of the fog.

"What the fuck?" Scooter tumbles backwards, a hand going into one of his pockets.

My heart only races in my chest this time. It doesn't try to derail itself like the first time I saw the undead. And that's what they are. They don't look like the creature Eric killed, but they're definitely not of this world. The stench gives them away.

One of the two has arms that hang below its knees and hands that end in claws. Its head is the size and shape of an oblong watermelon, its eyes glow red and its bare feet are webbed. The other one looks more human-like, but his eyes are dark pits that show no emotion and no sign of life. But it's his hands that gross me out. They're black like they've been burned and now are peeling, leaving oozing skin dangling from bone.

"Himself is waiting," the one with the lifeless eyes says.

Don't they know anything else to say?

"Get behind me, Lis," Scooter says.

"There's nothing you can do," I say, resisting his push.

He looks sideways at me. "I can cut them up real bad." A knife blade gleams dully in his hand.

My mind flashes to another night and another flash of shining metal. "That's not going to do any good."

He ignores me, probably thinking as a girl I can't possibly know what I'm talking about. "Damn, they're ugly. Even their mothers couldn't possibly love those mugs."

He hasn't gotten it yet. "They're not human, Scoot."

"Huh?" He takes his eyes off the pair and stares at me like I've lost my mind.

I've been wondering if I have. "They're not alive and that switchblade won't do jack."

"And you know this because..." His eyes are rooted on the pair as he moves back a couple of steps, pulling me with him.

The demons don't move. Is it because they know they can easily catch us?

"I've seen them killed before."

"What?" Scooter's eyes are bright and disbelieving in his thin face.

I don't look at him, but watch the demon pair. What will they do if we run? Chase us? Can we outrun them?

Then it comes to me. They want me, not Scooter. If I run, they'll chase me and leave him alone. But there's one problem with that scenario. Scoot won't leave me. And they'll probably tear him to pieces if he stays with me. I can't let that happen.

We're about five blocks from the Royal Street police precinct. If we can get there, Scooter might live. Not that the police can do anything against these creatures, but the bright lights might make them slink away. The only other option is to fight, and somehow I don't think demon fighting is one of my newfound skills. I wish telepathy was. Where is Eric when I need him?

"If I come with you, will you let my friend go?" I direct my question to the one with the dead eyes.

"What? Uh-uh," Scooter says. "You're not going anywhere without me."

"Himself wants only you," Dead Eyes says. "We will let the other one live."

"Come on mutha fuckers." Scooter bounces on the balls of his feet.

He has no idea what he's dealing with, but I do and I don't want my friend to die. I touch his arm. "I want you to watch out for *Grand'mere* for me."

"What?" He blinks several times probably unsure he's heard me correctly.

Before he can fully process what I've just asked him to do, I take off running blindly into the fog, praying I'm headed toward the police station. Praying also the demons will be so surprised they'll chase me and forget about Scooter. The fog is thick, and I'm practically running blind.

Please, please, let them follow me. Let Scooter be safe. The air pushes out of my lungs, and my side burns like Scooter's switchblade has sliced open my flesh. Sweat pours down my back underneath my sweatshirt, even as the moisture from the drizzling rain slides down my face.

Even though I expect them to chase me, when I hear the sound of feet slapping against pavement, the pit of my stomach drops.

The fog has distorted the sound. Are the footsteps in front of me or behind? My heart beats in time with the footfalls.

Then one second I'm running, the next my legs are pumping in mid-air. My breath hitches in my throat when I glance down. The red-eyed creature smiles at me, revealing razor sharp teeth as he holds me above his large cranium.

Tucking me close to his funky body, he takes off in a lope. Wind and rain batter my face. I'm cold from the rain soaking through my sweatshirt and from the fear of what's to come.

Is this how I die? I want to laugh at my grandmother's prophecy that I'll be a great Voodoo priestess. I won't live that long. I pray Scooter got away.

The creature slows its sprint to a slow jog as we move through a dark alley. Glass crunches beneath its webbed feet. Where are we? Where is he taking me?

My head swims from the pain of its sharp claws digging into my body and the stench wafting off his dead flesh.

We enter an abandoned building and the smell almost overpowers the one coming from the creature-almost. The building stinks of unwashed bodies, urine, and shit. My head bobs with each step the creature takes as we descend into the black, inky depths of the building.

He stops. Shifting me in his grasp, then reaches out and touches a wall at the bottom of the stairs. Glaring yellow light diffuses the darkness and the brick wall shimmers until a gaping hole appears.

Terrified of what waits for me, I punch, kick and claw at any part of the creature's body I can get to. He howls when my nails scrape away some of the tough skin on his side. I reach for its bulbous red eyes, but he holds me away from his body and shakes me until my brain feels like it's bouncing around in my skull.

Even though I'm dizzy and nauseous, I realize that this must be the entrance into Saarel's world. If I travel through this portal, my life is over. He will never release me. I start punching and kicking again, but it doesn't do any good. The creature just grips me tighter and steps through the hole.

The opening reseals with a hiss.

**

Flying through traffic lights, Eric's car ate up the distance between his house and Lisette's. A fear like hunger gnawed at his gut. His instincts told him she was in trouble. He couldn't explain it, but since he'd been in this dimension, intuitively, he'd been able to divine almost every instance in which she'd needed him.

He'd been so preoccupied by this feeling of impending danger that when Michele asked for a ride home from school he'd given her an absentminded okay. When she'd practically climbed into his lap while he drove, he knew Lisette had made another charm to reverse the first one.

What Lisette didn't know was that no charm she made would affect him. One, he was immune to such things, and two, he had never been in love with Michele. He had used her to get to Lisette. When he'd entered Haverford, he'd needed to attach himself quickly to a group and be accepted as one of the crowd. With Michele's inflated opinion of herself, it had been easy to make her think he cared. It allowed him to watch and wait for Lisette's arrival at Haverford without calling attention to himself. Arranging for her to have the locker next to Michele's had taken a little more manipulation.

Maybe because he was preoccupied with his thoughts of the amber-eyed girl or maybe because the mist was thick, he almost missed the body lying face down on the sidewalk. His first inclination was to keep driving, but at the last minute he steered his vehicle over to the curb. He scanned the street. No traffic-foot or car. Cautiously he approached the prone figure. Living under Saarel's thumb had taught him a situation was never what it appeared.

Pulling his blades from their scabbard, he touched the body with a steel point. Nothing. But there was a faint lingering scent, an odor that hadn't been washed away by the rain. The odor of sulfur. He stepped back.

"Hey, get up."

Still nothing. He was wasting time. Turning to go, he cast one last glance at the prone body. The male's pants were low enough to reveal his boxers. Eric almost smiled. Definitely not one of Saarel's minions.

He didn't have the time to waste. Saarel could have Lisette. But he couldn't leave a defenseless man lying on a New Orleans sidewalk. The male's wallet, visible in his back pocket, would make him a target. Eric dropped to his haunches and pulled the wallet from the jeans. Marik Gardner.

"Hey, Gardner." He poked the prone man again.

The prod brought forth a groan. None too gently, Eric flipped him over. Gardner came up swinging. Eric blocked a right jab.

Gardner's eyes opened wide when he focused on Eric's face. "Cemetery… you're the guy…"

Had he been in the cemetery when Eric rescued Lisette? He pulled the guy to his feet. "Where's Lisette?"

Gardner swayed on his feet. "Strange dudes…" With a shaky hand he pointed into the fog. "Tried to keep up…but too fast. Must've knocked me out. " A look of outrage clouded his features. "Gonna get those mutha-"

Eric gripped the guy's shoulders and shook him. He didn't have time for Gardner's rantings. Time was running out.

"What path did they take?"

The male pointed into the fog.

"Listen, Marik-"

"Scooter, man. Nobody but my mama calls me Marik."

So this was Lisette's friend. The one Hancock had approached.

"Go home, Scooter. I'll find her."

"No way. I'm coming-"

Scooter collapsed under Eric's fist. He couldn't have Scooter slowing him down. Dragging the guy off the sidewalk, he deposited him behind some hedges. Under the cover of the fog and the greenery, Lisette's friend would be safe.

Leaving his car behind, Eric broke into a run. There were two portals to his world, one in the cemetery where he had rescued Lisette and the other in an abandoned warehouse on the edge of the Quarter. The warehouse was the closer of the two.

When he reached the lower portion of the building and touched the wall, his hand came away coated with slime.

From the heat radiating from the walls, the creature had been here mere minutes ago. And he had Lisette with him. Eric could smell the freshness of her skin body, mingling with the rank odor of sulfur and death.

The portal opened at his touch and he stepped through. He didn't turn to see if it sealed behind him, but took off at a sprint. He knew this world better than anyone other than Saarel. He cut across the sand hills, hoping to beat whoever had Lisette before they delivered her to the Overlord.

When he reached the multi-storied building, he didn't smell Lisette. Good. He had arrived first. He needed to put this time to good use. He must search Saarel's quarters and be quick about it, for the dead did not sleep and Saarel was all-knowing. Eric's goal was to find the doomsday book that foretold of the coming of the Voodoo priestess.

He approached the Overlord's quarters, skirting the thin, emaciated bodies and the misshaped forms that littered the grounds. For the first time in eons, he felt remorse and sadness for these pitiful beings. This hell would be their last home. He refused to let it be his.

Saarel resided at the top of a twisted and dilapidated high rise. The stairwell curved on itself as Eric climbed the twenty stories to the top. When he arrived, he studied the entrance. Unlike Lisette, he knew no spells or charms to force his way in. There was no door handle to turn, so Eric placed his hand on the thick wood and pushed. The door opened. He laughed. How arrogant of the Overlord to believe he didn't have to protect his quarters with locks or magic.

When he stepped over the threshold, bug creatures called Blattopterans rushed to block his entrance. No taller than his kneecaps, their antennae twitched as they communicated with each other. He hoped they weren't summoning Saarel.

One stepped out of the pack. "The master is away."

"I'll wait."

Eric strode into the room with more confidence than he felt. In two millennia he had never been in the Overlord's quarters. He needed to find what he sought quickly before Saarel returned. For the demon to find him here would mean certain death.

He knew nothing about Saarel, who he had been before he was banished to this Realm of or what caused his exile. But the quarters surprised Eric. He had expected a hovel. The place lacked color or warmth, but was clean and spare. Eric glanced at the bug servants, wondering if they were responsible for the order. They watched him with curiosity and suspicion. Their protruding black eyes followed his every step.

There appeared to be only two rooms, this large central chamber and one to the left of the main entrance. He needed to get into that room, because beyond large boxy furniture there was nothing here. When he started toward the doorway in question, the slaves moved as a unit to block his way. There was something in the other room he wasn't meant to see.

He unsheathed his sword. Just as he moved forward intent on killing bugs, if necessary, the air began to shimmer. He cursed.

Saarel materialized, blocking Eric's path. He had lost his chance to view the doomsday book.

"Ah, *Eric*," he placed emphasis on the false name, "so good of you to visit." He lifted his face up and drew in a deep breath. "Another visitor."His lips curled in a smile, showing sharp teeth. "The Awaited One." He turned his hideous smile on Eric. "I'm pleased."

Going on the offensive, Eric asks, "Why send your minions? Didn't you think I can do the job?" If he could keep Saarel talking, maybe he could figure out a way to get Lisette out of the Fifth and away from Saarel.

Saarel strode casually around Eric. Fear causing his heart rate to accelerate, Eric turned to keep the Overlord in his sights.

"Call them my backup plan. But do not blame me. Lisette opened the portal in the cemetery with a chant. Since I cannot," bitterness tinged his words, "I took advantage of my slaves' ability to move between worlds."

"Why not close the portal?" Eric asked.

Saarel's limitations became clearer to Eric. If he could keep the Overlord off balance maybe he wouldn't need the doomsday book. Maybe he would learn everything he needed to know from Saarel himself.

"Because," Saarel said, "only Lisette can close the portal. Why, Eric, do you want to know so much?"

Before he could blink, Saarel had taken possession of Eric's sword and placed it at his throat.

**

Watermelon head lumbers a short distance, then drops me. I land on my hands and knees in grainy yellow dust. Any thought of escape is smashed when his huge hand clamps down of my shoulder, and he pulls me to my feet. I sway, dizzy from the shaking.

The air is a thick and hot like soup. When I struggle to breathe, I feel like I'm inhaling particles. I blink once, twice to clear my vision. It doesn't help. There is a yellow haze that covers the atmosphere.

This is not the world of my dreams. It's different. This land is an endless yellow desert. There's not a building or abandoned car in sight, definitely different from my dream. For the first time I begin to hope.

The creature shoves me forward. My feet sink into the fine powdery ash that covers this world. It makes movement hard and dangerous. I slip several times as we move toward the distant horizon. Dust irritates my nose and coats my tongue, making me cough. Without giving me a chance to recover, the creature clamps his claws around my neck. His sharp nails bite into my flesh, sending white hot daggers of pain into my head.

He grunts and gives me another push.

"Okay. I get the idea."

Trying not to breathe too deeply, I lift my heavy legs and take one step at a time. After what seems like forever, we crest a hill.

My stomach plunges and I begin to shake uncontrollably. Spread out before me is the high-rise city from my nightmare.

**

With a fisted claw, the creature bangs on the apartment door of my dream. Everything seems exactly the same. It's as though I've actually been here, not just dreamed about it.

The force of his pounding blows the door open on a scene so unreal I have to blink several times.

The serpent-tongued human from my nightmare, is holding a sword to Eric's throat.

When my brain is sure it's not hallucinating, my knees buckle. The creature's claw biting into my arm is the only thing that keeps me from falling.

What is Eric doing here?

Seeing us in the doorway, the demon lowers the sword. I release the breath I've been holding.

The creature pushes me into the room.

"Ah, Lisette, at last. Come in, come in, my dear."

Bug-like creatures-the cockroaches from my dream-huddle in the corner of the room with their antenna quivering. I can't stop the shudder that racks my body.

My attention is drawn back to Eric. I can't get my mind around the fact that he's here. Why?

There is some message in his eyes I can't read, but I sense the anxiety radiating from his body. I know the concern is for me. I try to smile to let him know it will be okay, but I can't. My legs wobble, and I have to lock my knees to keep from falling.

Holding the sword at his side, the demon moves between me and Eric. He's blocked out my sun.

"Let me formally introduce myself. I am Saarel, Overlord of this wondrous place called the Fifth Realm." Although his thin lips lift in a parody of a smile, his blue eyes are cold and watchful.

"Welcome to your new home. I have waited hundreds of years for your arrival."

Hundreds of years? Of course, he knows of my birth from the Book of Truths. Through my blanket of fear, I know I should speak but I can't. I keep seeing the sword at Eric's neck.

Saarel reaches out to touch my face. I jerk back. The revulsion must be written on my features, because his eyes narrow and he steps closer.

Can he hear my heart pounding in my chest? Yes, I think he can, because his eyes fasten on my neck. The thumping becomes so loud it drowns out all the sound in the room. It's like I'm locked in a void.

"My reward, Master?"

Saarel's attention shifts to the creature behind me.

I'd forgotten about watermelon man.

Irritation flashes across Saarel's face. "Yes, of course."

He raises his hand and a burst of blue light shoots out from his palm.

My captor is caught and engulfed by the light. I stare in horrified fascination as the creature catches fire, sizzles and burns in the blink of an eye. He smells as bad dead as he did alive. When the air clears, a pile of white ash is all that remains.

I stare at the spot, until the feel of a rough hand on my face tells me I'm not dreaming. This nightmare is real.

"Get used to my touch." Saarel says. "You are mine."

Eric's face is dark with anger and his body coils. He's about to attack. *Don't do it.* I know with certainty Saarel will kill him if he tries to defend me.

The three of us are locked in a vacuum of silence broken only when Saarel snaps his fingers.

My head jerks toward the entrance when the door bursts open and slams against the opposite wall with a bang.

Two burly creatures, one with greenish skin and the other with a long reptile-like face, step into Saarel's quarters.

"Take him away." Saarel points at Eric. "I must be alone to become better acquainted with my bride."

Eric's eyes lock on mine as the guards drag him from the apartment. There is pleading in their depths.

Tears slide down my cheeks. Eric has been my savior, my protector and now I'm alone with this demon from my nightmare- this demon from Hell.

Saarel catches a tear with the tip of his finger. He brings the finger to his mouth. "Hmm, I love the taste of fear."

The air waves and folds in on itself and his form blurs, then with a crack disappears. My mouth drops open. Saarel has morphed out of his human form into what I know is his true form. A four legged claw toed creature with scaly red skin. Only his eyes remain of his human self-blue and watchful.

I want to scream, but I start to laugh instead. Wild, crazy laughter spills out of me. All the time I'm backing up until my body hits the wall. The bugs stop hissing. They're clustered together in a corner watching me, their antenna twitching.

This being before me has a face as red as Hellboy's. I laugh again and keep laughing until the red thing raises up on two legs and slaps me, its claws raking my skin. My ears ring with the force of the blow, and my face stings.

"Are you afraid?" the red-faced thing with Saarel's voice asks. His breath comes in quick pants. To my horror, I realize, he's excited. My fear excites him.

My stomach heaves, and I fight the urge to puke. I pray that God will let me wake up in my small bedroom.

"What do you want?" My voice comes out in a squeak.

He smiles. "Nothing. I have everything I want. I have you."

"You can't have me."

Saarel's face splits into a grin. His teeth glare white against his red skin. "That's better. I want a mate with spunk."

Mate? The idea of mating with this creature tightens my stomach and the urge to hurl returns. "I'm not your mate," I say from between clenched teeth, disgusted at the thought. If I wanted to be anyone's mate it would have been Eric's. "Where's Eric. What do want with him?"

Saarel grips my chin with scaly fingers. "You are concerned for Eric? How touching. But do not worry about him. He will be well taken care of."

Remembering the sword at Eric's throat, I start to tremble. Why does Saarel wish to harm him? Eric who has only been my protector.

Saarel cocks his head and studies me. "You care for Eric?"

The tone of his voice makes me hesitate before speaking. I have a feeling anything I say will be the wrong answer.

He snaps his fingers, and without turning says, "Bring the infidel to me."

One of the bugs separates from the pack and scurries away.

Saarel moves until his face almost touches mine. I hold my breath and will him to back away. Even though his teeth are white, his breath smells like rotten meat. I stare in horrid fascination at his mouth, expecting at any moment that his lizard tongue will dart out and touch me.

Eric is hustled back in, a guard gripping each arm. The guards are so tall Eric's feet dangle above the floor. His face is pale, but his eyes are on fire. His gaze sweeps over my face and body. I give him a weak smile, trying to hide the absolute terror that grips me.

Still holding the sword, Saarel moves slowly toward Eric and places it at his throat again. "Have you touched her flesh?"

I flush. Why is he asking Eric this? It's none of his business.

"Have you?" Saarel's shout shakes the building. A shower of tiny insect-like creatures fall from the ceiling and scurry around in blind confusion, then disappear in the crevasses of the room.

"I have not." Trying to keep his throat from being pierced by the sword's blade, Eric's words are low and almost indistinct.

"I think you lie. I think you have had knowledge of my bride." Saarel glances at me, while still holding the sword at Eric's neck.

"Has he laid hands on you?"

I want to shout, *what business is it of yours?* But one look at Eric's face tells me my temper will only hurt us. I shake my head.

Saarel studies me for a long time.

I can't hold his gaze.

"But you wanted him to, did you not?"

I hesitate. As I do, Saarel pricks Eric's skin with the sword. Blood trickles down his neck.

"You wanted him to have knowledge of you?" Saarel repeats.

I hold Eric's gaze with mine. *Oh, yes. I wanted to feel his hands on me.* Even though, I don't say the words, they must be imprinted on my face, so I nod.

Saarel lowers the blade. "Good. Honesty is good." He throws back his head and howls.

Goose bumps rise on my arms. I tense, waiting for Saarel to change shape, because such a sound could only mean something bad is about to happen.

Then his cry stops as suddenly as it starts. He walks toward me, a smile lingering on his ugly face. "You mortals are so predictable." He spits on the floor by my feet. The saliva sizzles and burns through the floor. "This is what I think of honesty."

Whirling, he throws the sword. It turns end over end in what seems like slow motion. When it stops, it's embedded in Eric's throat.

I blink one, twice, then slide into darkness.

Chapter 22

I float out of sleep. Strange, my bed feels hard and that smell... Has Scooter taken off his shoes again? I open my eyes. It takes a moment for my brain to compute I'm not in my bedroom. In fact, I'm not in my house.

I lay in a corner of a small room on top of smelly tattered rags. The room resembles a storage closet with ornaments, swords, knives, books all covered with a heavy layer of yellow soot. I squint. There's a... there's a mummified body in the opposite corner propped against the wall. Oh, God. I shut my eyes and will myself back to sleep. Maybe when I open my eyes the next time everything will be normal again.

A scratching noise makes my eyes spring open and draws my attention to an open door. A beady-eyed inhuman face, with wiggling antenna peers around the corner. Then it all comes back to me in every horrifying detail, the trip through the portal, Saarel and the sword piercing Eric's neck. This is not a dream. Eric is dead.

I can't even cry. It's too unreal. I close my eyes and lay back on my rancid pallet. I can't deal.

When something touches my face, my eyes fly open. The cockroach thing is at the edge of my sleeping area, watching me with its protruding eyes. We stare at each other, me trying to make sense of what's happened, and it, probably trying to make sense of what I am.

"Eric is dead," I whisper, more to myself than to the insect.

The bug tilts its oblong head. It says something. The syllables are so drawn out I'm not sure what I hear.

Tears leak from my eyes and run down into my ears. I don't bother to wipe them away. The cockroach unfolds its long barbed appendage and touches its own face, then studies me again.

"Azsurrrr," it repeats.

Maybe it's trying to communicate with me. I don't know. I don't care. If I had a knife I'd find Saarel and hack him to pieces. I'd cast a spell that made him die a slow death. I'd- I'd-

"Eric," I wail. My tears come faster now and my breath catches in my throat.

The cockroach rushes toward me and tries to push pieces of the filthy cloth into my mouth. I bat it away. Is it trying to kill me? Wrinkles appear on its bulging forehead and it glances toward the doorway, then back at me.

I stop sobbing and watch it, trying to understand what it wants.

It steps back to the edge of my pallet, casting glances toward the door.

"Azsurrrr," it says again.

I frown and shake my head. What's it trying to say? Sitting up, I throw up my hands in what I hope is the universal gesture of confusion.

"Eeericcc," it says.

Frustrated, I lean against the wall. "I give up. I don't know what an azsur is or an eericc-"

Holy Mother of God. I scramble to the end of my smelly pallet. "Eric? Are you trying to say Eric?"

The bug repeats "eericcc azsur."

"I don't care about azsur. What about Eric?" Then my pulse gallops with a possibility. Maybe he isn't dead. But I know he's dead. I can still see in my mind's eye the blade in his throat. No one can live through that.

If only I'd been strong enough, brave enough to tell him how much I cared about him. Maybe after making that second charm, I should have fought for him instead of crying and hiding in my room like a child.

But it doesn't matter now. He's dead, and I'd never get the chance to tell him I love him. I need to see his grave and say goodbye.

"Take me to Eric," I demand.

The insect creature glances in what I can only assume is panic toward the door. It's listening for something or someone. Saarel.

Stiff with fear, I cautiously move toward the door, expecting Saarel to leap out at any moment like the boogey man. I don't see anyone, only the cockroaches moving in animated movements to and fro in the other room. Whatever I'm going to do, I need to do it fast. Somehow I don't see Saarel leaving his intended mate alone for too long.

I stop. What if this cockroach isn't speaking of Eric? Maybe it's a trap. I sigh. What difference does it make? I'd rather die trying to escape than spend my life, what time I might have, here in this hell. I need to see Eric for one last time.

I glance over my shoulder at the bug. "Lead on."

My guide leads me to a section of wall near the mummified remains and gestures for me to help it shove some of the debris out of the way. Keeping my eyes averted from the corpse, I do as commanded.

We uncover a small opening, like a doggy door, near the bottom of the wall that's just large enough for a small person, like me, or my insect companion, to squeeze through.

Once I'm on the other side of the wall, my breath catches in my throat and my stomach plummets. I'm on a platform. A spiral staircase, suspending from nothing that I can see, leads down from our location, in a dizzy descent.

I learn something new. I'm afraid of heights. I stand at the top of the stairs and actually consider crawling back through the hole in the wall and spending my last days in that room. Maybe that's the decision the mummified corpse made. Only the visual of me dying and drying in that room and leaving *Grand'mere* alone makes me turn around and crawl backwards down the stairs like a toddler. I take one step at a time, sending a tentative foot out each time to search for the next step. It takes a long time to reach the bottom, probably because the steps are littered with decayed material I won't think about.

The air is filled with the sulfur smell I've come to associate with this world and now the lurid stench of dead and decaying flesh.

As I pick my way down, I wonder why my guide is helping me. After the last several days, I know nothing is what it seems. So I follow this creature, all the time keeping an eye open and an ear cocked for the sound of pursuit. For Saarel.

After what seems like forever, my feet touch solid ground. My guide, who has been waiting patiently for me at the bottom of the staircase, watches as I attempt to stand on shaky legs. "Where to?" I ask.

Without fanfare, the insect points behind me. Tucked in a corner of the building at the rear of the stairs is a crumbled form. I move slowly toward it, my steps hesitant and my pulse thudding loudly in my ears. I want to see him, but I don't know if my heart can stand it.

Eric's dear sweet face is turned toward the wall, so I can't see his last expression. I'm grateful for that. It gives me time to adjust to his death. His body lies in relaxed repose as though he's asleep. I drop to my knees in the dust, little whiffs of it flying up around my face. It already coats Eric's body.

I stare at the mortal wound. It's a tear-shaped hole at the base of his throat. Around the edges of the gash, the skin is dark and jagged.

I look away and instead concentrate on wiping his face clean of the yellow dust. His skin is unbelievably soft. I gently straighten his head. His eyes are open and stare up the suspended staircase. My breath comes in short gasps and my eyes sting.

If only. If only what? If only he and I could go back a few days and avoid this path? If only I'd been brave enough to tell him how I felt about him? I take a deep, shaky breath. It's too late for that now.

You can bring him back. I whip around and stare at my guide. "What did you say?"

But I know it didn't speak. The voice was female. The voice was my mother's.

If only I could. I stare at Eric's lifeless eyes. Healing the wounds on my hand and resurrecting a dog are a lot different from bringing a human back to life.

I run my hands lovingly over his face, touch his lips. I can at least allow myself one kiss. A farewell kiss. I lean down and touch my mouth to his. His lips are cold. Cold as death.

As I straighten I study his face again, memorizing it. I smooth the hair off his forehead, trail my fingers down his nose, then brush the yellow soot that's collected on his eyelash. I pull back in surprise. His eyes are no longer brown but blue.

You can bring him back. I can bring him back. For the first time since I learned of my destiny, I want to use my powers. I'm desperate to use my powers. But I don't know how. I don't know what to say. I don't want to fail.

It's the intent. It's what's in your heart. My uncle's words ring in my head. And my heart wants badly to see a living breathing Eric to have him touch me, kiss me.

Resting on my heels, I extend my trembling hands until they hover over his lifeless body. Uncertain what to do and doubting my ability, I withdraw, resting my palms on my jeans.

My insect companion shifts restlessly behind me, its feet making scratching noises in the dust.

You can do this. I take a deep breath and this time rest my hands on Eric's chest. I close my eyes. Thoughts of failure, sadness and desperation run through my mind like water running through a sieve. This isn't going to work.

Opening my eyes, I withdraw my sweaty hands again and wipe them on my pants, leaving streaks of yellow dust. I can do this. But first I need to erase these negative thoughts. Remembering my uncle's words, I need to concentrate on the love I feel for Eric.

I place my hands on his chest again and clear my mind. Taking another deep breath, I gradually allow in the memories, him saving me in the cemetery, the creature in the alley, our brief kiss by the river and then I smile, thinking of him with Toto. My nerve endings tingle as the warmth of those feelings flow through my fingertips to Eric. I don't say any words like the pathetic chants I made over the love charms. The emotion that pours out of me is what I feel from the deep recesses of my heart.

After what seems like forever, I remove my hands and sit back. Eric is still dead. I bow my head and the feelings of helplessness and despair rush over me like water breeching a damn. I've failed. I touch him one last time, then rise and face my insect companion.

"Thank you for bringing me here," I say, trying, but failing to clear the lump in my throat.

But the creature doesn't acknowledge me. Its odd bug-like eyes are staring past my shoulder. I turn to look back at Eric's body. Nothing has changed. He still lies sprawled on his back, one leg tucked under the other. I step closer drawn by his beauty. My body jerks in surprise. The skin at his throat is smooth and unscarred. The ragged wound is gone and color is beginning to infuse his face.

I cover my mouth, but that doesn't stop my cry of happiness. He's alive. Eric is alive. I sink to my knees beside him.

"The prophecy is correct, you have great power."

I stop breathing. Slowly, I turn. I don't want to but I do.

The blonde, blue-eyed Saarel of my nightmare stands in front of me.

Mouth dry, heart pounding slowly in my chest, I look for my buddy in crime. But the slyness in Saarel's grin tells me I've been had. He was my cockroach companion.

Chapter 23

Eric groans.

Without a thought, I plant my body in front of his. Saarel will have to go through me to get to him. Which, from the scowl on his face, he's quite prepared to do.

"Leave him," Saarel orders. "The time has come."

I don't know what he means, but I don't like the sound of it. "No." I gather Eric in my arms. "I'm not leaving him."

Saarel snaps his fingers.

What does he think-

The stairwell disappears and I'm hurled into space. My stomach dips like I'm on the downward plunge of a roller coaster.

Just as suddenly, I land with a thud on a hard surface. Hot fingers of pain shoot up my spine. Taking shallow breaths to mute the throbbing, I stare into darkness. What happened? Where am I? Where is Eric?

My eyes search for any hint of grayness in the black space. Nothing. Nada.

Ignoring the agony, I roll to my knees and start to crawl. Moving slowly at first, I inch forward. A sudden jolt of electricity measuring eight point five on the Richter scale shoots through my body. It sends me flying through the air. I land on my back again. My heart beats wildly in my chest, I'm twitching and I can't blink. When I catch my breath, I crawl in another direction. I'm shocked again.

Saarel has erected some kinda force field around this space. He's imprisoned me. Am I going to die here? All because he thinks I have some super human power he wants to possess? I close my eyes and allow the pain to wash over me. Why is this happening to me? I don't deserve this. I'm just so tired. I want to lie here and sleep. Maybe when I wake up it-this dream-will be over.

I don't know how long I sleep, but when I open my eyes, twirling ribbons of blue streaks pierce the room's darkness. Am I hallucinating? With a groan, I roll over.

A brilliant white beam in the distance reveals an elevated pedestal in the center of this dark space. With the blue lights flashing outside the circle of white, the area resembles an arena awaiting the arrival of Lil Boosie.

A hand touches my shoulder. I jump and let out a squeak.

"Shh," Eric's soothing voice comes out of the blackness. I close my eyes in relief. He's okay. Where did he come from? Has he been here this whole time? Then I realize maybe the time I've been here has been shorter than I thought.

He touches my shoulder, and then gently turns my head.

With the next flash of the strobe-like beams, Saarel stands just outside the field of light. He raises a foot to take a step into the beam. Sparks shoot out from the contact point, but his foot doesn't penetrate the light. He stares down at the offending appendage as though he can't believe it failed him. He kicks at the wall of light, and as before, his foot doesn't break through. Fisting his hand, he punches at the beam. I can almost see the vibrations climb up his arm from the force of the failed punch. Howling in frustration, he morphs into his Hell-boy persona, then starts to chant.

"What's he saying?"

The white beam casts enough illumination for me to see Eric.

"He's speaking in the old tongue."

I frown in confusion. "Okay, but what's he saying?"

"We need to leave." Eric speaks softly, but I hear the tension behind the words.

"Don't you think I know that?" Fear and irritation makes my tone sharp.

A flash of bright light explodes in the room. For a moment I see dots in front of my eyes. When I'm able to focus again, a large black book sits on top of the pedestal.

"What's that?"

"*The Book of Truths.*"

I jerk in surprise, staring at Eric. How does he know that? I thought he'd never heard of the Book? I want to question him, but now is not the time to ask him why he lied. We need to get out of here.

The chanting increases in speed and volume.

Eric grips my arm. "We must leave *now*."

"And how do you propose we do that?" I snap.

"I don't know."

The chanting is so loud it hurts my ears. It sounds like a cross between a mass and how I imagine an exorcism would be-all fire and brimstone, and loud rants.

Then Saarel turns in our direction. Still intoning the strange language, he practically glides toward us, toward me.

I look around for somewhere to run, but there isn't any place. We're in a black void, suspended in space. I don't even know where we are. How can I run?

My thoughts chase each other in a circle. What can I do? Nothing. I cast an anxious glance in Eric's direction. His gaze is fixed on Saarel. I wipe my sweating palms on my jeans, and when I do I feel something lumpy in my pocket. The gris-gris my great-grandmother gave me. I'd forgotten about it. I almost laugh. What will a charm do against this demon?

I pull it out of my pocket. I don't have time to weigh the consequences. I just lob it. As it leaves my hand, I remember the shield. Shit. But the gris-gris doesn't bounce back. It goes through the shield and lands at Saarel's feet. He stares down at it in bemused silence.

The air fills with smoke, making the darkness luminescent. He's consumed within the fog.

"Run," Eric shouts.

Run where? But I don't have time to think, because Eric pushes me out of our prison.

"Hurry," he urges.

Using the bright light from the pedestal as a beacon, I dash toward it. I clear all the fear from my mind and focus my energy on putting one foot in front of the other as fast as I can. I must save *Grand'mere*. I must save myself. I must save Eric. This is my mantra.

Fully expecting to be repulsed like Saarel, I launch myself at the field of light like a bullet leaving a gun. I barrel through the beam without breaking a sweat and narrowly avoid plowing into the pedestal head first. As I stop my forward movement with my hand, electrical pulses of current swim up my arm.

Without stopping to question why I got through the light and Saarel didn't, I push up to my feet, then I step up on the podium. The book is closed. Without touching it or opening the volume, I say a quick prayer. I beseech God to give me the strength to protect the ones that I love and to defeat Saarel. I open my eyes and place my hand on the Book.

A tingling rush of warmth courses through my body, leaving in its wake feelings of love and something close to ecstasy. Holding my breath, I open the book.

Soft, radiant light flows up from the Book's surface, so much light I can't read the page. I blink and try again. Random words jump off the sheet. Veil-I puzzle over this, but read on. The words are blurred and the writing almost indecipherable, but Toussaint stands out in blaring detail. My breath catches in my throat. This is my prophecy!

A sense of urgency breaks through my excitement. I don't have time to investigate this wondrous book now. I close it and clasp it to my chest. The leather-bound text is surprisingly small and lightweight. I thought it would be this massive volume since it contains the futures of all mankind. I laugh with happiness. I've succeeded. I have the book. I've saved *Grand'mere*.

Smiling in triumph, I turn and search the darkness beyond the beam for Eric. As though on cue, he steps slowly out of the smoke. I hold up the Book for him to see, but he doesn't react. As he continues to move forward, a shadow forms behind him. Saarel. He holds a sword to Eric's back.

"Oh my God, Eric!" All the euphoria drains from my body.

"The Book, my dear Lisette," Saarel says. "Or I will cut off his head and your little bag of tricks will not be able to put him back together."

I lock eyes with Eric. He gives a little shake of his head. I ignore him. I won't lose him again. But if I turn over the Book how can I protect *Grand'mere? Do you really think Saarel will let you live?*

"If I give you this book, you'll let him go?"

"Of course."

The lie rolls too easily off his tongue.

What do I do? Even if he releases Eric, how will we get out of here safely? Saarel could capture us at anytime. Since we're probably going to die, I might as well get answers to my questions.

"Why do you want the Book?"

Saarel smiles easily. The gesture wrinkles the red skin. "He who possesses the Book rules the world."

Wrong answer. Now I know he shouldn't have the book. But how do I get the Book to safety and save Eric and myself in the process?

Use the force, Luke. Okay, now I know I've lost it. Thinking of movie quotes in the middle of a life and death situation is crazy. So, why did that thought pop into my head? I don't have any special skills except healing. Somehow I don't think that's going to get Eric and me out of this situation. Unless...

I step out of the protective shield of the light, carrying the Book of Truths with me. Eric's eyes widen in shock or disbelief or both.

"Let him go."

One second Saarel is behind Eric, in the next instant in front of me.

"Give me the book."

Like a child holding on to a precious toy she doesn't want to share, I shake my head and clutch the text closer to my chest. "No."

He reaches out and tries to pry my fingers from the book. A laser beam of light shoots out from the book and straight into his body. The charge blows him several feet away. I look down at myself. There's not a mark on me. I feel fine, great even.

"Hurry," I shout to Eric.

I pull him into my arms just as Saarel rises. Or, I should say, drops to all fours. Two pairs of red eyes stare at Eric and me from a bulbous face of rough alligator hide. How many different forms does he have? And it's about to charge.

My stomach is cramping and for a moment everything flies out of my head. Think. Think. Think. I remember the scars on my hand after my nightmare and how each morning my wounds are healed. I understand I healed myself, but suddenly I know why I have the scars. I'm not dreaming each night. I'm actually transporting somehow to this dimension, and Saarel is actually raking me with his razor-like teeth. An image of my bedroom flashes through my mind and I grab hold of it. I want to be there.

Saarel is charging toward us. His red eyes are all I can see in the semi-darkness beyond the pedestal's bright lights.

I grip Eric's hand. "Home. I want to be home."

A maelstrom of wind sweeps through the massive chamber. I feel myself lifted off my feet, but I hold tightly to Eric. We're caught in the jaws of a sucking vacuum of whirling, stinking air. My stomach drops. Gravity pulls us down, down and at the same time twirls us around and around like a child's spinning top. My ears pop and I swallow to relieve the pressure and to keep bile from rushing into my mouth. What's happening? I open my mouth to scream, but the sound is sucked away.

Chapter 24

Like a baby ejected from its mother's womb, I'm literally popped out of the vacuum. I land on a hard gritty surface that scrapes my face as I skid to a stop. Skin burning, I roll over and turn my face up to the rain. Clouds move across a starless nighttime sky. Grateful for the water cooling my skin, I lie sprawled on the sidewalk.

"You okay, honey?" A deep baritone voice asks.

I turn my head. The face blurs and then comes into focus. A Black man in a shiny suit leans over me. Raindrops glisten in his greased hair. Behind him are three other men dressed in suits with an air of concern on their dark faces. At their feet lays an open guitar case.

"Where am I?"

They look at each other.

The one who leans over me says, "You're in the Quarter. St. Peter and Bourbon, to be exact." He extends me his hand. "Let me help you up, little lady. You took quite a spill."

When he says the word "spill," everything comes rushing back-Saarel, finding the Book. I jump to my feet so quickly my head starts to swim. Where's the Book?

I glance down at the spot where I lay. The Book isn't there. "Oh, no." I turn wildly in a circle, my gaze skimming the ground in either direction.

Even though the man who extended his hand is at least six foot to my five foot two inches, I reach up and grab the damp labels of his suit. "Have you seen-"

An explosive sound like the percussion of thunder fills the air and a jagged hole opens up in the night sky. Lightening shoots across the heavens as the Book drops out of the hole. It lands in a puddle of water where it continues to emit sparks.

"Holy shit," one the men says. I run toward the Book, but not quickly enough. One of the trio gets there first.

"Don't-" But it's too late. He picks up the volume and I can literally see the electrical charge race up his arm. His eyes bug and his hair sizzles.

I try and pull the Book from his grip. His hand is frozen to the leather.

"Static electric," I say as I pry his fingers loose. Once I free the book, I clutch it to my chest.

Almost as one they turn and stare up at the sky. The hole has now closed. When they turn their gaze on me, fear and suspicion has replaced the goodwill in their expressions.

It's time to leave. I turn and take off at a run. Did Eric come back with me? *God, I hope so.* I need to find him. But more importantly, I need to get home.

**

Still swaying slightly in the wind, the front door of my house wobbles crazily on its hinges. I want to race right in, but my brain cautions me, so I slip silently into the house.

Odors of sulfur and something more foul lingers in the air, causing my stomach to pitch and roll.

Grand'mere's treasured antique furniture lies broken and twisted like rubble from Katrina. Glass crunches under my feet.

"*Grand'mere?*" My voice, thin and squeaky, echoes through the house.

She doesn't answer.

Placing a protective arm around my waist where the Book is hidden, I creep slowly through the living room. Even though I sense she's not here, I kneel to check every crevice for her presence. Splinters of wood embed themselves like sharp needles into my hands and knees.

In the kitchen, spilled spices and flour paint the walls in swirls of white and brown. I turn in a circle, the stench of demon in my nostrils. "Oh, God. I'm too late. I'm too late." If only I hadn't gone walking with Scooter.

Even before the thought has completely formed in my mind, I'm out the door. Joy blooms in my chest. I told Scooter to take care of her. She's with him.

I dash through Mrs. Joyner's yard. Nappy barks excitedly at this intrusion into his space. I don't stop, but race on to Scooter's house. I bang on the door until Boogie opens it.

"Is my *Grand'mere* here? Is Scooter?"

Boogie wipes a big hand over his face and then tiredly through his dreads.

Without answering, he turns and shouts over his shoulder. "Hey, Ma. Lisette don't know where Scooter is either?"

I grab his arm. "He's not here?"

Boogie shakes off my hand. "We ain't seen him since he left for your house last night."

"Last night?" I say stupidly. Everything that's happened to me has happened in less than twenty-four hours? How can that be? "But you've seen my grandmother, right?"

"Ain't seen her either."

I stare at his wide mouth waiting for him to take back the words. Waiting for him to tell me he's joking. That both Scooter and *Grand'mere* are sitting in the Gardner's living room.

But reality crashes down on me when I see Mrs. Gardner's large body suddenly fill the doorframe. Her chocolate skin is now gray and her brown eyes, hollow and bloodshot. "Marik ain't with you?"

Fighting back tears, I shake my head. "No, ma'am."

"This ain't like my boy. This one, yeah," she smacks Boogie in the back of the head with the palm of her hand. "But Marik always comes home or calls. He ain't called."

She studies me as though I'll provide more answers. I can, but what I know isn't going to sound sane to her. I was the last one to see Scooter. What if my attempt to draw both creatures away didn't work? What if the one with the dead eyes took Scooter? Bile rises in my throat and I don't dare look at Mrs. G. How can I tell her I might be responsible for her son's disappearance?

**

How could I have been so stupid? The splintered plates swim in and out of focus through my tears. *He'd never have left me.*

I jump up, wanting to destroy something, anything. But as I look around at *Grand'mere's* wrecked kitchen, I realize someone has beaten me to it.

If only I hadn't gone walking with him, then he and *Grand'mere* would be safe.

The harsh sound of my laughter echoes off the flour-coated walls. What am I thinking? I couldn't have saved her. The creatures-demons, whatever they are, would've come to the house looking for me and still would've taken her. But at least Scoot would've been safe.

The sound of footsteps brings my head up in a flash, and I look frantically around for something I can use as a weapon. On the floor is one of the kitchen knives, partially covered in flour. I reach for it, crouch, and wait for the attack.

The footsteps stop just outside the kitchen.

"I've got a knife, and I know how to use it." I don't, but whatever is on the other side of the door doesn't know that.

"Lisette."

Breathing a sigh of relief, I drop the knife as Eric slowly pushes open the door. His clothes are dirty, and his hair wet and matted, but he looks so good to me right now.

I fling myself at him. He closes his arms tightly around me, and I bury my face in his wet shirt. I try to block out my fear, but the sulfur smell from Saarel's hellhole still clings to his clothing, bringing back the horror.

After a minute, he gently disentangles my arms from around his neck.

"Are you okay?" His dark eyes search my face.

"N--No." I clamp my teeth together to stop them from clattering. "I—I think Saarel's got *Grand'mere* and Scooter."

Broken dishes crunch under my feet as I take a step back so I can see his face. "Do you remember my friend— the one Hancock was helping?"

Eric stiffens, then nods slowly.

"That's Scooter."

Some emotion flashes briefly across his face then quickly disappears behind a mask. Fear? Anger? I can't tell. He hides his feelings so well.

He moves away from me and starts to sift through the debris, touching surfaces. He holds up his hand and a slimy substance dangles from his fingers. "Demon drool."

"Yuck."

He wipes his hand on a dishcloth. I guess flour is preferable to demon snot. Moving quickly, he eases the back door open and slips out, leaving me standing in the middle of the kitchen.

Just as quickly he's back, motioning to me. "We need to leave."

"But—" I glance around the room. I don't know why. What am I planning to do? Clean house while Saarel holds *Grand'mere* and Scooter hostage? *She's going to be so mad when she gets back. If she comes back*, the voice in my head says. I slam the door on that thought.

Removing a slicker from the coat hook at the back door, Eric wraps it around my shoulders, then gives me a gentle push. "We must leave. Now. After you're safe, then I'll find your grandmother and Scooter."

It takes a moment for his words to sink in. I can only attribute my slowness to shock. Resisting his push, I turn to face him, my chin going up. "*We* have to find them."

He blows air forcibly out of his mouth. I reach up and grip his face, forcing him to look at me. "We," I say again.

Without replying, he takes my hand and pulls me from the house. Submerged beneath dirty rain water, the backyard looks like a wading pool.

We jog toward his parked car. After we're safely in the vehicle, he turns toward me.

"Lisette, it is too dangerous for you to go back. Saarel won't let you escape again."

I square my shoulders. "It's too dangerous for *you*. I won't be there to bring you back from the dead if Saarel decides to kill you again."

Then the questions that have been running through my mind since I saw him with the sword at his throat return. "Eric, why were you there? How did you get there? Were you kidnapped also?"

One hand plows through his thick dark hair. "I was there against my will."

"But why? Why did Saarel want you?"

He studies his hands that are now both tightly gripped around the steering wheel. "I don't know. Maybe he thought he could lure you there if he kidnapped me.

We will speak more of this later." He pauses, "After we find your *Grand'mere* and Scooter." He relaxes his grip on the wheel. "Do you have The Book?"

I nod and pat my stomach. "Right here."

He looks at my waist. Suddenly I'm very conscious of how dirty I am and probably how smelly. But I can't worry about that now.

He starts the car and pulls slowly away from the curb. I glance at my home. It sits despondent, waiting for its owner to return. *Please, God, let her be okay.*

"I understand why you might think Saarel has your grandmother, but why Scooter?"

"He was with me when the creatures-"

Eric's head jerks in my direction. "There were two?"

"Yes. The other one-the one you didn't see-was a zombie or something. The one Saarel killed, chased me, then forced me through the portal to the underworld. Just before I ran, I asked Scooter to watch over *Grand'mere*."

Eric nods. The car comes to a traffic light, and he makes a right turn away from the Quarter.

"So you think he was at your house with your grandmother when the demons came?"

"I don't know. His family hasn't seen him since he left to come to my house. And I did ask him to watch over *Grand'mere*."

"I was the last one to see him." Eric glances at me before the road demands his attention. He explains how he found Scooter and Scooter telling him about my capture. "And you are *his* best friend?"

I nod, then realize he's not looking at me, and say, "Yes."

He accelerates the car up the entrance ramp to I-10. "Is he the type of person to leave when his best friend is in trouble?" Eric's dark gaze holds mine briefly.

I groan and sink further in the leather seat. "Oh, my God. He followed."

Eric nods. "And probably the second one came back for him. Or--"

"Or what?"

"Nothing." Once again the curtain that hides his thoughts descends over his features.

Why does he shut me out?

His gaze goes toward my stomach, where the Book rests. "Have you studied it?"

I shake my head.

While he negotiates the traffic, I pull the Book from its hiding place and open it. Taking a deep breath, I flip one page, then another, then another. My stomach plunges to my wet sneakers.

"What's wrong?" He glances at me before turning his attention to the road.

"They're all blank."

"What?" The car weaves slightly out of its lane.

I look down at the Book in disbelief. "The pages are all blank."

"That can't be," he says.

My hands stop fumbling with the pages. I don't look at him, but instead keep my gaze on the open Book. "I thought you'd never heard of the Book of Truths. How do you know what should or shouldn't be here?"

He pauses before speaking. "Before seeing it when you did, I had not heard of it."

I shake my head. "You knew Saarel was calling for it when he spoke in that foreign tongue."

"I understand the language, but I know nothing of The Book."

I've had enough. "When will you stop lying, Eric?"

The silence that fills the car is like the air in a tomb, heavy and dark.

He sighs, then maneuvers the car over two lanes and pulls onto the shoulder. Gripping the steering wheel as though his life depends on that anchor, he stares out the rain streaked windshield.

"My name is Assur Semiramis. I was born two thousand years ago."

Chapter 25

"Quit the shit, Eric. This is not the time for jokes. In case you've forgotten, my *Grand'mere* and my best friend have been kidnapped."

"This is not a joke, Lisette. I speak the truth." His eyes are piercing and very serious. "I'm two thousand years old."

What kind of game is he playing? No one lives to be two thousand years old.

"I was a soldier when Cyrus the Great invaded the region now known as Iran. His legion numbered in the hundreds of thousands. Our meager troops..." His lips tighten. "We stood no chance against such insurmountable odds. I lost everything that day, my honor, my family-"

"I thought your family was in Europe?"

"I have no family. They have been dead two thousand years." His face is like granite, not a muscle moves. "I killed them."

His words drop like stones in the silence between us. I swallow, unable to get my mind around what he's told me. His voice is so convincing. He really believes what he's saying.

"How-how did you kill them?"

"I betrayed the location of my camp to Cyrus so that he would spare the life of the villagers-women, children and old men. He didn't. He placed a curse on me, then killed my troops and slaughtered everyone in the village."

His story is so bizarre I don't know whether to wait for the punch line or believe him. One of us is crazy-him for telling such a sick story or me for listening. Either way I can tell he's in pain. So I do what only a friend can do and place my hand on his arm. "Oh, Eric. I'm so sorry."

After a moment of awkward silence, I ask, "Why didn't he kill you?"

Eric keeps his eyes straight ahead, his body rigid. "I don't know. Maybe he felt a better punishment was for me to live forever in this half life, knowing I caused the death of all those I held dear."

I squeeze his forearm. Even if he's delusional, the agony in his voice is real.

For several heartbeats the only noise inside our vehicle is the swish of wiper blades against the windshield and the drone of other cars' tires on the wet road.

Playing along with him, I ask, "Where have you lived these past two..."

He finishes my sentence. "Two thousand years?"

I nod, still unable to believe he might really be-well...old.

"Everywhere." He studies me, maybe waiting for a response to all he's told me.

I don't know what to say. My mind is going in circles. Sometime between the start of this conversation and this moment, I've begun to believe maybe there's truth to his story. It would explain why sometimes he acts so much older than the other boys at our school. Not to mention the demon-killing thing.

"How long have you lived here in New Orleans?"

"Just a short while."

Something occurs to me. "If you've lived this long, why are you still in high school?"

He laughs and a dimple shows briefly near his mouth. "What else would a seventeen-year-old do?"

I shrug. "If I'd lived that long, I wouldn't be in high school."

Just then a tractor trailer speeds by, spewing a fountain of water over the windshield. I feel like we're in a car wash.

"I know you saw Ashley Crandall running out of the cemetery and came in to investigate, but why were you in the alley when that creature came for me?

"I started following you after the incident in the cemetery."

Strangely, the fact he followed me doesn't scare me. "Why?"

"I've seen many things in these two thousand years. Someone who raises the dead is not an ordinary person. I was curious. Fearful for you, I started following you." His voice is quiet.

I remember almost stumbling over him outside St. Peter's in the Quarter.

"You heal, you raise the dead, and you make love charms." He stares out at the road as though he knows what he's saying makes me uncomfortable. "What are you?"

Do I tell him the truth? It can't seem any stranger than what he just told me. But it's so hard to say the words out loud.

I clear my throat. "I'm—my mother's family—my mother's family is into Voodoo." I glance at him from the corner of my eye, trying to gauge his reaction.

He doesn't say anything so I continue. "They think I'm going to be this great Voodoo priestess."

"And you don't?"

I shrug. "I don't know. I don't know anything. I can barely make it through school each day." Laughing, I wipe the condensation off the windshield with my palm. "If I were this great priestess, don't you thing I'd turn your girlfriend into something, a donkey, a hyena?"

"Michele is not my girlfriend."

This has me turning in my seat to stare at him. "Sure, she is."

"She's not."

"You're with her every single day. That makes it look like she's your girl."

The corners of his mouth lift in what for someone else could be mistaken for a smile. "I'm with her so I can be close to you."

Laughter burps out of my mouth. I clamp my hand over my lips. When I'm sure nothing else is going to escape, I say, "Right."

His eyes bore into mine. "Trust me. I'm telling you the truth."

Liar.

"So you don't have the ability to turn people into animals."

I shake my head. "According to my great-grandmother, I haven't fully developed into a priestess. There are stages, and I haven't completed them all."

"How many are there?"

Another shrug. "I'm not sure. Four, I think."

"And you're completed how many?"

I count on my fingers. "Raise the dead, heal, and activate charms. So three."

"Four," he says.

"Four?"

He nods. "Travel between dimensions."

My eyes widen. I hadn't thought about the jump from the Fifth Realm back home. Gripping his arm, I'm practically leaping out of my seat. "Maybe this means I'm a priestess. Maybe I have all the skills I need to rescue *Grand'mere.*"

But then my high spirits deflate like air from a balloon. "If I've completed the transformation, I'd know it. And I don't feel any different than I did before I made the jump."

"That's something you can ask your great-grandmother when you ask her about the Book."

He pulls the car back onto the highway.

Until this moment, I hadn't given any thought to where we were headed. But Eric is on the stretch of highway that leads to the bayou.

How does he know where my mother's family lives?

Chapter 26

He maneuvers the car off I-10 onto the exit for the bayou.

We pull into a bait shop parking lot, where Eric rents a boat.

"Do you need a guide?" the shop's owner asks.

"No," Eric says.

I wait until he has the boat untied from its moorings and we are on our way. "Did you follow me here, too?"

A flock of water fowl takes flight in the wake of the boat's passage. Beads of rainwater glisten on their wings like pearls.

"Yes," he says, steering the small boat around fallen logs that jam the waterway. "I needed to watch over you."

I stare at the passing trees and wildlife while I alternate between anger and confusion. When will I be able to protect myself?

The day is dark, as it has been for the last week or so. The sun seems to be hiding until it's safe to come out. I'd like to hide, but I can't do that. I have to rescue *Grand'mere*.

When we arrive at my great-grandmother's dock, she and my grandmother and a group of women dressed in white and soaked from the rain are already there. Standing up in the boat, I wave, relieved to see their faces. Eric places a hand on my arm to restrain me as I move forward.

"He is not welcome here," my great-grandmother barks.

There isn't a smiling face among the group. A fleeting thought races through my mind. How did they know we were coming?

"He's a friend," I say.

"He's the devil's spawn," my great-grandmother says.

Confused, I study her face. "Why do you say that? You don't know him."

"The aura of evil surrounds him," she says.

Okay, maybe senility has set in. I look at my grandmother to see if she feels the same way. Gone is the sparkle in her brown eyes, they're as cold as death.

I don't have time for whatever's got their panties in a wad. No disrespect intended. *"Grand'mere's* been kidnapped. I need your help."

"You can have our help," my great-grandmother says. "But he," she points at Eric, "needs to leave my property before I bring the spirits down on him."

"Why are you being so rude?" I ask. "Eric has saved my life. He wants to help *Grand'mere.* He's come here to help me plead for your help."

I glance at Eric. Instead of nodding in agreement, his face shows no expression.

"Say something," I hiss at him.

He bows to my relatives. "Please forgive my intrusion. No matter what I might appear to be, let me reassure you I mean neither Lisette nor her family any harm."

Is he poking fun of my relatives? His speech is a little over the top. But his expression is as serious as our situation.

"Leave." My great-grandmother's chest heaves with each breath. She looks like she might stroke out.

Even in rain-soaked garments, the women look formidable with their strong brown bodies. I can believe they could take on Saarel and win.

Evidently Eric thinks so too, because he says, "I leave Lisette in your capable hands."

He gives me a little nudge. "Go," he whispers.

Drawing back, I look at him in bewilderment. "What are you saying? We need their help."

"And you'll get it without my presence," he says in a low voice.

With one eye on the boat, my great-grandmother shouts over her shoulder, "Olnick, Pasquale."

Two burly men come running from the direction of the house.

"Help my great-granddaughter out of the boat. And you," she points her cane at Eric, "don't move a muscle."

The men move cautiously into the water. A roll of thunder cracks the late afternoon sky, startling one of the men, making him loose his balance. He slides down into the murky water. Surfacing quickly, he looks sheepishly up at the women, then joins his partner and approaches the boat.

"If Eric leaves, I'm going." I say, arms crossed over the Book.

"Take her," my great-grandmother commands.

And they do. They pick me up bodily as I kick out with my feet. My abuse rolls off them like the sting of an annoying gnat.

"Eric!" I twist and struggle, looking behind me. He's turned the boat and is headed back the way we came. "Come back here, Eric," I shout.

My stomach drops as I watch him maneuver the boat around a bend in the bayou and disappear. My hope for rescuing *Grand'mere* just vanished with him.

"Come," my great-grandmother commands.

I shoot her a hateful glare. I'd rather stay on the dock, cold, wet and shivering, than accept her hospitality.

She shrugs, turns and with everyone else following her, lumbers slowly toward her house.

The waves from the boat's passing gently lap the shore. "You promised to help me," I say softly as though my words could be carried on the wind and bring him back. "How will I rescue *Grand'mere* now, without you?"

**

Alone and pacing on the dock the better part of an hour ranting at my great-grandmother and then at Eric, I finally give in and enter the house.

Standing in the doorway to the kitchen, I slip the book from beneath my shirt. Even as warm as the kitchen is my body feels bereaved without the sensation of the leather against my skin.

Maybe fearing an attack from "the devil's spawn," the women from the dock haven't dispersed to their own homes. My great-grandmother must have retired to her room. I guess bats need their sleep.

Almost as one, the women stop their preparation. It's as though someone has waved a wand, freezing them in time. I can hear the kitchen's clock tick.

My grandmother turns slowly our eyes meeting across the room. Her gaze goes to the book held tightly in my hand.

Keeping her eyes locked with mine, she says to the women, "Leave us."

They scatter like leaves in a strong wind.

After the last one departs, my grandmother, motions to the book. "What do you have?"

Not being in a cooperative mood, I say, "A book."

She nods, not at all fazed by my belligerence. "The Book."

"How did you know?"

"It hums."

I stare at the leather bound tome. "It vibrates for me."

"Is that why you came?"

I place a hand on my hip, something I would have never done in front of *Grand'mere*, and stare at my grandmother defiantly. "All Eric and I wanted was your help."

She ignores my reference to Eric and my attitude. "Where did you find it?"

"In the Fifth Realm of Hell."

Her brown skin pales, and she lowers herself into a chair. "He captured you?"

As *Grand'mere* would say, *I got my back up.* "I was kidnapped by some kind of creature. Eric rescued me."

"This friend of yours, how long have you known him?"

I glower down at her. "What difference does that make?"

She sighs. "Your great-grandmother sensed something evil about him. She was afraid for you."

I sit down across from her and look her in the eye. "I thought I'm supposed to be this great Voodoo priestess.

If that's so, shouldn't I be able to tell if someone is good or evil?"

"If your transformation is complete, you should. But your great-grandmother is not certain you have completed *l'exploit*."

I frown.

"The change," she says. "It is possible you can't see him for what he really is."

Heat rushes to my face. "Maybe I can. You don't know him like I do. He's saved my life twice."

"Another time before this one?"

"Yes."

"Tell me."

I tell her about my encounter in the alley with the creature-the Nian-sent by Saarel.

She draws back in surprise, her face tight with anxiety. "If he kills demons, then he's a demon slayer." She goes on. "Humans cannot kill demons." She studies me. "At least not living humans."

I don't tell her about Eric's admission that he is two thousand years old. It kinda plays into the feelings she has against him.

I push the book toward her. As I do, it falls open to the page I think is about me. She reads it and looks at me in something close to awe.

"I have heard about the foretelling of your birth, but there was always a little doubt in my mind."

She turns the page and like me turns another and another. She glances up at me in confusion.

"They're all blank," I say. "That's why I came. I hoped you could help me understand why all the pages except mine are empty. I have to find Saarel's page so I can figure out how to defeat him."

Shaking her head, my grandmother looks up from the book. "I have no idea." She rises. "Let us wake your great-grandmother."

**

It's close to midnight as I lie on the sofa in the living room, pretending to be asleep and plotting my getaway.

The man called Pasquale is patrolling the grounds. I have two means of escape-the road or the bayou. As much as I fear the bayou, it's quicker and I've lost too much time as it is. There will be no help from my great-grandmother or the other priestess who make up the small enclave of Voodoo worshipers.

My great-grandmother has no idea how to solve the mystery of the blank pages. Forgetting or not caring that I'm fighting for my *Grand'mere*'s life, my great-grandmother commands me to stay in the bayou. I cannot. I will not. I must rescue *Grand'mere*. I must go back. With Eric gone, I'm on my own.

The house has been silent for the last hour. If I'm going to do it, now is the time.

Some good has come from this trip. My grandmother has given me a pair of boots that fit. I leave my wet sneakers behind as a parting gift, and, boots in hand, creep silently toward the front door. Peeping through the sheer curtains, I watch for Pasquale. From my position on the sofa, I've timed his tour of the property. It takes him exactly ten minutes to complete his circuit. I have that long to make it to the dock, unhook one of the pirogues and push it far enough into the water so I won't be detected. It sounds simple, but once in the water, I'm at the mercy of whatever lives in the murky depths of the bayou.

I ease the door open and slip silently out into the darkness. I watch for Pasquale's flashlight. When I no longer see it, I assume he can't see me. I make a dash for the dock. Using the protection of the trees, I dart from one to the other. Thank God for the rain. It's kept the moon hidden behind the clouds. Of course that will work against me as I make my way down the bayou. I won't have the moonlight to guide me.

Stubbing my toe on a large tree root, I almost lose the Book and my boots in the darkness. I bite my lip to keep from crying out. Not having time to nurse my pain, I limp toward the dock, toe throbbing. The closer I get to the water, the darker the night becomes. Scenically beautiful during the day, the canopy of trees that lace the waterway now block out what little light there is from the peek-a-boo moon. Maybe that's why I didn't see him.

I find a boat just where I expect it to be. I untied it from its moorings and am ready to push off, when his voice comes out of the dark.

"I was afraid you might take the road instead."

Eric covers my mouth with his hand just before I let out a yelp of surprise.

"Shhh," he whispers in my ear. He guides me to the boat.

"I'm glad you came back. I thought you'd deserted me." These are the first words out of my mouth when we are a safe distance from my great-grandmother's house.

At first, he doesn't respond, just carefully poles the pirogue through the waterway's dark maze.

"I said I would help you find your grandmother. I wouldn't go back on my word."

I can't stop the smile that spreads across my face from the sincerity of his words. "Thanks for coming back."

"Our fates are bound together," he says.

I don't know if that's true, but I'm relieved he thinks so.

"They didn't have any answers for me," I say.

"That doesn't surprise me. This is the way the Book protects itself. Lesser beings are not meant to view the future. It would destroy the world."

But there are those who would destroy others to know the powers revealed between the pages of this small volume.

The silence stretches between us, a silence filled with uncertainty and fear.

"First we must find the correct portal to enter The Fifth Realm again," Eric says.

"Does it make a difference?"

Something splashes in the water, making me jump.

"Yes," he says. "The entry changes every so many cycles of the earth's moon."

"Eric?"

"Hum?"

"Do you think they're okay? Has- has Saarel harmed them?" I can't bring myself to say killed.

"They're safe."

The conviction in his voice makes me feel better. I sag with relief. Then doubt enters my mind again. "How can you be so sure?"

"Because it's you he wants. He won't harm them until he has you in his control."

"Oh." Although subconsciously I knew it would be a trade-off, me for them, it's just now hitting home. "Will he kill me?"

Eric hesitates too long. My stomach churns. Thank goodness I haven't eaten in a long time. I'd embarrass myself by up chucking over the side of the boat.

"I won't let that happen."

But how can he prevent it? He couldn't protect himself from Saarel's anger. I stare out into the darkness, trying not to let fear and hopelessness put me into a deeper funk. It will be fine. We will find them and everything will be okay. I repeat these words over and over to keep from dissolving into a whiny, crying mess.

When we arrive at the bait shop, we retrieve Eric's car.

Though it's close to 2 am, as we near the city, the carnival-like atmosphere takes over. It's Fat Tuesday, the last day before Lent. Even the periphery of the Quarter, the normally quiet area, is thick with partiers.

It becomes impossible to drive.

"We must walk," he says, and pulls the car into the driveway of a bar's loading dock, where we abandon it.

Laughter, music, voices combine to produce a deafening cacophony of sound. Holding tight to my hand, he shoulders through the crowd with me in his wake.

We're running out of time.

Chapter 27

Feeling Hancock's watchful gaze like hot coals digging into his back, Eric picked up one blade from the kitchen counter, tested it and slipped it into its scabbard. He turned, wanting to read the other man's expression after he asked his question. "Will you watch Lisette until I return?"

"What am I, a nursemaid? First the dog, now the girl." Hancock's body stilled, his eyes became shadowed pools of wariness. "Why? Where are you going?"

Eric studied the man closely before speaking. "To Saarel."

"Why does this not surprise me? You are not planning to fulfill your duty, are you?

"No." He could have elaborated, but why bother. The outcome would be the same.

He delayed picking up his jacket in case Hancock decided to attack. Eric hoped he wouldn't. As much as he wanted to kill Hancock, he needed him.

"It is your duty," Hancock said.

Eric thought it ironic that Hancock, who was a cold hearted bastard, felt he owed allegiance to Saarel-another cold hearted bastard.

"My duty is to someone more worthy of my loyalty."

"Your duty is to Saarel. You gave him your word you would bring the girl to him."

Yes, he'd given his word, but that was before-before he'd met Lisette. Before he'd found out what a caring person she was, what a gift she had for helping the weak, the elderly- and in his case-the damned. "Why, so he can kill her?"

"You knew that would be the outcome when you agreed." Barefoot and legs spread, Hancock looked ready to do battle.

"Agreed?" Eric snorted. "When did I agree? It was either do it or be tortured."

"No good will come of your going without her. So why march back for what will surely be your death?"

"To kill him."

The other man jerked in surprise. "Kill Saarel? No one can kill him." He paused, studying Eric. "Is this a suicide mission?"

"I hope not." Eric's mouth tightened in grim determination. "I will succeed." *I must succeed.*

Hancock laughed. "What do you want me to do with the girl after you are dead?"

Eric had made one big mistake in his life, trusting Cyrus the Great. Was he making another trusting Hancock? But what choice did he have? Taking Lisette would mean certain death for her. At least with Hancock her chances were marginally better.

Pinning Hancock with what he hoped was a determined gaze, he said, "You didn't answer my question. Will you protect her until I return?"

Hancock's mouth tightened into a mutinous line. "Why should I?"

"Because it's your chance to do something honorable."

"Honor is an overinflated virtue." He held Eric's gaze. "And if I do not agree?"

Eric shrugged nonchalantly, even though his body was tight with tension. He knew leaving her with Hancock was the only way to keep Lisette safe. "Then I must take her with me. Once there, I'll decide how I'll protect her."

"How do you know you will return?"

"I'll return." Hands fisted at his side, Eric waited.

After what seemed like an eternity, Hancock sighed. "Aye. I will watch her."

**

Somewhere in Eric's house, a clock gongs nine times. What's taking him so long to hide the book? Did he have to dig a six foot hole first to bury it in?

A creaking sound makes me jump. The skin on my arms prickles. I have this reaction whenever Hancock is nearby. When the creepy one doesn't appear in the doorway, I relax, but not too much. I know he's somewhere close.

I take a deep breath. This is as good a time as any to ask him what he knows about Scooter's disappearance. What can possibly happen to me with Eric in the house?

Gathering my courage around me, I walk toward the back of the house. I assume it leads toward the kitchen, which is where I hope to find Hancock. As I move closer to the end of the hall, I hear angry voices.

I slow down until I'm tiptoeing. *Grand'mere* would be upset to know I'm about to ease-drop on someone's private conversation. But I have no choice. I must find her and Scooter. If it takes spying on Hancock, then I'll do it.

Certain I can't be seen, I stop. White cabinets line the deep green walls of the kitchen's cavernous space.

"Will you watch over Lisette until I return?" Eric asks.

A flash of heat rises into my face. *He's leaving me here? No. Way.*

I hear the swish of metal on metal. Eric's blades?

"Where are you going?" Hancock asks.

"To Saarel."

"You're not taking the girl?"

"--I am leaving her in your care."

My skin feels like fire ants are crawling over it. I'm *not* staying here with Hancock.

There's a rustling of clothing.

"It is your duty," Hancock says.

"My duty is to Lisette- to save her."

"Your duty is—"

Hancock says something that's lost as their footsteps move away from my hiding place.

"-- Will you protect her while I'm gone?"

I can't hear Hancock's reply.

"Here's your chance to do something honorable." Eric says.

More indistinguishable words. Then I smell rain. Someone opened a door. Eric must be leaving.

I hustle back to the sunroom, planning to dash through the courtyard to intercept him. But the squeal of Eric's tires tells me I'm too late.

Shit. I lean my forehead on the cool glass of the French doors.

"Hmmm."

I swing around so quickly my head swims.

Hancock stands in the doorway to the sunroom. "The young master says I'm to escort you to the Fifth Realm."

I will myself not to show any reaction to that lie. What kind of game is he playing?

"Where—where is Eric?" My tongue is thick and doesn't want to work. My mouth is dry.

"He went ahead to prepare the way."

Prepare the way? For what?

Hancock smiles, the smile of a snake.

I shudder. This stinks worst than Saturday morning garbage after Friday night's fish dinner.

I'll be safer on my own. I pat the door behind me, searching for the handle.

"You want to see your friend, do you not?"

I stop dead. "My friend?"

The cold dark eyes watch me like a hawk ready to pounce on a mouse. "Yes, the one you call Scooter."

I knew it. "Where is he? What have you done with him? Do you have *Grand'mere* too?

Hancock smiles again, teeth flashing like an alligator. "Yes. They are together. If you want to save them, you must hurry. Time is of the essence."

I know going with him is stupid, that I might be walking into a trap, but what other options do I have? I can't sit around and wait for Eric to return. What if he doesn't? What if Saarel kills him? I block the thought from my mind. "Let's go."

**

After a silent ten minute walk through flooded streets, Hancock and I step into an alley. It stinks of overripe garbage. I cover my nose with my t-shirt. Rain and unidentified gook make the pavement slippery. As we walk down the alley, I feel eyes on me. I search the darkness, seeing only sodden cardboard and tattered blankets piled over grocery carts, but no faces.

"In here," Hancock says, as he strains to push open a heavy creaking door.

It's the same abandon warehouse the demon brought me to just last night. It seems like a lifetime ago. I move through the open door scared shitless.

"Watch your step," Hancock says.

I look down at the floor. Fast-food wrappers litter the warped boards. Something skitters across my feet. I jump and let out a screech.

"It is just a rat."

"*Just* a rat?" I shudder. As we move through the warehouse, I study the ground for more rats instead of watching Hancock.

He opens a door, then jams it with a block of wood. I know this door leads down into a basement. He descends the same steps the creature took me down just the night before. I follow slowly, knowing what waits at the bottom.

He presses his hand against the wall. Mumbling something under his breath, he places his palm on another spot.

"What's wrong?" I glance back up the stairs. I swear I hear something moving up above. This place is giving me the heebie-jeebies.

"It doesn't open."

"What?" My attention is divided between Hancock's frantic search and the feeling someone is walking around above us.

"The portal is closed."

"Okay, then let's get out of here. I'm getting a bad feeling about this place. There has to be another portal."

I don't wait for Hancock, but sprint up the stairs. I can't spend another moment in this dark, dank place.

When I reach the top, I hear Hancock's heavier tread behind me. My eyes quickly scan the large space. The warehouse is a mass of shifting shadows.

I hear a swish, then a thud. Hancock's head rolls past me along the debris littered warehouse floor, leaving a trail of blood. I whirl around in time to see him slowly crumble. When his body hits the floor, it convulses, spraying bright red blood inches from my feet.

I stare, not able to breathe, not able to think.

Sword drawn with Hancock's blood dribbling from the blade, Eric stands not two feet way.

My mouth is open. I can feel the strain of the scream tearing at my throat, but nothing comes out.

"Come," Eric says, holding out his hand to me.

Eric just killed Hancock.

I back away from him.

He grips my arm and gives it a powerful shake. "Do you want to save your grandmother?"

I thought I knew this guy. I don't. *How could he kill a defenseless human, no matter how heinous Hancock was? What kind of monster is Eric?*

I open and close my mouth. I've seen him kill demons, but this is so different. This was a person I knew. I spoke to.

Eric shakes me again. "Do you want to save your grandmother?" he repeats.

I've got to get a grip. There's Grand'mere and Scooter to think about.

I nod.

"Then we must go now." He turns and hurries toward the open door.

I stumble after him. "Why--why'd you k-kill him? He was taking me to Scooter and *Grand'mere.*"

Eric pulls me out of the warehouse. We're half way up the alley before he answers.

"Do you want to live?"

I nod stupidly.

"That is why I killed him. He wanted to give you to Saarel."

"But-but..."

"Hancock is a soul gatherer. He collects souls for Saarel. He wouldn't have taken you to your grandmother. He would have given you directly to Saarel."

"A s-soul..."

"Gatherer."

I stop walking. "Then why'd you leave me with him?" I don't care that he knows I was ease dropping.

Eric turns and walks back to me. "It was the lesser of two evils. Take a chance on Hancock or take you with me to the Fifth to a certain death."

My stomach sinks. "Has he...has he taken Scooter's soul?"

Eric gives me a look filled with pity. "We won't know until we find your friend's body."

How does he know so much? Unless... "Are you— are you like him?" I hold my breath, afraid of the answer.

Eric doesn't break stride. "No. We're nothing alike."

The night seems to have grown colder just in the few minutes we were inside the warehouse. Rain, our constant companion, falls in heavy sheets, making visibility poor.

As though sensing my confusion and shock, Eric reaches out to take my hand. I hesitate, realizing this is the hand that held the blade that chopped off Hancock's head. But I remember he's saved my life several times already. If he wanted to harm me, he's had several opportunities.

His touch is cool but dry. Trying to warm my fingers, I curl them into his wide palm. "Where're we going?"

"To find the other portal."

"How do you know so much about the portals?"

Without breaking stride, he says, "It's how I entered your world."

We exit the alley, find Conti St. and make our way due north. "Where is it?"

Without breaking stride, he glances at me. "You know."

I do?

My steps falter as we approach St. Louis Cemetery #1, site of the fiasco with Ashley Crandall.

Eric has dispensed with the hood to his slicker and his dark hair is now plastered to his head. "I think the other portal is here."

My mouth is dry. "But why here?"

He gives me a sympathetic look. "This is where you opened it."

I stare at him dumbstruck. "I opened a portal?"

He nodded. "The creatures were sent to do Saarel's bidding, but they were only able to leave their dimension because you opened a portal. This one."

"Oh, my God." My knees tremble and I stall at the entrance. I've created this nightmare that's resulted in *Grand'mere* being taken. I wondered if I had something to do with the creature's appearances, but I really didn't want to believe I was the cause.

"Why doesn't Saarel come for me himself?"

"He cannot leave the Fifth Realm." Eric grips me by the elbow. "We have to go. Every minute is precious."

I swallow and nod. I don't have time for a meltdown, not if we're to find *Grand'mere* and Scooter alive.

We enter the cemetery and make our way to the spot where I gave Ashley the charm. The sense of dread makes my steps slow and awkward, but I force myself to keep walking.

I've been too afraid to come back to the cemetery since the incident with the charm, afraid of what I might find.

The toppled angel still remains buried in the earth, its wings pointing up toward the sky. And the crypt door remains open and the crack in the ground is still there. I glance around the cemetery, expecting to see a demon behind each grave marker.

Eric opens wide the burial chamber's door and motions to me. My feet remain firmly planted.

"Lisette, hurry."

The urgency in his voice breaks the spell. I move forward just as he disappears into the darkness of the crypt. I hesitate just at the opening, close my eyes and say a prayer, then I step inside.

When I open my eyes, the darkness beyond the crypt door is absolute. I take my first deep breath, and completely forget the gloom as damp, stagnant air enters my nose. There's something else in the air, something that coats my mouth and throat, something that makes me want to gag.

It's the scent of death.

Chapter 28

A pinpoint of yellow light sizzles, then cracks as it expands into a large jagged oval. The edges of the hole sparkle, but beyond the hole is darkness. Eric wants me to step voluntarily into that? No way.

"Hurry," he says, coming back for me and pulling me toward the opening. He probably knows this is the only way I'll step through, with him by my side. Gripping my hand tightly, he and I leap through the portal together.

Each portal must deposit you in a different place, because this spot looks entirely different from where I first entered with Watermelon man.

Stunted trees litter a barren landscape. Their leafless branches extend up to a sky, purple with mutinous clouds. The clouds move swiftly, as though any moment, they'll shed copious amounts of rain. I say as much to Eric.

He studies the sky, frowning. "Those are not clouds. We must find shelter quickly. They are flesh eating creatures called Gersthops. Like locusts from your bible."

As soon as he says flesh-eating, I start looking seriously around for a hiding place. There are no buildings, no haven.

"Come," Eric calls to me from a fallen tree. "We will climb in here."

When I reach his side, I look dubiously at the hollow tree and shudder. After passing through a crypt, the idea of another small dark place doesn't appeal to me. "Can't we find something else?"

"Look around, Lisette. Can you see anything else we might use for protection, short of burying ourselves in the earth?

I shake my head.

A loud ominous hum fills the previously silent atmosphere.

"What's that?"

"Get in," he orders. "They're coming."

I burrow like a small animal into the cavity of the tree. He crawls inside, then wriggles into the space next to me that should only comfortably hold one squirrel. I try to breathe shallowly to fight the panic. I'm not successful.

I inhale the pungent smell of wood. With my face turned to the side, I think of the spores and bacteria I'm breathing into my body as my heart races away in my chest. He pulls the slicker over our heads, turning so he faces me. We breathe each other's air.

"I left the Book in the media room of my house. It's stored among the Xbox games," he says. His breath caresses my face.

"Why are you telling me this?"

"Because if something happens to me, you'll know where it's hidden."

"You will come back with me," I say with conviction. I don't want to think about any other outcome.

When they come, it's like the roar of an airplane's engine. They seem to sense our presence and immediately land on the slicker.

My breath comes in rapid pants. Only the calming presence of Eric beside me keeps me from climbing out and running.

Will they eat the cloth and then start in on our flesh? My breath grows even more rapid.

"Shh," Eric whispers, then his lips close over mine.

If he's attempting to take my mind off the Gersthops, he's doing a great job.

His lips are dry but soft. I want to move closer to him, but I don't want to disturb the slicker. So I must be content with the taste of his mouth and dream of more. Concentrating on the feel of him, my breathing slows.

I'm aware of the droning, but it seems light years away. I've never been in love before. Most of the boys I went to school with were either too childish or they weren't interested in me. Maybe I was too nerdy or my body wasn't thick enough.

All I know is I've never felt this way before, like I could melt and become one with him. His closeness relaxes me.

The next thing I know, he's throwing the slicker off and backing out of our refuge. When I crawl out, I blink at the harsh light. Then I remember the kiss. I look at Eric. He's brushing dirt and tree pulp off his pants. He turns and reaches for my hand. He smiles and his brown eyes shine down on me.

"We need to go," he says. His gaze once tracing my features now studies the desert-like landscape.

"Do you know where we are?"

"No, but if we keep moving, we should reach his domain eventually."

I stare out over the dunes. "Maybe I should try that thing I did. You know-the jump."

He frowns. "How can you jump if you don't know where you are going?"

"Good point."

His mouth quirks up at one corner. I know he thinks I'm an idiot.

"How will we rescue *Grand'mere*? I can't believe he'll just let us dance right in and take her away."

"No. It won't be easy, and I don't have a plan." He glances down at me. "Do you? Have you gained any more powers?"

I shake my head. "I might have everything I'm going to get." Remembering something, I frown. "Saarel said I should have all my powers since I'm almost sixteen. Do you think he got that from the Book?"

"I'm not sure," Eric says. "We need to get moving."

He supports my arm as we travel up and over a sand dune. "When is your birthday?" He asks.

My stomach sinks when I remember today's date. "Tomorrow-Ash Wednesday."

"One way or another," he mutters under his breath, "by tomorrow, this will all be over."

If that was supposed to make me feel better, it doesn't.

We continue, traveling over small hills and flat landscape. I feel his eyes on me, watching me for what? Fatigue? I'm not tired, but I'm very thirsty and my skin feels so dry. This place is sucking every bit of moisture from my body. "Where can we find water?"

"We don't."

I stop walking. "What do you mean, we don't?"

"Water doesn't exist in this Realm. We-they don't feel thirst."

A chill runs down my spine. I walk around so I can see his eyes.

"You said, 'we'."

I wait for him to deny it, but he doesn't.

"That's how Saarel knows you. You. Live. Here." I poke him in his chest with each word.

His face suddenly appears tired, defeated. He nods. "I tried to tell you in the car on the highway that I lived in the Fifth."

I can only stare at him, my mind unable to process his words. Slowly, the truth filters through my thick brain. He lives in Hell. He's dead.

I must have spoken the words aloud.

"I'm actually neither alive nor dead."

I frown. "What does that mean?" My eyes travel over his face, looking for some sign that tells me he's different. I can't find anything.

"I will explain later. Now we must continue." He starts walking. I follow.

"After Cyrus the Great murdered my troops and village, I thought he would kill me. He didn't. Maybe he thought it would be more painful for me to remember my treachery over and over. There was a sorcerer that traveled with him. Cyrus had him say the words that would banish me here."

"For how long," I whisper.

"Forever."

Forever. For Eric to be banished and to live in this-this hell for hundreds, no, thousands of years must be beyond awful. I wonder if his years are as long as the years in my dimension. I study him out of the corner of my eye. He doesn't look thousands of years old. Odd.

To take my mind off the coming ordeal, I study the barren trees, the smog-clogged air, the sand-like ground, the stillness. Then it comes to me. There are no birds, other than the destructive locust types, no insects, no animal sounds. All the wonderful things that make my world so special are missing.

"Do you think I'm a freak?" he asks.

"No." Funny. That's the word I use to describe myself. It sounds strange to hear the word coming from him. Just as strange and heart-tugging as *Grand'mere* trying to say 'jiggy.' I smile at that memory, and I walk faster. We must hurry. Her life is in danger.

Out of the corner of my eye, I see his lips tighten.

Should I have said something else? Been more convincing? But I don't know the right words to say. No, I don't think you're a freak, but my other friends, Scooter and the guys at my old school, would definitely think you're a freak.

Eric grips my hand. After my less than spectacular declaration I would think he want nothing to do with me. But his eyes aren't on me. He stares out at the horizon. Well, as much of a horizon as this place has.

Coming toward us is a huddled form.

The grip Eric has on my arm tells me he's expecting trouble.

"Who is it?" I whisper.

"I don't know. But it is always wise to be cautious."

As the shape gets closer, I see it is human, a woman, in fact. She carries a bundle of rags. When we get closer, she drops to her knees with a cry and extends her package toward me.

"Help us." Her voice is deep and cracks. She starts to cry, burying her face in the mass of rags. Her hair is matted with the yellowish-brown soot. I can't distinguish her features because they're caked with grime.

My stomach gives a painful twist, and I move toward her. Eric jerks me back.

"What's wrong with you?" I ask as I try and ply his fingers from my arm. "Can't you see she needs help?"

He ignores me and instead addresses the woman. "What do you want?"

I watch him not her. I've never seen Eric sound so harsh.

"Mercy, mercy for us, Master."

My attention switches from him to her then back to him. "Why does she call you master?" I ask.

Instead of answering, Eric grips my hand and starts to walk away from the woman.

"Mercy, please, Master."

The woman is screeching now. The sound tears at my ears and my heart. I dig in my heels, tug my hand out of Eric's and start back to the woman.

"Lisette. We must go if we are to find your grandmother."

I halt, but the woman's haunted eyes pull me toward her. I sink in the earth beside her.

"What's wrong?" The words escape before I think. What's wrong? Duh. She's living in Hell.

She doesn't look at me, but casts worried glances in Eric's direction.

"It's okay," I say. "Tell me what's wrong."

"The Master." She bows her head, but cuts her eyes in Eric's direction.

I smile at her even though she isn't looking at me. "He's not your master."

She glances quickly at me then at Eric, then bows her head. She doesn't speak again.

A worm of dread slithers up my spine. Rising slowly to my feet, I turn to Eric. His face is a statue carved in stone. "Why is she calling you master?"

Lips compressed, he doesn't answer. Even though my heart is frantically pounding in my chest, I walk around him, studying him. Waiting.

"I'm not Saarel," he says, teeth clenched.

"Right. You've fooled me once before."

"I'm Eric." He reaches out to touch me, but I back away.

"How do I know that?"

He moves toward me, then stops. "Ask me anything."

I shake my head. "Eric says you are all knowing. You could know everything he knows."

His face twists with some emotion. He shakes his head. "I love you, Lisette. Saarel is incapable of love."

As much as I want to believe those words, I know they wouldn't fall so easily from Eric's lips. If this is Saarel, then he has me right where he wants me. So it doesn't matter what I do. I go to the woman. Her need is still painfully written on her face.

Ignoring Eric/ Saarel, I ask her again. "What's wrong?"

Wordlessly she extends her bundle. I reach out to take it.

"Don't touch it, Lisette."

I ignore him, whoever he is.

As I grip her bundle, I'm surprised to find that it has form. There's something inside. I lower the filthy package and begin to unwrap it. The cloth disintegrates in my hands in puffs of dust. My fingers slow as I realize what I'm holding. I recoil in horror. It's a baby, a dead baby with strips of withered skin hanging from the bones of its small skeleton.

She picks up the dead child in trembling hands and places it to her shriveled breast. "He will not nurse." She is smiling and cooing to the dead infant and smoothing the wisps of hair on its shrunken skull.

Eric touches my shoulder, then gently pulls me to my feet. "Come, there is nothing you can do." He holds me in his arms, stroking my shoulders. Yes, this is my Eric. Saarel wouldn't care that I'm distressed. But it's not my distress that tugs at my soul. I stare at the poor woman, singing an off key tune to her dead child.

"The baby has been dead a very long time," Eric says. "There is nothing you can do."

The mother's cries start up again. "Save him, please."

Eric pulls me away and forces me to walk with him.

"We can't leave her."

He doesn't look back, but continues in the direction we were heading.

"Pleassse."

"I have to do something," I plead. Ignoring Eric's look of displeasure, I head back to the mother, not knowing what I could say to her to ease her pain.

I drop to my knees in front on her. Gripping her chin in my hands, I raise her face so I can look into her eyes. "I'm so sorry." Those are the only words I can think of to say, but they are wrenched from the depths of my heart. "I'm so very sorry."

She stares at me wordlessly, then tears pool in her crusted brown eyes and begin to slide down her face, leaving tracks of lighter skin in their wake. I stroke her dirty hair and murmur comforting words to her. She leans into my body, her sobs shaking both of us. I hold her for a long while, the stench of old cloth and death between us.

"I left him alone."

At first her words don't register, but she repeats them.

"I left him alone."

Pulling away from her, I gaze into her pain-filled eyes, listening to her words.

"He was sick and I needed money for food and coal. So when the soldier showed me his silver and told me to put my crying baby in another room, I did. I had only the stable. It was cold that day and the babe was already sick. When the soldier was finished with me and asleep, I went to get my baby."

Now she started to cry in earnest, body whacking sobs. "When I went to get him, he was dead. My baby..."

I wrap the mother's pitiful body in my arms and rock her. I stare at Eric over her head. He stands looking out over the dune, not at us, but his face is taut with emotion-pity.

"I killed my baby."

How she must have suffered. How she must have blamed herself.

"It's okay," I say. "He forgives you. He knew you loved him. What you did was for him." I didn't say that her decision was not the smartest because at this point it doesn't matter. It won't bring her baby back. "He forgives you," I croon again to her.

I continue to rock her with thoughts of my own mother running through my head. A mother's love is a powerful thing. The last few days I've felt closer to my mother than I ever did before. And today, holding this weeping mother, I feel something release inside. "I forgive you."

And I know I'm forgiving my own mother for leaving me, though she didn't leave me of her own free will. But you can't rationalize with a small child. To me, it felt as though she'd abandoned me. Now I say a silent prayer of thanks to my mother for being there for my first four years of life. My own tears flow and mingle with those of this young mother.

"Lisette?" Eric's voice intrudes on my thoughts. And yes, I know it's Eric. Saarel would not have the patience or care enough to allow me the time to grieve with this poor mother.

"We must go," he says.

Nodding, I pull away from the woman and her child. I look into her eyes and give her a hopeful smile. She returns it. Then before my eyes, she and the baby shimmer away in a halo of white light.

Stunned, I can only stare at the spot where she'd sat, then a warm rush of certainty infuses me. She is at peace.

I glance up at Eric and smile. "Let's go."

He grips my hand and pulls me to my feet. As I stand, a wave of dizziness washes over me. I sway.

"Lisette? What's wrong?"

I hear Eric's voice from a far off place. Something clutches at my gut and I feel like my insides are being pulled out of my body. Groaning, I drop to my knees and heave.

"Lisette?" From a long way off, I hear the worry and concern in his voice.

As I glance up, his body wavers in front of my eyes. Frightened and sick, I reach out to him, needing to touch him. My hand slips right through his body.

Blackness flickers around the periphery of my vision. Then everything goes dark.

**

Eric landed with a thud. Pain shot through his body like a hot poker and dust flew up his nose. Before he could get his bearings, hands jerked him to his feet. Two burly human slaves pinioned his body between theirs. He broke free from the restraint of one of the guards, and landed a fist in the slave's jaw.

Then pain exploded in his head. He dropped to his knees as his vision faded to black. By sheer willpower he forced the darkness back. He had to stay in control. He had to get back to Lisette.

From far away he heard clapping.

"Well done, Assur."

Thrusting away the pain, Eric lifted his head. Black dots swam in his vision. His head throbbed and bile surged in his throat.

Clapping his hands in a parody of applause, Saarel sat atop a throne made from the stunted trees that dotted the acrid landscape. The usual degenerates, beggars and thieves littered the ground at his feet, alternately fawning or pleading. Saarel stepped on their bodies as he strolled toward Eric.

"What do you want, Saarel?" Eric's voice slurred. He had disobeyed the first rule of the Realm- speak only with permission. But his anxiety for Lisette overruled his caution.

Yellow smog swirled around Saarel's blond, human persona. "Do you know how I reward traitors?"

Eric held his tongue. One indiscretion might earn him torture, but a second might cost him his head.

Saarel's eyes were like blue flame, scorching in their intensity. "I knew what you planned. I have not been master of this domain for thousands of years without knowing what goes through my minion's minds."

Eric flinched. He was no minion.

"It is not too late to save yourself," Saarel said. His hot breath burned Eric's face. The demon was so close Eric could see his eyes change from blue to magenta.

"Just bring her to me," Saarel said, his anger building at Eric's silence. His human shape quivered. A sure sign he was about to morph into another form.

Eric needed to know Saarel's plan for Lisette. He had to find some way of saving her, even if it meant his own demise. "You would kill her," he said.

Saarel's jaw bunched. Eric braced himself for the hailstorm of the Overlord's wrath. It didn't come.

Saarel stepped back with his hand at his heart-if he had one-pretending to be hurt. "You wound me, Eric. Why would I want her dead? She's too valuable to me alive."

What new scheme was he hatching? He was too serene for someone who had been betrayed by an underling. Eric preferred Saarel foaming at the mouth. This calm signaled trouble.

Despite words to the contrary, Eric knew when Saarel tired of Lisette he would kill her. Eric wouldn't be the instrument of her death.

Something important flickered through his mind. Why didn't Saarel just go get Lisette now that she was in the Fifth? Why did he still need Eric? Could it be that there were boundaries the Overlord couldn't cross? Hoping this was true, Eric said, "I will not help you." Maybe he could keep her out of the clutches of the Overlord and get Lisette safely back to her dimension.

Saarel snapped his fingers at the guards. They tightened their grip on his arms, pinning him between them.

Saarel was in his face again. "Oh, you'll help me," he said coldly. He motioned to one of his slaves.

The guard dragged a small woman forward and dropped her at Saarel's feet.

"Remind you of anyone?" Saarel asked.

It was like looking into the face of his grandmother, dead these past two thousand years. That small, defenseless woman he'd sacrificed.

But this elderly woman's eyes were amber, not gray. And Eric knew the plea in those eyes was not for her life, but for the life of her granddaughter, Lisette.

He was caught in the same quagmire that had ended his existence. He had to sacrifice someone. Would he make the correct choice this time?

Saarel must have read the capitulation in Eric's gaze.

"Good." Saarel smiled. "You have one hour to bring the girl to me. For every minute you're late, I'll cut off parts of this old one's body, starting with her legs."

Chapter 29

"Lisette."

"I don't want to get up, *Grand'mere.*" I search for the sheet to pull over my head, but it flows through my hand.

"Wake up, Lisette."

When I recognize Eric's voice, the fog recedes. I open my eyes. Pain, like bolts of lightning, shoots straight to my brain.

"Let me help you up."

"Where-" I wet my lips and taste grit, then the foul smell of sulfur fills my nose. Now, I remember. I'm in Hell, Saarel's hell. Groaning, I close my eyes. "What happened?"

"You fainted."

My eyes snap open. "Fainted?"

He nods and places an arm around my shoulders, lifting me to a sitting position.

And then I remember just before I blacked out Eric disappeared.

"Where did you go?"

He frowns. "Go? I didn't go anywhere."

"You disappeared. My hand went right through you."

Shaking his head, he helps me to my feet. "I think you imagined that."

I start to shake my head in denial, but immediately stop. My brain feels like its sliding from one side of my skull to the other.

"I didn't-" Swaying on my feet, I decide for the moment to give up that train of thought. It takes too much concentration.

He steadies me then takes my face into his hands. "Do you trust me?"

His eyes are so dark they're almost black. A look of intense concentration mars his face. He no longer looks like Eric, but a caricature of the guy I love.

"What's wrong?"

"Nothing."

But the lie is in his eyes. I try and pull my face from his hands, but he's too strong.

He leans closer, his breath warm against my already heated skin. "Lisette, this is very important. You must do exactly as I instruct. The life of your grandmother and you depend of it."

He has my attention. I listen closely to his words.

Then the trek begins. We walk until my trembling legs threaten to collapse. I'm so weak and tired I don't have time to wonder about the words he whispered to me.

"Just a little further," he urges. "Just to the top of this mound."

I stare up, up, up. This isn't a mound, it's a freaking mountain. Mustard colored dust swirls around the peak of this monstrosity.

I can't climb it. My limbs are stuck in the sand like metal legs stuck in concrete.

Sliding his hands up to grip my face between his palms again, he stares down into my eyes. This time his voice is gentler. His gaze travels over my face as though memorizing it. "We're running out of time. Remember, no matter what happens that I love you."

Before I have a chance to savor the moment, he scoops me into his arms and charges up the hill. I bury my face in his neck, inhaling the scent that is uniquely Eric-spice and musk.

When we crest the mountain, he places me on my feet. I'm aware of a sound that builds until it's a roar that vibrates through my bones.

Coming toward us on a wave of shimmering heat is a ragtag group of zombies, demons and half humans-some walking upright, some dragging their ravaged bodies through the sifting sand. They stop some distance from us and two creatures of ginormous proportions separate from the masses.

In the blink of an eye, they're in front of us. I step back, but lose my balance and fall, sending puffs of dust up around me. One of the creatures reaches down and with a hand the size and smell of an overcooked ham, tosses me over his shoulder.

From my upend position, the dull browns and saffron yellows of this world whiz together in a blend of color as we race across the wasteland. I'm dumped in front of two cloven hoofs. My gaze drifts up a black wide pant leg, until it stops on the Saarel's smiling face. My heart is like a runaway train that's jumped the tracks. Only a supreme effort keeps me from throwing up on his hoofs.

Even stranger is the crown on his blond head. It glitters with the lights of hundreds of multi-colored jewels.

He pulls me to my feet.

"My bride, you have returned. How touching. Did you bring the Book?"

How stupid of me. I could have traded *Grand'mere* and Scooter's life for the book.

My expression must give him the answer, because he says, "Too bad. Now I'll have to kill the old woman." He snaps his fingers.

"Noooo..." I grip his arms. As I do, two guards rush forward. He stays them with a hand.

"What is it, my lovely? Come to your senses about being my bride."

A shudder runs through my body. He must see it or feel it because his face contorts into an ugly scowl.

Before he can respond, I say, "I know where the Book is. I'll go back for it, just don't hurt her."

When he smiles, I see a flash of his sharp lizard teeth. "Now you want to bargain."

I peer around him at the group of followers. "Let me see her. If she's okay, I'll bring you the Book. And what about Scooter?"

"She is alive. And so is the other one... in a fashion.

My stomach dips. "In a fashion?" I have a bad feeling about this.

"He bartered his soul to gain his brother's freedom."

"Noooo!"

"Oh, yes. And now it is your turn to fulfill your ancestor's debt." He holds out his ghostly pale hand to me.

If Claudette weren't already dead, I would gladly kill her at this moment. I back away, needing to stall for time. Eric's instructions run through my mind.

"I want to see my *Grand'mere* and Scooter."

"Then will you come willingly?" Saarel asks.

I nod, keeping my face blank and hoping my eyes don't betray me.

He snaps his fingers. The crowd parts and a small hunched figure stands alone. It takes me a second to recognize her. "*Grand'mere.*" I start to run toward her, but the monstrous creature that deposited me at Saarel's feet holds me in place. His double trudges to her, picks her up and brings her to Saarel.

Weak, she crumbles like a rag doll when he releases her. I gather her into my arms and feel her tremble like a wounded bird. I turn on Saarel.

"How dare you mistreat her! Let me take her home."

He laughs, a big gut-busting sound that sends his subjects scattering, tripping over each other, fear distorting their misshapen faces. "You bring me the Book, I'll let her go."

I study his features. Right. Like I'd believe him. Anyone who'd kidnap a defenseless old lady is not to be trusted.

"I want to see Scooter, also." *Then what?*

I resist searching for Eric. I want to keep him out of Saarel's thought as long as possible.

"I'm here, Lis." Scooter's voice floats on the air.

Holding *Grand'mere* tightly to my body, I search the crowd. I don't see him. Frowning, I glance up at Saarel. "Where is he?"

The demon Overlord smiles slightly. "He's here, just not as you remember him."

What kinda of game is he playing? "What do you mean?"

"His soul is here, but not his body."

My gaze flies to the Overlord's face, not sure I heard him correctly. "Wh—what?"

"A body is useless. I have too many as it is. He flings his hand in the direction of his subjects. "All I desire for my purposes is the essence of a being."

A pain slices right through me. *Oh, my God, Scooter. What have you done?* "Wh—where is his body?"

Saarel shrugs. "I do not know or care."

"How--how did you get his soul?"

Saarel shrugs. "It doesn't matter. I have it on good authority that the soul gatherer is dead."

Hancock's head rolling on the warehouse floor flashes through my mind. I can feel the blood drain from my head, leaving me faint and nauseous. *Hancock is dead.* I may never find Scooter's body. My knees buckle, threatening to send both *Grand'mere* and me face first into the malodorous dust.

Scooter, why? Why, Scooter? I hold tight to *Grand'mere* rocking us both in a dance of agony. Pain guts me, tearing a hole from my stomach to my back, making me double over with it. "God, Scooter."

"God has nothing to do with this," Saarel says, a sly smile pulling at the corners of his thin lips. "Soon I will be God of all the heavens."

I rise, anger buzzing inside my skull like a swarm of enraged bees. Hot blood rushes to my face, filling my head with its roar. I'm drowning in my grief.

Vaguely aware of Eric shouting my name, I ignore him.

"Never. You'll never-"

In a blink Saarel is standing in front of me. He grips my hair and jerks, the pain like shards of ice plunging in my scalp. My eyes water.

Rational thought flees when Saarel pushes his face so close to mine I can smell death.

His lips turn up in the grin of a predator. "I will be God with your help."

Saarel pulls me up by my hair, until our eyes are level and my feet no longer touch soil. I can't break his hypnotic gaze. I'm powerless to resist as he draws me toward him. He places his hard mouth to mine.

He doesn't kiss me, but rather sucks the air from my lungs, drawing more and more from me. Something tears loose inside me, like a boat yanked from its mooring.

My brain feels as though it's being crushed by a giant pair of pliers. My throat aches with a need to scream. I want to fight, but I can't break away from the power he has over me.

Vaguely, I hear Eric's enraged voice and then his grunts of pain. *Grand'mere* screams my name. The fear in her voice helps me rip my gaze away from Saarel's mesmerizing blue eyes and my mouth from the parasitic kiss. Swaying on her feet, *Grand'mere* pounds on Saarel's back. He swats her. The power of the blow sends her flying through the air to land in a crumbled heap. She doesn't rise.

Grand'mere!

Fear and rage pump through my veins. A howl like a freight train fills my ears. Heavy and pounding, my head feels like twice its normal size. Bodies of half human creatures, their mouths open in surprise and terror, swirl and spin in a funnel of wind. Colors and sounds blend. I see Eric's face before he flies away. I also see Saarel, his face twisted in unholy glee. He, too, flies away. When Grand'mere spins by, I reach out and pluck her from the whirling wind into the vacuum with me. I clutch her tightly to my chest.

Then as though someone has flipped off a switch, the sucking, swirling motion is gone. I land with a bone-jarring crash.

**

Rain pelts my face as I lie in a puddle of water and stare up at a sky filled with dark angry clouds. I reach out for *Grand'mere*, but my fingers encounter only stone. Using every bit of strength I have, I pull my bruised and batter body off the rocky ground. I'm back where it all started- in St. Louis Cemetery.

"*Grand'mere!*" My voice ping pongs off the tall mausoleums as my eyes frantically scan the cemetery for her. There are hundreds of crypts, but no *Grand'mere*. Panic makes it hard for me to catch my breath. I call her name again. Where is she? The last thing I remember is wrapping my arms around her fragile body. I've got to find her. She's here, I know she's here.

A shadow moves in my peripheral vision. I pivot so quickly my head swims.

Hair matted to his skull, Eric trudges toward me through standing water. Rain drips off the ends of his dark hair and runs in rivulets down his face and neck. Even though I'm glad to see him, my first thought is: she's not with him.

He tries to pull me into his arms, but I won't go. "Where's *Grand'mere*?"

Looking around, as though she should be standing with us, he then swings his gaze back to me. "I don't know."

"I've got to find her." I turn to go, but his hand on my arm stops me.

"Are you okay?" he asks. The words are almost lost as he succeeds in pulling me into his arms and presses his mouth into my hair. The warmth of his breath sends welcome tingles down my spine at the same time his comfort makes me angry. I don't have time for this.

"No." The sound comes out muffled against his body. "What happened?" My voice sounds weak and unsteady in my ears.

"You brought us back."

At his words, the whirling, sucking maelstrom of my emotional meltdown flits through my mind. Then what he said sinks into my battered brain. "Who is 'us'?"

He pulls back to look into my eyes. "You, me, and Saarel."

My body jerks in horror. "Saarel? No. No way."

Please, God, say it isn't so. I search Eric's face for some sign that he isn't sure. But there is only certainty in his eyes.

I shudder, remembering the last moments before the jump- Saarel's face. Then the ramifications of Saarel being here plow into my brain. "Where'd he go?"

"I don't know."

"Are you sure he came through?"

Even as I say the words, I know Saarel is here. Something feels off in the world around me.

I'll worry about him later. Thoughts of Scooter pushed through my fear. I push them down. I'll worry about him later also. Now, I have to find *Grand'mere.*

"Lisette?"

I turn impatiently toward Eric. "What?"

"You have to send Saarel back."

I stare at him, dumbfounded. "*Me*? Don't you mean *we*?"

He shakes his head. "Only you have the power to send him back to his dimension."

I draw away from him, thinking he's lost his mind. "I can't send him back. Did you see what he was doing to me? He would have killed me.

Did you see me putting up much of a fight? No, you didn't, because Saarel was draining the life out of me. And now you tell me I have to send him back to Hell? If you're relying on me, you'll be waiting a long time. I don't have what it takes."

I walk away.

Eric's next words stop me cold.

"Lisette, I think you've completed the transformation."

Fear and hope batter at my defenses much like the rain and wind now pummeling my body. He doesn't know what he's talking about.

He catches up with me and places one warm hand on my shoulder to slow me down.

"After we have found your grandmother and dealt with Saarel, then we can find your friend."

I stare into his brown eyes. It doesn't do any good to mention if Eric hadn't cut off Hancock's head we might have better luck finding Scooter's body. What's done is done. "Promise?"

He nods. "Promise."

I continue walking, weaving between crypts, calling *Grand'mere's* name. While I search, my soul and body ache for my best friend. For now, I have one task: find *Grand'mere*. Saarel can rot.

For every step I take, the wind drives me back two. Rain batters my body. So much rain has fallen in the last week the river should now cover the city. The standing water is about a foot deep in spots.

As much as I try not to think about Eric's words, my mind goes back to them. What if I'm a Voodoo priestess? No, no. I'd know it. Wouldn't I?

I stop and reluctantly turn to face him. "How do you know I completed the metamorphosis?" The wind almost rips the words out of my mouth.

"Because Saarel knew. That kiss... And because-"

I frown. "Because what?"

When he doesn't answer, aggravated, wet and scared, I turn to walk away again.

He grips my arm to stop me, and then stares at me in silence.

"What?" His silent assessment makes me angry, but underneath the anger lurks a suspicion that he's right. I've changed.

"Your eyes-"

"What about my eyes?"

"One is brown and the other is blue."

"What?" I stare at him in stupefied horror. Have I become more of a freak than I already was?

"I noticed it when you became ill, after you touched that mother."

I shake my head and try to pull away from him. I don't want to hear any more. I'm tired of being different. I've been different all my life. "I need to find *Grand'mere*."

"Lisette. He-- Saarel has absorbed some of your power. That's the only way he could've traveled back with us. We must find him. He must be sent back. He will destroy this world."

Somewhere in the distance, a church bell gongs the new hour. I start to tremble. The idea of facing Saarel again paralyzes me, but a certainty fills me. I don't have to look for him. He'll find me.

I stumble over *Grand'mere* lying face up, thank God, in a pool of water.

"*Grand'mere*." I drop to my knees and touch her face. It's cold. My fingers tremble as I search for a pulse in her neck. My own blood pounds so rapidly through my veins I can't be sure if I feel her pulse or mine. I place my face next to her mouth. The faint warmth of her breath fans my cheek. I close my eyes in relief and briefly lower my forehead to hers. If I had lost her...

Eric's touch on my shoulder reminds me we must hurry. I raise my head. Even as I place my hands on her body to start the healing process, I wonder how I can keep her safe.

Closing my eyes, I let go of all my fears for Scooter's safety and doubts about my ability to defeat Saarel and concentrate on sending good energy through my fingertips to *Grand'mere*.

Bright light pierces my eyelids. At first I think it's another manifestation of my new powers.

"Lisette." The tone of Eric's voice makes my eyes fly open.

Crisscrossing through the cemetery are the beams from several high powered flashlights, startlingly bright against the darkness. Criminals don't announce themselves, so it's either tourists out for nighttime kicks or the police.

Chapter 30

I'm hoping it's the police. If it is, it might be a way of keeping *Grand'mere* safe while we hunt for Saarel or he hunts for us.

"Let me handle this," I say to Eric. "Over here," I shout, standing up long enough for them to get a fix on us, then dropping back down to *Grand'mere's* side. I use my t-shirt to clear the water from her face, even though it's more for my peace of mind than hers.

Two police officers converge on us from different directions.

"What's going on here?" one of the officers asks. He wears clear plastic rain gear over his uniform. He drops to his haunches as soon as he spots *Grand'mere* on the ground and presses his fingers to her neck.

"I think she's had a heart attack," I say.

"What are you three doing here this time of night and in this weather?" This comes from the second officer who stands back, hand resting on his hip just above his gun.

"She wanted to pay her respects to our family member." I cast a quick glance at the mausoleum *Grand'mere* lies in front of-Moriel. I breathe a sigh of relief. The Moriel family is a politically connected family in New Orleans and our ancestral name. Maybe this will carry some weight with the officers and they won't question my story.

"I'm calling for an ambulance," the first officer says. "She's in a bad way." He speaks into the radio at his collar.

"But why at 11pm?" the second officer asks.

So there's one hour left before midnight. One hour before my sixteenth birthday. One hour before Saarel arrives to finish me off. I resist the urge to glance at Eric.

"She wasn't feeling well earlier today, but she wanted to pay her respects while the spirits were about." I almost laughed at the comical expression on the second cop's face. He probably thinks he's dealing with devil worshipers.

He turns to Eric. "What about you, buddy?"

I hold my breath not sure what he will say.

"I am visiting this country."

"From where?"

Eric opens his mouth, but I speak up before he can say Iran or worst yet-Hell. "Spain. He's visiting from Spain."

The officer asks for our names and addresses. I tell him Eric is staying with me and give him my address.

"Ambulance is here," the first officer says.

We can see flashlights bobbing and weaving through the maze of tombs. Within minutes EMTs have *Grand'mere* strapped to the gurney, a water proof blanket over her and an I.V. started.

"I'd like to ride in the ambulance with her," I say this to one of the EMTs.

"'Fraid not, miss," the second officer says. "I'd like you and your friend," he nods at Eric, "to ride over to the station with us."

"Why?" My attention is divided between the gurney being pulled away and the presence of the two police officers. I shiver as the wind blows rain in my face and apprehension makes my stomach cramp.

"We'd like to talk to you two about some disturbances in this cemetery in the last few days," the first officer says.

"What disturbances?" I fake an innocent stare. They obviously didn't buy my story about visiting deceased relatives.

"We'll talk down at the precinct," the second officer says.

"Where are they taking her?" I ask.

"Charity Hospital," says the first officer.

Grabbing Eric's hand as we're escorted out of the cemetery, my first thought is to transport us somewhere else. But where? With my lack of skill, I'd make the jump and bring the policemen along for the ride. My second thought is we'd be safer in police headquarters. Then I laugh to myself. We're talking about Saarel. There's nowhere Eric and I will be safe.

"We need help," I whisper to Eric as the four of us wind our way out of the cemetery. The faint sound of music floating through the air from the Quarter gives a surreal feeling to the night. Jazz, demons, cops and the clueless-Eric and I being the clueless-mingle together in a pot of supernatural stew.

A squad car waits outside the entrance to the cemetery. Second cop opens the door and motions for Eric to get in. When he glances at me, I give him a reassuring nod. Confidence I don't feel.

"Could you drive us to the bayou before you question us?" I ask the first police officer before getting into the squad car.

He shakes his head with a slight grin as though my request is ludicrous. "We don't run a taxi service. The first place you're goin' is to police headquarters."

"Please. It's a matter of life or death."

"Right." Protecting my head with his hand, he gently pushes me into the back seat of the cruiser.

As the police car pulls away from the cemetery, Eric slips his fingers through mine. I glance over at him. I must look afraid because he leans over and whispers in my ear. "Have faith."

I pull my cross from beneath my t-shirt and worry it with the fingers of my other hand. I haven't been without it since the incident in the cemetery with Ashley. I smile weakly at Eric and turn to stare out the window.

Graffiti and plastic cups, now sodden in the rain, litter the streets. Driving is slow-going because the streets are a wall of drunken, shouting partiers and standing water.

Inside the car, the mood is somber; the windshield wipers are a metronome for my thoughts. My brain is going in useless circles like a rat in a maze. I can't defeat

Saarel. He's lived for thousands of years. I've only been around for fifteen as an ordinary girl, not a demon-fighting machine. These last few days have been crazy. It's like this has been happening to someone else and I've been watching the story unfold from the sidelines.

The police radio squawks, breaking into my thoughts.

"Disturbance at Bourbon and Toulouse. All units in the area respond.

Officer number two picks up the mike. "Officer Roger and Lyons in the vicinity."

The radio crackles. "We have a report that someone dressed like Hellboy is assaulting tourist.

Officer number one shakes his head. "Damn drunks."

Eric and I exchange a look. Saarel.

Although the interior of the police car is warm, my hands feel cold and there's a fine sheen of sweat on my upper lip. My hand tightens convulsively around Eric's.

Officer number two turns to us. "Get home. It's getting crazy out here. And stay out of the cemetery."

The back doors unlock, and Eric and I spill out into the crowd.

The cruiser now sends out intermittent bleats of its siren. Like the parting of the Red Sea, the crowd slowly divides to allow the police car to pass. It drives on, lights flashing, siren blaring. They have bigger problems than us.

The hole in the crowd immediately closes and we are engulfed. Eric grabs my hand and pulls me toward the edge of the horde.

"We have to follow that police car," he shouts. "Then we have to lead Saarel back to the cemetery."

"Why?"

"Because the portal needs to be sealed after he goes through it."

Like a running back, Eric clears a path for me through the crowd.

I tug on his arm. When he stops, I shout into his ear. "How will we get him to the cemetery?"

"You're going to lead him there," he shouts.

Stunned, I don't move.

"Come on," Eric says. I can't hear his words, but rather read his lips.

I follow him like a sacrificial lamb.

When we find the patrol vehicle, the doors stand wide open. The two officers are nowhere to be seen. Strange. Aren't they supposed to lock their police car?

Eric spares one glance for the abandoned vehicle and pushes on through the crowd with me following close behind. We pass two alleys with Eric cautiously approaching each one, peering down one, then another and moving on. He keeps me behind him each time. At the third alley, he whips back so quickly he knocks me into the building, abutting the alley. My breath comes out in a whoosh.

"Is it him?" I whisper, struggling for air.

He nods. He tries to keep me from looking, but he's just a little too slow.

What I see makes me freezes. It's like something out of a science fiction movie. Saarel is holding someone dressed as a jester by the shoulders. The jester twitches like electrical current shoots through his body. But what holds me glued to the scene is the bright stream of yellow light that passes from the man's mouth to Saarel's. Or at least I think that's the direction it's flowing. Is this how it looked when Saarel gave me that kiss? Was my essence passing from my body as a stream of light?

Eric pulls me back behind him, but not before I see another costumed tourist slumped against one of the buildings, his face white as a sheet, his eyes open and blank.

I swallow convulsively, and a shiver of revulsion and fear passes through me. For just a second I allow myself the luxury of leaning on Eric and drawing in his strength.

"What's he doing?" I whisper. The words come out choppy as my teeth clatter.

Eric pulls me into his arms. "I think he's draining the life force from that person."

"Don't you know?" I ask. "Haven't you seen him do it before?"

"I am only guessing because there is no life force to drain in our dimension."

"Oh." I glance at him, apologetic. "Sorry."

He smiles, but there's no humor in the lift of his lips. "I must draw his attention."

I grab his arm before he steps away from the protection of the building. "Are you crazy?"

"I have to stop him, Lisette, before he kills again."

"What about your plan for me to lead him back to the cemetery?"

"I've changed my mind. It's too dangerous for you."

I study his grim face. "We both know he can jerk your chain at any moment."

"It's something I have to do," Eric says, touching my face briefly with cold, wet fingers.

"No you don't. Let me save *you* for once." I smile a smile without humor. "I thought I was this big bad Voodoo priestess. Either you believe it or you don't."

I have him now. I hold my breath, hoping he buys my plan.

I'm not sure I can send Saarel back to his dimension, but I'm willing to try, if it will save the people I love.

I lean in and place my lips lightly to his. "I love you, Eric. Believe in me."

Indecision plays across his face. I see the moment he decides to let me try, it's reflected in his eyes.

"I love you, and I know you can do it," he says.

I let out a sigh of relief. "I want you to tell him I'm at the cemetery. Then make sure he gets there. I don't care how you do it. My guess is he's gathering the life force of enough souls so he has the strength to overcome me." I laugh. "Imagine him getting ready for me." I shake my head in wonder.

"If I can hold him off until midnight, I'll be okay." I'm bluffing because I haven't the slightest idea how I'll be different at 12:01, but Eric doesn't need to know that. "Give me a five-minute head start."

Without giving him a chance to protest, I take off toward the cemetery. The crowds are thinning as the midnight hour approaches, and the partiers disperse back to their hotels or homes to rest for Lent.

I make good time and reach the cemetery in ten minutes. From the clock in the window of a business I pass, it's now 11:50 p.m.

To my surprise the gates into the cemetery are being guarded by the same two officers who escorted Eric and me out of the burial grounds not thirty minutes earlier.

I smile in relief, but then in alarm. Saarel will rip these two apart.

"You've got to leave," I say, running toward them. I know anything I say will sound bizarre, but I have to warn them. "A demon is coming. You got to run."

One of the officers nods. "Yes. Himself is coming."

My heart stops.

Chapter 31

When I look into their blank eyes, I realize they're already dead. They're zombies like all the rest of the creatures that Saarel has sent for me. They're just fresher and newer.

There's a hitch in my breathing. I will myself to calm down. I don't have time to panic. If I live through this, I'll have a breakdown later, but now I have lives to save-starting with my own.

Somehow I must get into the cemetery and to the portal. I search my memory. Is there another entrance? Of course, my brain is not the most reliable at the moment. Something about facing one's own death does that to a person.

Can I make the jump to the cemetery? I've only done this twice and both times it was to travel from one dimension to another. Will it work moving within this dimension?

I back away from the officers. They don't seem inclined to follow me, thank goodness. I close my eyes and visualize the crypt that houses the portal. "I need to be there," I whisper to myself. No sucking or swirling feeling. I open my eyes. The officers watch me with dispassionate eyes. I try once again. Nothing. I'm still outside the cemetery. I want to scream in frustration, instead, I stomp my foot. Water bounces up onto my pants. I have to think.

I shift slowly toward the entrance of the cemetery. Will they try to stop me going in? They close ranks, blocking the entry.

Maybe I don't have to do anything just stand here and wait. At midnight I'll have these mystery abilities that will make me a powerful priestess. It doesn't matter I don't know what they are or how to use them.

Hearing the mocking tone of my thoughts makes me realize, I don't believe there will be a transformation. I've never believed. It's something I've been told will happen, but I never bought into. And yes, I can wait until midnight and I might be safe from Saarel, but he'll still be here draining the life force from every human in the city, in the world, until my world will look like his. People like in my nightmare, soulless zombies.

I square my shoulders and march up to the officers. They come to attention.

"You will let me pass."

"We must wait for-"

"They must wait for me."

My heart sinks like a stone to the bottom of the Mississippi River.

Time's up.

I whirl. Saarel stands in front of me. His whole being is brighter, his eyes brilliantly blue, and his blond hair is almost white it's so bright. I know instinctively he's lit from within by the life force of the people he's murdered.

Before I allow myself time to think, I pivot and dash between the police officers, heading for the cemetery entrance. Before I reach the entry, Saarel is standing in front of me again, smiling.

"Going somewhere, my little bride?"

I blink in disbelief. One minute he was behind me and now here he is in front of me. I never saw him move. He's faster than I am, definitely more cunning than I am, and stronger. What in the world makes me so powerful? According to my mother's family, I'm supposed to be just short of Christ-like. Yet in this moment, Saarel could snap me like a twig.

I can't even figure a way to get into the cemetery. How can I defeat him?

"Come, my mate, let us end this dance," Saarel says, as he practically glides toward me.

"Yes, let us end this dance," Eric says, standing behind Saarel just inside the cemetery. His dark wet hair is plastered to his head. "You can't have her, Saarel. I'll fight you with everything I have."

Saarel doesn't turn, but smiles. The smile is not for me. "Such a stupid boy."

He moves so quickly Eric has no time to prepare. He backhands Eric and sends him flying further into the cemetery. Then Saarel charges after Eric, picks him up and lifts him until his feet dangle off the ground.

"Is this how you repay me?" he shouts. "I gave you a gift-time away from the Realm. All I asked was that you deliver her to me in a timely manner and this is how you repay me?"

Deliver me? My brain is slow to make sense of the words. What does he mean- "deliver me?" My gaze flies to Eric's face. He doesn't meet my eyes. He also doesn't deny Saarel's accusations.

Eric was supposed to deliver me to…Saarel? Why? My body goes cold. I wrap my arms around my waist, waiting for Eric to tell me Saarel's words are a lie.

Eric says nothing. His silence condemns him.

Moaning, I bend at the waist, feeling the pain of Eric's deceit. I loved him. Thought he was my friend. Were the moments we shared together just a lie? Was he pretending all this time to like me? I don't want to believe Saarel, but it would explain why Eric was always so evasive, never answering my questions. And why he knew so much about Saarel. He was Saarel's slave. His job was to deliver me so that Saarel could drain my life away.

I'm numb. Eric's face quavers in my vision. I feel the tears, but I don't have the energy to lift my hand to wipe them away.

"You sniveling coward," Saarel says. "You betray your troops, your family and now you are disloyal to me."

And he's betrayed me.

"You have-done nothing to warrant my loyalty," Eric says, each word a struggle.

Saarel punches Eric hard enough to send him flying several more feet into the cemetery. Even though I want to hate Eric, my heart feels every blow Saarel delivers.

Only a tombstone stops Eric's backward skid. He rises slowly to his feet, blood spurting from his nose. "You will never rule this world."

He leans heavily on the stone and slowly turns his head in my direction. There is something in his eyes, some message. I don't want to look at him. I hate him. But I can't look away. He cocks his head, listening.

A church bell sounds the hour-the midnight hour. My breath catches in my throat. I understand the message.

Eric is trying to hold Saarel at bay for the minute it takes to reach a new day, for me to be sixteen. But is Eric doing this because he wants to save me or save himself?

It doesn't matter, because Saarel might have been tricked by Eric once, but not twice. With a roar that shakes the earth beneath our feet, Saarel morphs into his demon form, hooves and all. Mud and water fly as he pivots and lunges for me. His speed leaves me no time to prepare. I'm caught like an animal in the headlights of an oncoming train.

He doesn't collide with me, but leaps into my body, becoming one with me. His thoughts merge with mine as my being expands and black corrupt thoughts fill my mind, my heart- his thoughts.

"Do not resist." Saarel's voice echoes in my head.

Lisette.

Maman?

Fight, Lisette, my mother's voice urges.

"Death is so peaceful," Saarel says. "Surrender to me."

I can't breathe.

His voice is so soothing. I thought this fight with him for my soul would be a battle instead of this drifting away. I just have to close my eyes and it will be all over.

Fight, my mother whispers again.

For just a moment a flame flickers in my soul. But it's extinguished just as quickly, when a familiar voice says, "You do not deserve to be the next priestess."

The voice is so jarring and out of place, my eyes fly open. The part of me that is still Lisette Beaulieu recognizes my grandmother, Chante, standing before me. Her cloak flies around her in the wind. *Why is she here?*

"Because *she* wants to be the next priestess," Saarel's sly voice says from somewhere deep inside me.

The flame that flickered briefly, extinguishes. My own family betrays me.

"Yes, let go," Saarel says.

"I thought you were a fighter?" This time it's Eric's voice I hear. "I waged a battle against this devil for you. Fight him, Lisette."

Saarel's voice booms in my head. "My Gods, I believe the Book of Truths lied. She's a weakling, not the chosen one."

His laughter clamors in my ears. "When I finish with you, conquering your world will be nothing. But first I will deal with your sweet grandmother, then I will find your little cocky friend's body and destroy it. He'll never be able to return. Imagine him trying to barter with me."

From somewhere deep in my core, I try to find my essence- that which made me Lisette Beaulieu. I try to remember what little I know about Voodoo. The spirit or loa must possess the body. Is that what I must do? Allow the loa to enter my body to fight off this demon? Which loa is the correct one? I don't have time to figure that out. I must open myself up to them and hope the right one comes to my aid. I must hurry. My vision is darkening.

I compartmentalize my thoughts so Saarel can't read them. Then I begin. "Enter almighty ones, spirits of my ancestors. Help me fight this demon. Help me so I can help others."

From a long way off, Eric shouts my name. I hear my mother calling my name. Voices. There are so many voices. They blend together until they are one, chanting.

A bright light fills my soul. I'm dying then. This is the end. They were wrong. I'm not the one.

A prayer of forgiveness floats through my mind. I'm sad because I won't be able to say goodbye to *Grand'mere* or to Eric. But I'm happy because I'll be able to see my parents.

I will myself to open my eyes to catch a last glimpse of the city I love.

The night is as bright as day. Light so bright it sears my eyes. I close them quickly. I thought the other side would be calmer, the light would be muted.

Not wanting to die in darkness, I open my eyes again and force them to stay open. Strange, Saarel is standing in front of me. When did he leave? He's bending backwards as though a great force is pulling at him. Trees whip and bend in gale-like wind. Another hurricane? I don't feel the wind. I just see the effects. Bodies fly past me. One is the long-limbed demon of the other night. Where did it come from?

Eric is holding onto a pedestal that sits atop a crypt. He's clinging to it for dear life, but he's laughing, laughing like a madman. Has he lost it?

Then I finally understand. I'm the cause of the wind and the light. I'm making it happen. I turn my full attention on Saarel. His teeth are bared in a grimace. His cloven feet are spread wide.

I take a deep breath and focus my energies on him. I still don't know what I'm doing or how this Voodoo priestess thing works, but I'm faking it for all it's worth.

Should I kill him? *Thou shalt not kill.* The bible proverb rings in my head. So, my only alternative is to send him back to the Fifth Realm. And as Eric told me, seal the portal so Saarel or no other demon can ever escape.

I lift my arms, and by sheer force of will, I drive Saarel further into the cemetery. He howls like the wind, cursing me as he goes.

The crypt that held the portal no longer exists. A black hole widens where the stone once stood, sparks shooting from its edges. It's like an explosion ripped a hole in the fabric of time.

"No," Saarel roars as he gets closer to the hole. "This. World. Is. Mine."

"Sorry, Saarel. This world is not big enough for both of us. I'm sending you home where you can rot forever." I must hurry. My limbs feel like they're encased in concrete.

"Noooooooooo." Saarel tumbles head-over-heels toward the portal. "If. I. Go. So. Does-"

Eric's bloody body hurls past me toward the portal opening. "No!" I grab his booted foot just before he reaches the hole and hold on with all my strength.

At the same time I hear Saarel's scream of rage, Eric's boot slips from my nerveless fingers and he hurls toward the gaping hole.

"Youuu must ssseal-" The wind whips the words out of Eric's mouth as he tumbles toward the hole.

I scream and run toward the portal, grasping for any part of him I can reach. In an act of desperation, I leap. My out stretched fingers brush his boot as I plunge to the ground, landing in mud and water. I jerk my face out the muck just in time to see the portal seal, sending both Saarel and Eric back to the depths of Hell.

Chapter 32

From the third floor of *Grand'mere*'s Charity hospital room, New Orleans looks brand new. White clouds float across a peaceful blue sky. The sun glitters off lingering pools of water, but the River is calm-full but calm.

Everything is right with the world, except Scooter and Eric aren't in it.

Not wanting to upset *Grand'mere*, I cough to cover the cry that escapes my throat, but I can't stop the tears. She's very fragile and doesn't remember anything of what happened in the Fifth Realm-which is a good thing.

"Lisette?"

I swipe at the tears, but don't turn around. "Yes, ma'am?"

"Are you keeping the house clean?"

"Yes, ma'am."

Boogie helped me cleared the debris from our small house. It took a day and a half. He thinks we were hit-burglarized-big time. I let him think whatever he wants.

Mrs. Gardner has filed a missing persons report on Scooter. I don't have the heart to tell her I know where he is-at least where his soul is.

My uncle came by the house this morning just as I was taking Toto to Leticia's house. My great-grandmother wants to see me.

When hell freezes over.

I'm not ready to see her or anyone who's connected with that family or with Voodoo. That's what's gotten me into this mess. I sent him away. He'll be back.

I wonder what my grandmother, Chante, has told them. Did she tell my great-grandmother she was in league with Saarel? Did she mention that she tried to destroy me? No, I'm not going back.

"Excuse me."

I spin from the window to see a tall, pale man wearing a dark blue suit, standing in the doorway.

"Yes?" Is he in the wrong room?

He smiles slightly and bows his head in greeting. "Are you Lisette Beaulieu?"

Frowning, I say with caution, "Yesss..."

He reaches into the breast pocket of his pin striped suit and pulls out an envelope. "This is for you."

I reach for it. Before I can ask him what it is, or who he is, he's gone-his footsteps fading down the hospital corridor.

"What is it, Lisette?" *Grand'mere* asks. There's a thread of fear in her voice which makes me think that maybe she does remember something of her ordeal.

"I don't know."

My fingers tremble so much it takes me two tries to get the sealed envelope opened.

I pull out two sheets of official looking documents. It's a deed. The deed lists Lisette and Evangeline Beaulieu as owners of a house in the French Quarter.

Icy fingers skip up my spine. The house is Eric's.

Chapter 33

Déjà vu.

Grand'mere and I stepped over the threshold into the sunroom of Eric's house. Spinning through my mind is the image of me entering the same room two weeks ago, dripping water onto the polished wood floor. And of Eric's face gravely watching me.

A drawn-out breath of air escapes *Grand'mere*'s lips. It's the same reaction I had when I first saw the house, except Eric was at my side.

While I daydream, she's moves on to the foyer. "Tell me again why this boy left you his home?" She's turning in a circle taking in the grand staircase, the massive cut-glass chandelier that hangs over the high polished black and white marbled entry.

It's the umpteen time she's asked that question. And it's the umpteen time I've lied to her. "He is—was an orphan. No relatives. And I guess—I guess he liked me."

"Huh." She makes this doubting sound deep in her throat. Her fingers trail up the staircase banister. She glances at her fingers. "No dust," she whispers more to herself than to me.

I've been thinking the same thing. The French doors opened as though on oiled hinges. Eric's plants are still alive, and in fact, are thriving. Someone is taking care of the house. But who? I think about Hancock floating through the house, and I shudder. That's impossible, because I saw the butler's head roll across the floor of a debris-littered warehouse. No, he's definitely dead. Eric killed him.

"We can't live here," *Grand'mere* says, as she stares up the long winding staircase. "We could never afford to pay the utilities."

I don't tell her that isn't an issue. That there's a trust fund set up for the care of the house. I don't tell her, because that will bring on questions I can't answer. Besides, Hancock lived here and he's responsible for the disappearance of my best friend. I could never live in a house that man inhabited.

"You're right. We can't live here." I move toward the front door, a massive mahogany structure. But she's not behind me. I hear her soft footfalls fading away.

In a panic, I spin around. She's halfway down the hall heading toward the back of the house. Toward the kitchen.

"*Grand'mere!*" But it's too late.

I get to the doorway just in time to hear her say, "Oh, my."

Her face looks like a kid on Christmas morning. It's all bright and shining and her eyes are big and round. Her hand skims over a steel six burner stove. Then on feet as swift and light as a young girl's, she seems almost to race to a steel refrigerator that towers over her small frame. She pulls open the double doors. The interior is brightly lit but empty, as though straight from the show room. She opens the freezer compartment that rests at the bottom. It's also empty.

Then she spots two coordinated doors that rest under butcher block counters. She pulls open one door. "Oh." It's a dishwasher. I'm the dishwasher back in our four room bungalow.

She frowns as she stares into the interior of the other appliance, then she glances at me for an explanation.

"Trash compactor." I don't want her to get too attached to this house. Cause as she said earlier, we can't live here.

Grand'mere hums to herself as she spins around the kitchen, opening cabinets and marveling over the counter top. The humming increases until it vibrates inside me. Then I realize the hum is centered in the house not coming from *Grand'mere*.

I move out of the kitchen and toward the front. As I climb the winding staircase, the vibration gets louder. Opening one door then another, I find myself in Eric's room. His scent still lingers-Irish spring soap, and...a musk that's all his own. Sitting on the bed, I run my fingers over the silkiness of his duvet-browns and golds. For the few months he was here, he tried to experience a life time. The banging stereo, the fast sports car, the luxury of this house...

A dark spot appears on the brown section of the duvet, turning it mocha. Another spot appears and another. It takes a moment for me to realize they're my tears. I swipe at them, but they fall faster.

"Don't cry, Lisette."

The sound of his voice makes my breath hitch in my throat. "Eric?" I jump up and turn in a circle, searching the room.

"Eric?" This time my voice borders on hysterics.

"*Shhh.*" The sound carries on the sudden gentle current of air that flows through the room, even though there's no open window. His voice calms me, allowing me to feel the wind like the touch of his hand on my face and feel the beat of my heart. My body still vibrations.

I know what that feeling is now. *The Book.* I'd forgotten about the book. Eric had placed it in a safe place. Where did he hide it? Think! Think!

And then I remember-- the media room.

Once I have the Book calmness spreads through my body. Somehow this Book will help me find the answers to bring Eric and Scooter back home. I know it will.

I clutch it to my chest and go in search of *Grand'mere*.

Epilogue

Today is my first day back at school and nothing's changed. The fluorescent lights are still too bright, the banging of lockers too loud and strident voices bounce off the walls like ping pongs. Pushing and shoving, my classmates hurl insults across the hall at each other and move around me like I'm invisible. Nothing has changed.

My chest expands and I take a deep breath as visions of the last week flicker through my mind like strobe lights. Demons, Saarel, portals, the bayou, death and destruction, and in the middle of all this is me, Lisette Beaulieu, Voodoo priestess. No—everything has changed.

Michele stands at her locker surrounded by her wannabees.

"Excuse me." They're so busy gossiping, no one hears me.

"Excuse me." When no one moves, I put my shoulder into the back of the nearest girl and shove.

"WTF?" she shouts.

One by one the crowd parts for me, and I move unhindered toward my locker. Oblivious to what's going on around her, Michele, with her back to her friends, is having a one-sided dialogue with herself as she applies makeup. She doesn't realize she's no longer commanding the stage.

"He must've had a death in the family. Cause no way would he leave without telling me." Admiring herself in her pink locker mirror, she gives her hair a final flip.

A shiver passes over me. She's talking about Eric.

I spin the numbers on my combination lock and open the door. I sense the moment she spots me in the mirror. She pivots to face me, hands on hips.

"Where is he?" Her eyes shoot lethal daggers of hate. Gone is the pretense she knows where he is.

"He's in Europe—" one of her entourage attempts to say, but is stopped by Michele's hand in the girl's face.

"Where. Is. He?" She leans into my space. Her breath smells of cigarettes and peppermint.

"Who?"

Like, I don't know. Like, I haven't thought about him every minute, every second, of the past three days. Like I'm not heartbroken he used me.

"Eric."

I shrug. "Don't know." Her obsession about a boy who cares nothing about her seems childish. She has no clue as to who he really is. Couldn't she sense he wasn't ordinary?

The five minute warning bell sounds.

She grabs my arm as I try to get my books. "You know where he is, you slut-" She draws back from me, frowning. "Are those contacts?"

It's only then I remember that one of my eyes has changed colored. "Yeah, contacts to compliment my bleached hair." I run my hands over my uncovered mane. She doesn't get the joke.

I don't waste my breath explaining the Voodoo thing. She wouldn't get it anyway. Wonder if she even remembers being in love with Ashley. I smile to myself picturing her trying to explain her mental lapse to Eric.

Determined to ignore her, I turn back to shoveling books into my pack. She doesn't leave, but continues to glare at me as though that will make me talk.

Eric was secretive. I doubt he shared too much of himself with anyone—other than me. I close my heart against the remembered anguish in his voice as he told me about his village and his role in their death. Even now, I want to shut out his voice and all thoughts of him, but in the last few days I've come to understand his motives better. He may have started out working with Saarel to seduce me to their world, but in the end, Eric tried to save me.

Tired of her presence and the hangers on shifting restlessly behind me, I turn to face her. "Why do you think I know where he is?"

I see something move in her eyes. She would never admit I meant something to Eric. It would lessen her role as his girlfriend. He used her to get to me. But she doesn't know that. He had to blend in and how better to do it than with a narcissistic female who didn't doubt he was totally into her. Her ego wouldn't allow her to believe otherwise.

"You tagged along with him wherever he went." Her eyes narrow to slits. "But he didn't care about you."

She doesn't sound so sure. She looks to her audience for confirmation. They nod obediently.

"You're right. Eric went home," I say. And it's true, he did. Just not the home Michele imagines.

She blinks. She doesn't know where his home is and this bothers her. My former self would have smiled smugly at knowing I knew something she didn't, but not now. Her problems are small. Mine seem almost insurmountable. I have to find a way to bring Eric and Scooter back.

I've decided to put an end to this conversation. "Yes, I know where Eric is."

Her mouth opens and closes like a fish caught on a hook.

I step into her space. "And when he comes back, it will be for me... not you." *And I will bring him back.*

A smile splits my face. She's speechless. At last.

Tossing my gold twists, I step into the stream of students hustling toward class.

Dear Reader,

The past resonates through the French Quarter from its four-hundred-year-old warehouses, to cobbled streets and narrow alleys. Loving New Orleans as much as I do, I thought it would be a great setting for a book.

I hoped you enjoyed Lisette and Eric's story. Look for their adventure to continue.

Connie

CPSIA information can be obtained at www.ICGtesting.com
Printed in the USA
LVOW131936150413

329236LV00009B/1280/P

9 781479 231744